# The Broken Knight

# The Broken Knight

## Emmylou Kotzé

PINK HYDRA PRESS

2024

# The Broken Knight


The Golden Girl ........................................................ 1

The Christian Wedding........................................ 18

The Sea-Demon................................................... 50

The Faery Sword................................................. 85

The Burning Town............................................. 104

The River Queen .............................................. 115

The Deserters ................................................... 132

The Dark Priest ............................................... 152

The Secret Pool................................................ 183

The Sword's Legacy ......................................... 206

The Lost Lover.................................................. 232

# Chapter One
# The Golden Girl

*I think I hate rain.*

*Not for the chill nor the clouds that bring it forth, not for the damp, nor even the crash of the pagan thunder-god's hammer in the sky. The chill breeze refreshes me; the smell of the world becomes clean and cool and, of course, it is refilling my empty waterskins as I sit loathing it.*

*But I hate what happens in the rain. In the rain, I remember.*

*What a tragic life this person I was must have led, when his memories return to him only as the sky weeps. And yet, not all of these memories were built from pain . . .*

*The best of them is a memory of a young girl with brown hair in a walled garden, under a gnarled and sprawling apple tree. She stands* with her arms stretched out, and the raindrops fill her hands as she laughs. They dye the sleeves of her grey woollen dress black; they dance around her bare, wet feet.

I cannot bring to mind the features of her face, nor what she is to me.

I feel her eyes on me, I remember her laugh, her hands and feet—but I would not know her if I met her. Somehow, this is what disturbs me most of all.

To be sure, other visions of the past are more unpleasant by far. I remember swinging a heavy, rusty axe with such anger that there were tears in my eyes, and the groan of a great oak tree as it crashed to the ground. I remember riding along a muddy road at the head of a horde of men, the dull ache from long travel on horseback settling in my thighs and lower back, the stiffness of gauntleted hands in the damp and cold. I remember a wooden-walled fort bursting into flame, horses slipping in the mud and screaming in fear, the inexorable fire burning steadily even as the rain hammered down. I remember dying men shouting for me.

The name they shouted—I didn't even remember that name until someone else told me what it was. When the stableboy found me lying bloody, half-conscious, at the bottom of the dyke that encircled his lord's ruined hall.

'Thane Wilhelm,' he whimpered, pale eyes staring through the dirt that darkened his face. 'You're alive.'

Alive I was, but the lord I had fought for, along with every one of my own men, was dead. His thralls had scattered into the fields, returning later to loot the battlefield. I was a thane—a landed warrior in service to a higher lord, the stableboy had to explain to me, a concept I could barely recall. I had a fort of my own, with soldiers and lands, peasants working the fields, other freemen answering to my authority, but not near here. Somewhere else, on the sea, a tiny island off a wind-swept shore far north. That island might as well be across the great western ocean, for all I knew. I could remember none of it. The grubby lad was my only source of information.

'Did I have a wife waiting for me in this holding?' That was the first thing I asked.

The boy looked down at his bare feet before answering. 'My lord—your lady—she's dead. I heard you tell m'lord Egbert, once. I—I'm sorry.'

'Oh,' I replied hollowly. I had had a wife, and she had died, and I didn't remember her. 'Did I—I mean, do I—have children?'

'Not that I've ever heard tell of, my lord.'

The rain darkens the sky, bringing with it an evil wind that sets me to shivering and barrages my mind with strange new memories so that I cannot think. A vision of a lady laughs up at me, feathery black hair tickling my neck as she languishes in my arms. I am staring out into a snowstorm from the safety of a cold stone hall, waiting anxiously for a shadow of my father to appear against the mist. My back is hunched over a horse's withers, bunched muscles moving beneath my hands with the motion of her gallop, the two of us alone in a world of howling wind and torrential rain. My hands are red with blood, my own blood . . . I slowly sink to my knees and fall asleep with a dull red pain in my chest.

Still, what haunts me most is the face of the little girl I cannot re-member. Is hers the face of a childhood playmate, a little sister? Or even, may God be good, a daughter of my own?

You have no known family, they told me when they bade me flee the ruined fort. The stableboy and the old seneschal we found both said so. By all accounts, your father and mother died many years ago. There was no brother marching with you at the head of your host, nor sister sending succour throughout the endless campaigns. If rumour can be believed, you never spent much time in your own hall; you built yourself a reputation of prowess upon the field of battle, fighting for one lord against another all through the years. All across the lands of the Angles and the Saxons. Go home, Thane Wilhelm. Go back to your island, and raise there what you will. The defenders of this fort are gone. None remain of your own warriors. Go home. Go to heal.

*Go home, they said, but none wait for me there. There will be no dutiful wife, weaving tapestries in her lonely hours without me, praying for her husband to deliver her from the advances of greedy suitors. There will be no loving son who sets out to find his long-missed father, fetching him home to tend his lands and family. Dare I saunter into this alien world, come to my own holdings like a ghost to trouble joy, remembering nothing, passing over loyal servants I have known all my life, asking for directions to the dining hall where I supped as a little boy?*

*Memories haunt me, showing me nothing useful, resolving nothing. They play on to the clash of steel in the background, and the moans of dying men to the left and right.*

*I dare not even contemplate the violence that Thane Wilhelm was capable of. He lived by the sword and would have died by it but for— but for what? How did I escape with only a minor wound on the head, when my men all perished in sword and flame, and remain as food for the crows? How did I survive? Why did I survive?*

OUT IN THE SOGGY FOREST, somebody screamed.

Will paused with his hand on the cloth he had been using to polish the flat of his sword. The tiny fire he had built gently licked up the giant trees that formed the walls of his dry nook, leaving stripes of soot where it had kissed. Every now and then a drop of rain landed on the fire from above, making it crackle and hiss.

Long moments passed, and Will decided that the scream must have been his imagination. Perhaps he was hearing things, recollections of blood-curdling screams from memories long ago.

He listened through the drumming of the rain. Were those human footfalls he heard, off to the eastern edge of the wood? Raised voices?

Moving purposefully, Will picked up his sword and strode into the rain, following the distant sounds he could not ignore. No-one should be out in the woods on a night like this, and certainly not with such a commotion.

Through the trees, he espied the light of flickering torches, and now he could clearly hear the raised voices of the mob, just as he stumbled into the clearing.

They were poor men, he saw, peasant farmers or village tradesmen to judge by their clothing. A few women hovered at the edges of the mob, carrying the torches, their faces pale and vindictive. The leaders of the mob had just pounced upon a struggling figure who was wrapped up in rags like a leper, a child or woman by its size.

Will strode forward, carried by nothing more than an instinct to stop the violence.

'Stop!' he commanded, waving his sword, and the way

everybody came to attention at the shout was intensely gratifying. Three men froze holding the ragged victim, one with his arm around its neck, the other two grasping an arm each. The victim wriggled energetically, but their grip was relentless.

'What is the meaning of this?' Will demanded over the pattering of the rain. He pointed his sword at the three ringleaders. 'What are you doing with this child?'

'No child,' the man in the middle said, and pulled at a grey hood that obscured most of his victim's features. Will scowled. The grubby face beneath was female, perhaps as old as eighteen or nineteen. She remained silent, but her dark blue eyes burned defiance.

'She's witched!' shouted a woman shrilly, and stepped closer to Will. 'A heathen outsider with old ways—with evil ways.' She spat at Will's feet in disgust, and ineptly made the sign of the Christian cross with her left hand. 'She's used magic against our village, killed the pigs, made men die of terrible diseases!'

'This ends tonight!' exclaimed the man holding the girl's left arm. A ragged cheer went up from those not completely deafened by the driving rain.

'Aye,' another man shouted. 'And she's a thief. We caught her red-handed just now, stealing from honest tradesmen in the night.'

Will's scowl deepened. 'That's no reason to chase this girl down and murder her in the woods,' he said coldly.

There were angry mutters all around him, and his hand clenched harder on his sword. Someone shouted, 'But she's a pagan!' Agreements rose in a shrill chorus.

'And so were we all, once, pagans!' Will shouted back at them. 'Is there a priest amongst you tonight?'

There was a long, sullen pause.

'He's sleeping,' one of the women replied at last.

'You have no right to deliver divine justice without a priest's blessing,' Will hazarded.

'Well,' one of the men said at once, 'we'll have to wake him, then!'

Suddenly, the girl's eyes changed. She looked straight at Will, and her expression shot through his soul. She was alone here, as was he. Her gaze was pleading, desperate. She did not utter a word, but she clearly knew exactly what was to become of her, if he did nothing.

Will was her only hope, and they both knew it.

Quickly he moved forward, and his body remembered a thousand like experiences, instinct taking the place of the conscious memories he had mislaid. The sword seemed to become part of him, melting into his arm; it felt almost as though it were whispering to him, a steel song softer than the falling rain. It was as if he had rediscovered his life's purpose.

He laid the edge of his sword against the middle man's neck. The man froze and his eyes bulged as he felt the cold steel kiss his skin. The two holding the girl by her arms made squeaking noises and fell away as fast as they could.

Will grinned dangerously. The rain was already a damper on the spirits of a mob like this, and they had not expected to meet justice upon their dread crusade. Their fear took the atmosphere of horror and vengeance away, and transformed them back into a collection of wet, frightened village folk with no real weaponry between them. They registered Will's imposing height, caught a glance at his unkempt brown beard and hard dark eyes, and fell back, fearing and respecting him.

'Let the girl go,' Will commanded, and the man shakily released her, fright leaking from his eyes. The girl collapsed on her feet as she was released, but Will caught her deftly. He heard her surprised intake of breath as he easily supported her weight.

She hesitated, gripping his arm. Then, unexpectedly, she wrapped both of her arms around his waist and leaned her full weight on him, breathing shallowly. She was soaked through, and shivered like a leaf.

Will self-consciously put his arm around her shoulders to support her. Anger burned in him, and suddenly he would have liked nothing so much as to cut a bloody swathe through these people, these men who judged what they did not know of, and these women whose eyes were always moving and whose mouths were always busy, condemning outsiders with a single word, dismissing the wretched and needy with a single haughty glance. They disgusted him. He could almost imagine that the blade that was now part of his hand thirsted for their blood.

But they were no danger to him, and he lowered the sword.

The world returned, leaving him blinking and wondering what evil spell had briefly engulfed his mind. The faces before him were masks of terror. Not adversaries, but victims. Ordinary people, who cowered in fear before him.

'Get out of my sight,' Will spat. The leader of the mob turned and ran without looking back, followed by several of his fellows. Others remained, looking uncertainly at Will and the girl, who remained completely silent and motionless.

'Get out of my sight,' Will repeated. 'All of you!'

No-one moved, and Will's heart sank to his stomach. Then a burly man spoke tentatively. 'What about that which she stole?'

Cold fingers pressed into Will's hand. He looked down at the girl, who was hiding her face. He held out a small purse, heavy with coins. 'Is this what she stole?'

The man gave a nod. Will tossed the purse to him.

'There,' he said. He looked around at the pale, silent faces. 'What's yours has been recovered. It is finished. The girl will come with me.'

Some of those faces looked as though they might have liked to dispute his statement, but the rain was pouring and the torches were burning low. Wandering through the dark woods in search of a vagrant with a sword was not something these simple folk wanted to try. At home there was warm food and drink and a fire in the hearth. One by one, they turned to go home.

The woman who had made the sign of the cross lingered to the last.

'Beware, fallen warrior,' she said to Will. Her pinched face and hollow eyes were cadaverous in the guttering torchlight. 'The demon gods of this land are restive, and evil comes to walk in these last days.' Her eyes settled malevolently on the slight figure of the girl. 'Lures of the flesh are the means to undo the servants of the true Christian faith.'

With that, she turned sharply and joined the ghostly trail of little lights snaking back, leaving Will alone with the rain and a cold, crying girl in his arms.


ANGLO-SAXON THANES AND ATHELINGS, when they rode to war, did so with a full armament of weapons. They carried round shields and long spears, and wore swords on their belts.

They dressed in mail and boiled leather for protection. When travelling, they rode fast, highly-bred horses too precious to charge into battle.

A landed warrior of thane status required a contingent of servants to help him maintain his armour, keep his weapons sharpened, and tack up his horse with the regalia of his ancestors. He would never travel without at least half a dozen companions, to reinforce his noble status and help guard against outlaws. Horses were expensive, and so was anything made from good leather or steel. A steady flow of careless mounted warriors past his hideout was all the average bandit required to live comfortably.

When taken into custody by one of these elite warriors, one might reasonably expect a cosy campsite, perhaps with gay tents, goodly company, and plenty of food and drink.

Will had nothing of the sort. His own horse had been lost on the field of battle, and the old gelding they'd given him to escape on he'd sold in the first town he reached. Most of his armour had gone the same way, although he had kept his boots, chainmail tunic, and golden arm-rings. At the time of his departure, he had had a sword by his side and, when he checked, three knives in holsters at various places upon his person. Two of the three knives he had sold; the third and sharpest he had kept along with the sword.

Newly affluent in a busy town, Will had discovered the first thing about Thane Wilhelm that truly disgusted him. He'd walked past a tavern, caught the rich scent of golden beer, and been seized with such a longing to go inside and try some that he'd had to force himself to turn round and walk the other way down the lane, bombarding himself as he went with a series of stern admonitions. Sensibly, he had purchased instead a supply of provisions, bedding, fresh breeches and underwear, and a sack with carrying straps. It was hardly a lord's armoury, but it was more than what the average Welsh slave owned, and he felt he should be grateful for that.

Will stood with his back to the girl as she stripped off her sodden rags and wrapped herself in his only blanket. The night was chilly with the late summer rain, and she shivered as she tucked the blanket beneath her chin. With her inside the bare shelter formed by the two tree trunks growing into each other, he was obliged to stand in the rain outside. The foliage above him broke the force of the raindrops, sending them down to gently fall on his face. He was already soaked to the skin, and the cold of the droplets numbed his cheeks.

The excitement of the night was rapidly deserting him now, and he wished he could shut his eyes. The soft hissing of the rain on the leaves above seemed to make out a melody. Earlier, he had thought he would never get to sleep, that the disjointed memories of his life past would plague him the night through. But the commotion in the woods and the arrival of the girl had chased them away, for now.

His eyes closed for a moment, and he swayed on his feet. Opening them once again, he realized that the girl had appeared silently beside him.

*Where the hell did she come from?* Will hoped she hadn't noticed him jump.

She seemed insubstantial as a ghost as she stood there. His woollen blanket covered her from shoulder to knee, and she had made some sort of effort to tidy her hair. It was a dark, rich golden colour, a little past shoulder length, and more tangled than a nest of rodents. She looked shyly up at him.

'Thank you for saving me,' she said softly.

Will shrugged. 'Some would have said that I had a duty to,' he returned, offhandedly. 'Would you like some food?'

The girl's look of eagerness betrayed her thoughts instantly. She was nothing more than skin over bones, he thought, and gave her the best part of his bacon, bread, and dried fish. There were also apples, which he had picked earlier that day in the woods, and fresh water. She ate as though she were starving.

'Is there a stream nearby?' she asked him.

'Beyond the tangle of berry bushes there, a few dozen strides,' Will gestured. He had managed to place himself in between the fire and the outside world, leaning back on a tree trunk, and hoped that his hair would dry out sometime during the night. 'Listen, I hope you have somewhere to go, because—'

'Goldwine,' the girl said.

'What?'

'My name. It's Goldwine. You may call me Goldie, if you wish.'

'I'm Will. I was saying—' He hesitated. 'Goldwine? That's not the name of a peasant nor runaway thrall.' He appraised her with a fresh eye. 'Where are you from?'

The girl looked back at him with eyes the exact blue of the cornflowers he had noticed growing in the fields during these last few weeks of summer. Her tangled hair clung damply to her neck and shoulders. Will realized, uncomfortably, that she might be underfed and dirty right now, but that she was also beautiful—or would be, eventually, if she had access to a hairbrush and several regular meals a day.

'A long way from here,' Goldie replied distantly. The flames crackled to the sound of her voice and seemed to create sparks in the surface of her eyes. 'East and east and east again, across the narrow sea and the great forests. It was a land of mist and marsh, and rivers flowing through the woods. A wild place . . . a beautiful place. But my mother abandoned me, and I was taken in by a family who lived on the edge of the marshland.' She blinked her eyes, and suddenly the sparks were gone. 'They raised me, but I was never one of them. Just some girl they had shown kindness to . . . and expected her to pay it back.' Her fist clenched, and she quickly looked away from Will, as though she had said too much.

He tried to follow her eyes. 'You ran away from them?' He hesitated. 'You took a ship?' Strangely, he remembered more of distant history than he did of his own life. His ancestors had come from across the stormy sea, he knew, to find adventure and carve out little kingdoms for themselves on this island.

Goldie nodded, tight-lipped, and Will sighed. It didn't take much imagination to follow her story through to the end.

'So you've been living off the land, by thievery, and by your wits.'

'No!' Goldie protested. She bit her lip. 'Tonight was the first time I ever stole something—or *tried* to steal . . .' She scowled at him. 'I never would've tried if I hadn't met Rob Lightfingers and his band of outlaws.'

Will's brow wrinkled. 'You met *who*?'

'A band of robbers who steal from the rich to give to the needy,' the girl explained. 'They roam by hill and vale, forest and heath.' Her blue eyes were very wide when she looked back at him. 'I met them, stayed in their hideout for a while, but I wanted to move on. My destiny was not there.'

'So you were stealing,' Will said with a snort, 'to give to . . .'

'Few people are more needy than those who haven't eaten in five days,' Goldie said, sulkily. Her girlish air of affront, for some reason, struck Will as so ridiculous that he had to chuckle.

Goldie shifted her position. 'You laugh like a man who hasn't laughed for a year,' she remarked.

'What would you know about it?'

'I haven't been laughing much lately either,' Goldie said with a toss of her head. 'So—' She pointedly studied their surroundings, the thin blanket that was all he had to cover her for the night, the chilly breeze that swept through the woods, the dripping boughs that were the only shelter she had against the weather. 'Tell me *your* sad story, Will. Are you down on your luck like me, or are you a thane turned robber?'

Will turned his face away, leaned flat against his tree-trunk. The campfire was burning low, guttering into embers. 'It's time we went to sleep,' he said.

He closed his eyes, and all was silent for a moment except for the determined patter of raindrops on the boughs above. He could hear the movements of the girl as she settled in the dry nook. Despite his exposed spot, sleep was very close to taking him. But the girl spoke again, simply asking: 'Will?'

He managed a grunt, keeping both his eyes closed.

'Good night,' Goldie said in reply, 'and thank you, again, for saving me.'

Will cracked open one eye. All was nearly darkness in the embers of the dying fire.

'It was nothing,' he said to the darkness. 'Anyone would have done the same.'

She said nothing, but he heard a tiny snort of disbelief as she settled into her nook.

Will closed his eyes again, and drifted off into a sea of his own half-remembered nightmares.

GOLDWINE SAT IN THE DRY NOOK and watched the man's face as he fell asleep. Water dripped onto his head from above and ran in slow rivulets down his cheeks and through his beard. Apparently, he was sleepy enough to disregard them, for soon he began to snore loudly. She rested her head against the folds of the thin woollen blanket, pretending to be asleep herself.

But as soon as she felt assured that he would not wake, she flung aside the blanket, left him behind at the campsite, and strode out into the rain. She was shivering, though it was not cold, and she seldom felt the cold anyway. No matter how tightly she shut her eyes, she saw the men who had seized her, their faces only shadows, the flickering of the torches searing through her eyelids. It had seemed almost a fitting end; that she who was born of water should be dispatched by fire.

She remained silent, breathing deeply, until all she could hear was the gentle patter of raindrops on the forest canopy above. Will was still sleeping, heedlessly, a few paces away. *He is far too trusting,* she thought to herself. *I could slit his throat right now if I wanted to. As a warrior, he should know better.*

But there was something very comforting about that sort of trust. Her foster brothers would never have let their guard down like this around a stranger.

She glanced back towards the sleeping man as calm slowly descended upon her. Who was he, truly? She had only an abbreviated name to go by and what her own instincts told her.

He was in his early-thirties, or possibly late-twenties, the age at which men were most valued in war. He was clearly of some rank, to judge from his clothes and his mode of speech; his dark brown hair and beard had probably once been neatly clipped, but he had allowed them to grow shaggy, giving himself the air of a bandit, or possibly a soldier for hire.

Both possibilities seemed unlikely to Goldie, though. He was clearly travelling with some purpose, as a man might when he was returning home.

*A nobleman marching back from war, to his wife and his fertile fields,* she thought. She crept towards his sleeping figure. *You have everything waiting for you, Will. I have nothing.* Her foster family had thrown her out, and she could never return to her own people. She was alone, and she needed to survive.

It was but the work of a breath to dislodge his pack from between his legs, and the work of another moment to find his purse. It was not as heavy as she had hoped.

She turned to get up, but her mind was suddenly full of misgivings.

*You'll take the money, and what then?* she asked herself. *Another town, another mob, and soon you'll be burned alive.* She bit down on her lip to keep from shaking.

'I ran away to gain my freedom,' she said under her breath. 'No man holds me. I do as I please.'

*But that's not how this world works,* she knew. *A woman cannot wander for long on her own.* She glanced towards Will again. *He is strong, he has courage, and he doesn't want to hurt me.* She weighed the purse in her hand. *And he may have power. He may be a man of means.*

She remained crouched down, irresolute. Above her, the

rain continued to fall. She could hear the river in the distance, rushing on towards its destiny, not knowing where it might end up but determined to get there quickly.

*I have always swum against the flow of the river.*

# Chapter Two
# The Christian Wedding

*A warm day in the first month of summer.*

*A tiny hill-fort with an army advancing on either side, swords, battle-axes, spears flashing in the sun.*

*Something dreadful happened that day at the battle for Fort Horsa.*

*War is certainly not a new art to this ravaged land. People huddle together behind fortifications of wood and stone, and sharpen their axes by midnight hearths. I have seen girls no older than twelve shooting practice-arrows at a scarecrow in a field. I have seen more mounted warriors than I care to think about, and forts of warrior lords bristling with armaments.*

*But that day at Fort Horsa, that fateful day of which I remember only awaking, there was something unexpected. Something worse than fire-arrows or boulders flung from catapults. How else can I account for ranks upon ranks of charred dead? Warriors turned to ash where they stood, slain long ere they had a chance to engage with the enemy! They fell in agony, fleeing an unknown horror that stole the courage right out of their hearts.*

*I escaped with barely a mark on me. The loss of my memory seems of little account, when I compare it to the fate suffered by my men.*

*I have replayed the moment of my awakening in my mind a thousand times. I came to at the bottom of the keep's defensive dyke, not far from the ranks of burned dead, and the smell of roasted flesh was coursing through my lungs. It seems likely that I was running, like so many others ran, but that I lost my footing and fell, hitting my head. If so, my own clumsiness saved my life. The fiery weapon raged above ground, but I was safe at the bottom of the ditch.*

*Now when I sleep, I dream of ash, and the faraway laughter of a man-shaped shadow that stands over me. His black robes flutter in the wind, flicking out of my grasp, and as I try to crawl through the mud at his feet, I am surrounded by thousands of charred bodies.*

*Who are you, I try to cry, but my throat is choked with ash. Everything has burned away, like the shadow of the man I used to be. Like the memory of my wife. Like the memory of home, which now only stands in shadows.*

*Perhaps there is something even darker waiting at home for me. Some terrible secret I ran from. Something I tried to drink and whore away. It is a bitter irony that now I cannot remember what I might have wanted to forget.*

*But the only answers lie in that distant home, so home I go, leaving the shadow-man and his dreadful weapon of fire behind. I cannot face the army that wields such a weapon, no matter how much it preys on my mind. I am no hero. The monks may talk of how Christ saved the world despite His humble beginnings, but He was the son of God and I have no such aspirations to my own paternity.*

*Let the nobles and thanes of the south fight amongst themselves. I am going home.*

T HE NEW DAY DAWNED like the promise of redemption. Will opened his eyes and found that he was lying on a carpet of wet leaves. He had slid sideways during the night, and apparently fallen to the ground and curled up there. He felt cold and damp, but not nearly as much as expected. He came fully awake then, and saw that somebody had draped his woollen blanket over him as he slept.

He smiled for the girl's sake and then, because he was not totally naïve, checked to see if all his possessions were still where he had left them. His sword had ended up tangled uncomfortably beneath his legs, but his pack lay like a cushion in the crook of his knees. A desultory check through it assured him that nothing was missing.

There was no sign of Goldwine anywhere near the campsite, though there were a few of her rags hanging from the boughs of an oak nearby. Will examined the garments and decided that they must have been discarded; they were certainly good for nothing else. There was nothing that looked like hose, tunic, dress, or undergarments hanging anywhere . . . so, clearly, she must be wearing those.

Clearly she was gone already, journeying towards whatever

it was she hoped to find, out in the land on her own.

Mixed feelings fluttered through him as he sat back down and wondered what to do about breakfast.

*She could have said goodbye, at least,* part of him thought.

Another part, the person in him that Will suspected represented Thane Wilhelm, or at least the memory of him, said, *Good riddance to the dirty wench.*

And then a third voice, outside the confines of Will's own head, said, 'Hungry?'

Will turned around and saw Goldie.

He realized that he was seeing her properly for the first time, and his first impression was that she was even smaller than he had first thought. She was shorter than him by more than a foot, and as skinny as a rat. He had the impression that if she stood very still, he might take her for part of the forest. But she had clearly washed herself in the stream, and her hair was now the colour of ripe wheat in the summer, or of honey. It framed her face with the blue eyes he had noticed before, and her skin was sun-kissed like a peasant woman's. She was dressed in light-coloured rags that almost made her look like a boy, covering up the shape of her body: a loose, long-sleeved tunic and baggy trousers. There was also a cloak so thin that it could have been used to strain vegetables, and long strips of cloth for garters.

In her right hand she carried by their tails two large, juicy spotted trout.

'How did you catch those?' Will began, but she only grinned at him.

'Will you start a fire for us? I hate the taste of raw fish.'

When the fire was going and the fish were roasting, she sat down cross-legged and asked, 'So, which way are we travelling?'

Will froze.

'Goldie, child,' he began in his most paternal voice, 'I don't know what you thought, but there is no question of *us* travelling anywhere together. I am going my own way, and I will be happy to set you upon yours.'

'But you saved me,' Goldie protested.

Will shrugged. 'So what?'

She frowned and looked into the fire. 'I've nowhere to go.'

Will sighed and put a hand over his eyes.

'There's no way I can pay the way for both of us,' he said sternly. 'And besides—Goldie—there's no call for you to lead a life on the road from town to town. Take it from me, that's no place for a young woman.'

Goldie ignored his remonstration. 'I can fend for myself,' she said in a low voice.

'You were so starved you resorted to thievery,' he threw back at her.

'A moon ago, I was on the sea,' she replied sulkily. 'After that, in towns where no-one gives you anything for begging. I can survive in the wild—I caught two fish today in less time than it took you to wake up. I have skills. I could sew if I had the tools for it, and I know mushrooms and herbs. Where are you going, anyway?'

'To the north-western coast,' Will replied, frowning when he realized that the words had escaped his mouth without his mind (which was thinking longingly about the fat fish roasting in the coals) having any say in the matter. He focused his attention on Goldie, who had leaned forward expectantly at this answer.

*I may as well tell her*, he thought, and forestalled her next question. 'From there, I will obtain passage over the sea to the island of Mann. I have my own lands and people waiting for me there.'

Goldie sat up, her eyes gleaming. 'Take me with you! I could be a serving-girl in your fort. I can work. I know I'd be protected if I was on your land.' She swept her hair behind her ears and looked imploringly at him. 'Please? I've nowhere else to go.'

Will avoided her eyes, feeling something like shame sweep into his stomach. 'Not even sure I'm going to end up there,' he mumbled.

'What?'

Will gave up. *There's something about her eyes*, he thought. *As relentless as the river's flow.* Goldie was impossible to lie to. 'You guessed right before,' he admitted. 'I'm impossibly down on my luck. I—' He hesitated, and closed his eyes. Admitting this was painful. 'I can't remember anything about it.'

'What do you mean?' She had shifted all her weight towards him now, leaning so close he could touch her.

'I hit my head during battle, and I—I forgot everything.' Will clenched his jaw in frustration. 'They told me my name, told me of my life, the lands I own—but I can't remember any of it!' He wanted to laugh, all of a sudden, for no reason. He wanted to cry. There were tears in his eyes, he realized, and Goldie was looking at him with something unreadable in hers.

It was all going wrong. Goldwine was not the first person he had talked to since that day—Will had recently shared the road with a travelling monk who'd made quite an impression on him—but she was the first person he'd tried to explain this to. The monk had serenely accepted whatever curt answers Will had given him. But sooner or later he would have to make others understand what had happened to him, and as it turned out, he couldn't tell his story without falling apart over it.

He clenched his fists on his knees and stared at them. 'I—' he began, and found he could say no more. *Who am I? I would come to my own home a wanderer, an errant stranger, a—*

'I am a broken man,' he whispered, and felt the sting of tears upon his cheek.

Goldie shifted from where she sat. She crouched next to him and, tentatively, laid her hand upon one of his clenched fists. When he didn't resist, she took his hand in hers, clasped it, and drew him towards her. Too surprised to say anything, Will hugged her back as she held him. Their embrace lasted for only a moment, but when she disengaged, Will felt himself comforted beyond belief.

'I understand,' Goldie said softly. 'Be calm. You don't have to say any more.'

Embarrassed, Will wiped his eyes with his shirtsleeve. Goldie pretended not to see, busying herself with the fish, which were ready to eat now. She hesitated before speaking again.

'Clearly,' she said as she set the fish upon a bed of green leaves to cool, 'it would be to both our best interest to travel together. For myself a protector, and for you—' She broke off.

'Someone to stop me falling apart along the way?' Will tried to sound indifferent, and was aware that he failed miserably.

Goldie bit her lip and cocked an eyebrow, and suddenly Will found himself laughing again. She was so tiny, so absurd. *By all measures,* he thought, *I should be the one making travel plans and providing the fish.* He could see very little of the frightened, bedraggled girl he had rescued just the previous night.

'You never give up, do you?'

Goldie smirked like a cat in cream. 'And I never lose.'


As Will set off northwards out of the forest, Goldie kept close by his side, chattering cheerfully with scarce regard to the subject. He said little, allowing her to dominate the conversation. It was good to not have to listen to the voices in his head for a change.

They trekked through the woods until they reached a narrow, paved road that led westwards. A Roman milestone by the side of the road proclaimed that there was a settlement three miles away. Goldie expressed her surprise that Will could read the writing of the old Romans, since she herself could only read the script of the runestones.

'If the village still exists,' Will said, 'it will be a good place to stop and get our bearings.'

Half a mile on, they came to a small pagan shrine next to a waterfall where travellers could rest and refill their waterskins. Whilst Goldie stuck her head in the water—the girl seemed to be thirsty all the time no matter how much she drank—Will inspected the shrine. Fresh offerings of little blue and white flowers decorated the stone. There were wreaths of wild briar and bouquets of greenery tied together with raw wool.

'All you had to do was come a couple of miles west and you'd have been safe,' he told Goldie as they set off again. 'Looks like they're all pagans on this side of the woods.'

'There's that word again,' Goldie said.

'What word? *Pagan?*'

'I don't understand what you mean by it.'

'It's a Christian word,' Will said, 'and it means anyone . . . well, everyone, who isn't of the Faith. Them who worship different gods.'

'But every place has its own gods, does it not?' Goldie said. 'They are everywhere. You don't need to put names to them, but they abide wherever nature is.' She shrugged gaily. 'Which is to say, everywhere.'

'Well, Christians—' Will began uncomfortably, 'Christians believe that there is one God greater than all your small nature gods. Men should not pray to the wind when only He can save our souls. He sent us His son to make sure of that.'

'Save our souls from what?'

Will hesitated. 'From evil. False gods. Selfish desires.' He paused. 'To reach heaven. Where no-one will suffer as they have on earth.'

Goldie looked puzzled for a moment. Then she turned her head and asked curiously, 'Are *you* a Christian?'

'Yes,' Will replied. 'I . . . I try to be, at any rate.'

Goldie hesitated again, the look on her face half curiosity and half disgust. 'But . . . why?'

'My parents were . . . and their parents before them. My grandfather converted as a young man, and he never once looked back. I recall that much. But none of that really matters,' Will said hurriedly, seeing Goldie's brows furrow in puzzlement. 'After I lost my memory, I was . . . lost, myself. Everything was tangled up in my head. But then I met a man, a monk, who explained the true Faith to me . . . and I found a small measure of calm. When I prayed, I was able to . . . to think more clearly. To understand that there is something bigger than just myself.'

Goldie remained silent for a while, chewing at her bottom

lip. Then she said, 'I have heard things on my travels, about Christians. Your god is unnatural, they say. You disrespect all the proper ways, and you do no honour to the sprites and faeries.'

Will snorted loudly. 'No enlightened person would believe such silly superstitions,' he said, shaking his head. 'Faeries, indeed? Are you trying to make me laugh again?'

'Superstition?' Goldie repeated incredulously. 'The immortal ones exist, whether *you* believe they do or not.'

'How would you know?'

She ignored the question. 'The gods created the immortal races to help govern human affairs.'

'And how do they do that?' Will taunted. 'By pinching the lazy housewives black and blue? By making sure the milk does not curdle and by dancing on the hearth when the household is asleep?'

'You mistake common household imps and gnomes,' Goldie said haughtily, 'for immortals of true power. One of the greater faeries could blight a village or make it prosper. Could curse you or bless you. Could make a woman barren or see to it that she has a dozen children. They separate those who are beloved of the gods from those who have wronged them.'

Will patted her on the back. 'Look, here's the village. We'll have fancy-tales later, all right?'

Goldie made an unseemly face at him.


The broad wooden gates of the village were wide open when Will and Goldie strode in. Merry music came from somewhere within the crowd that milled about inside the gates.

Festively festooned maidens sashayed through the muddy streets, handing out garlands. Goldie found herself sporting a wreath of forget-me-nots that matched her eyes before long, and every one of the garland-throwers kept trying to catch Will's attention.

Will leaned over to ask a bystander what all the fuss was about, but Goldie tugged at his sleeve and burst out, 'It's a wedding!'

They were forced to follow the tide of the crowd along to the village square where, indeed, more girls were preparing an altar, and young men were carrying long tables to set down for an outdoor banquet. A fat minstrel sat on the low-hanging branch of a bushy willow tree, strumming at his lyre whilst three younger men at his feet vainly attempted to keep tune on their own instruments. And at the top of the square, in pride of place of it all . . .

'A Christian wedding,' Will remarked, astonished. There was no mistaking the low wooden building with the painted crosses, nor the aging, tonsured man in worn brown robes who stood bemusedly looking on at all the fuss going on around him. He held a silver chalice but appeared completely indifferent to whatever else was required of him. There was as yet no sign of either the bride or the groom.

Will strode up to the aged friar and bowed deeply before him, one knee going nearly to the ground. 'Greetings, Father,' he said to the surprised man.

The friar clasped his hand with immediate enthusiasm. 'Most fortunately met, good stranger, most fortunately met! What a great pleasure to meet a fellow of the Faith this side of civilization!'

'A noble follower of the Cross,' Will added. 'Thane Wilhelm.' Normally, he would not have been so free with his name and title, but there was something in him that had been stung by Goldie's remarks about Christianity, and wanted to show her some of the dignity of his religion.

The friar practically swelled with elation. 'I humbly present myself, Brother Francine, and my—congregation,' he said, with an apologetic cast to his expression. 'You find us on a most happy occasion, Wilhelm, a very happy day indeed.'

'Your congregation is very . . . boisterous,' Will remarked.

The priest sighed. 'One must forgive them, for we have not converted all of them to the Faith yet,' he said. 'They . . . well, I find this land very trying, if you must know. I studied in Rome, at the very heart of God's great civilization, but the Church willed that I go forth to serve parishes like these in this . . . this less enlightened part of the world. Alas, the community of Christian folk has actually declined since I started preaching. My congregation, sir, consists of but a single family. One family!' The friar sighed in despair. 'But where am I to find the time to gain their trust and convert them all? Me, at my time of life?'

'Is your congregation . . . the bride's family or the groom's?' Will asked politely.

'The bride's,' Brother Francine said. 'This village being too small to even have any thane resident, that's the trouble.' For a moment the look in his eyes was murderous. 'Brother Lucas in Easterling, now—he has all the luck, what with the thane there to set a fine example! But the bride's family insisted that they have the wedding *here*, ha! Half the folk from Easterling are coming here just to see—'

As Will tried to move away from the garrulous friar as

politely as possible, a worried-looking boy of about fourteen sidled up to Brother Francine.

'F-Father,' he began, not daring to make eye contact with anyone present, 'there's a—there's a problem, Fath—'

Francine stared at him. 'Well, what is it, Robin lad?'

'It's—it's m-m-my sister, Father,' Robin stuttered. 'Sh-she's not getting ready, Father, and she says—she says she's not going through with the-the-the ceremony, Father.'

Francine looked as though a thunderbolt had struck him.

'*What?*' he exploded. 'She can't do that! The thane's arriving at noon! Everything's ready!' He poked at Robin's chest. 'Your family agreed to the betrothal six months ago!'

Robin looked as though he was screwing up every ounce of his courage. 'Y-yes, but she-she-she's saying that she's changed her mind, Father.'

Brother Francine's shaven countenance turned as pale as milk. Robin seized his arm and gibbered, but the priest clutched at Will's sleeve, who was starting to regret talking to him in the first place.

'You're a good Christian man,' he said pleadingly to Will. 'This wilful girl will never listen to me. I beg you, good thane, you must help us. You must set her on the righteous path for us. Please.'

Will cleared his throat and tried to think of an escape. There was none. The friar's hand was entangled in his sleeve, and the boy, who was now supporting Francine's weight, looked more terrified than a trapped mouse.

'I—' he began, helplessly.

'Hi!' a bright voice piped out from his left. 'Pleased to meet you both. I'm Goldwine.'

The friar noticed Goldie for the first time. He stared at her as though she were some apparition, his mouth silently opening and shutting.

'You're not a leper, are you?' he finally managed to say.

'Do I look like a leper to you?' Goldie demanded. She flashed a huge grin at them all. 'Why don't I talk to the wayward bride, Will, and you take care of the priest?'

'Friar,' Will muttered automatically.

'Whatever.'


ROBIN, WHO SEEMED A LOT more articulate once he had been detached from the priest, led Goldie through the village to their family's abode.

'It'll be a disaster if Truda refuses to go through with it,' he whimpered, shaking his head. 'The man she's set to marry isn't just *anyone*. He's the thane's son!'

*Do these Christians hold beliefs about wives and husbands that are as narrow as their definition of godhood?* Goldie was mystified, and yet fascinated at the same time. *What would a Christian woman be like; as nervous as that trembling priest, or as reticent as Will?* It was this question that had prompted her to volunteer for this.

The longhouse where Truda and her family lived was clearly the pride of the village, larger than any other and surrounded by its own garden. Creeper roses decorated the front door, and bushes of holly and blackberry lined the path that led towards it. The inside was spacious, the walls decorated with plush tapestries. Goldie could not recall having been in a more luxurious dwelling. She could barely tear her eyes away from the tapestries, from following the delicate lines of weft and weave, the patterns shaping the bright scenes depicted. But Robin was ushering her away, moving towards the bedrooms, which were located off the main hall.

A middle-aged woman sat near the cold fire in the empty hall, sobbing noisily into a scrap of cloth. She waved them away. A couple of terror-struck girls younger than Goldie looked on as though the continuation of their lives depended on it. Robin ducked into a dark passageway, and Goldie followed him, not needing to crook her neck as he did.

Robin hesitated at the doorway of a small room towards the corner of the house. 'Gertruda?' he called. 'I've brought some-one to talk to you.'

There was no answer, and Goldie entered the room rather apprehensively. It was a cosy nest, the kind of place where one could curl up most comfortably in the winter. There was a nar-row white bed in the corner and a grey wolfskin upon the floor. A dress hung from a loom in the centre of the room. Some seamstress had gone to a lot of trouble on it, embroidering del-icate patterns on the pale blue cloth with golden thread, and layering the sleeves and skirt with a creamy white fabric. Goldie had never seen anything stitched quite so fine. All this was strange to her, but she had never been afraid of strangers.

She tentatively approached the figure that was sitting on the bed, chin in hand, staring at a tapestry on the wall. 'Gertruda? I'm Goldie.'

The girl turned around, surprising Goldie. She had been ex-pecting a weeping wreck, with dishevelled hair and red-raw eyes. Gertruda's face was calm. Her squarish jaw was set with a stubborn cast, and her violently curly ash-blonde hair was im-peccably combed and coiffed. Her eyes were completely dry. *I guess there is more of Will in this one*, Goldie thought, and felt quite relieved.

Gertruda looked critically at Goldie. 'You're not a leper, are you?'

'No.'

'You dress like one,' Gertruda said, watching Goldie's expression carefully. When she got no reaction, she burst out, 'Look, who are you? I was expecting the fat friar.'

Goldie shrugged demurely. 'They sent me to talk you into turning up for the wedding.' Gingerly she sat down on the foot of Gertruda's bed, and folded her hands on her knees. There was a long, pregnant silence. Goldie looked around, taking everything in. *I would certainly feel like a princess, if I lived here.*

Finally Gertruda burst out, 'Well?'

Goldie turned towards her and smiled. 'Well what?'

'I'm waiting for you to start.'

'Why should I need to say anything?' Goldie asked. 'I'm here to hear the story from *you*.'

'But you said they sent you.'

Goldie smiled again. 'I don't always obey the orders that men give me.'

'Then surely you understand!'

'You've told me nothing. How can I?'

Gertruda stared at her for a while. Then she said, 'It's the thane's son, you know. The thane's son that they want me to marry.'

'So I've heard,' Goldie said gravely.

Gertruda shook her head and buried her hands in her curly hair.

'It's all on account of Father being dead,' she began, her

words coming out all in a rush. 'I mean, I know all about responsibility. I know who I am and where we came from. My family's been here since the Romans ruled. When they left, my ancestor married his daughter to a Jutish mercenary in order to protect her and all the people of this village. *They* sacrificed things, I understand. With Father gone, it's only Mother and me and Rob—and he, well . . .' She rolled her eyes heavenward. 'I know what this marriage will mean to my family, to our village. And six months ago, I agreed to the betrothal, because of these reasons.' She broke off and stared desperately at Goldie.

'But?' Goldie encouraged her.

'But I hadn't met my bridegroom then.'

'Ah.' Goldie shifted towards the girl, interested. Gertruda did not have much of the obedience she had expected. 'And now?'

'I've met him now! And I *don't* want to marry him!' Gertruda flushed angrily. 'He's spoiled, and selfish, and cruel. And . . .' She stopped again, looking embarrassed.

'And?' Goldie prompted her. 'C'mon, you can tell *me*.'

'And I . . . I've met someone else.' Gertruda lowered her eyes and put her hands in her lap. 'And I love him, I think.' She clasped her hands to her heart.

*There's the heart of the matter*, Goldie thought. Her curiosity had been answered, now. *She is hardly that different from me, only tradition weighs on her more heavily.* She was starting to feel pity for the girl, but kept her expression neutral as she asked, 'And who is this man that you think you love?'

'His name's Doric,' Gertruda said, and Goldie could not help but register the dreamy note in her voice. 'He's a farmer's son. But he's a freeman!' she added hastily. 'His family owns their land. He's determined to acquire more until he gets the status of thane. He wants the best for me, for everyone. He's so kind, and thoughtful . . .'

'Gertruda,' Goldie said, cutting her off, 'I remember hearing your family are Christians, is that correct?'

'Yes.'

'Well, the priest also said that you are the only family in these parts that belongs to his church . . . So your young man, I must therefore surmise . . .' She glanced at the girl's suddenly stricken face, '. . . is a . . .'

'A pagan,' said Gertruda in a very small voice.

'Do you think you could give up your religion for him?' Goldie asked incredulously.

'No,' Gertruda said, looking down at her hands. She raised her eyes. 'But I think he would consider converting for me.'


GOLDIE FOUND WILL HOVERING over the stricken priest in the little church. Francine was blotting his forehead feverishly with a piece of cloth and gabbling at Will without pause for breath. Will nodded and frowned at intervals, and seemed much re-lieved when Goldie dragged him outside. The sun was nearing its midday zenith, and an air of expectation hovered over the celebrating villagers. Goldie glanced around with trepidation before delivering Will her bad news.

'You know,' Will said when she had finished, 'I don't think either of us should be interfering here.' He could not seem to look at her face, but stared away into the crowd. 'It's their own business. Their own *private* business. And we're complete strangers.'

Goldie blinked incredulously. *What is he playing at? He has to know that the matter of marriage can be life and death for a woman. Mortal women have to acquiesce to the will of their husband; it makes no sense to marry someone you can never agree with.*

She caught his gaze at last, and poured as much charm and supplication into her eyes as what she could. 'Will, I beg of you, you must do something. You must do something to stop this.'

'Me? Why me?' he demanded of her.

'My words would carry no weight with the thane, or the holy man, or the villagers,' Goldie said impatiently. 'I'm just a runaway orphan, a woman, a pagan. You are a thane, a nobleman—and you are a Christian.'

Will scowled and looked away.

'Will, if things go the wrong way, the thane could lay waste to this entire village. You must know that as well as I do.'

'She should have thought about that,' Will said coldly.

*How can he not understand?* Goldie felt as though she could burst with frustration. 'She loves another man.'


*WHY CAN'T I LOOK HER in the eye?* Will's gaze roved everywhere but towards Goldie, and he felt a coward without fully knowing why. Taking himself forcefully in hand, he looked at her.

And then, it was no longer the golden-haired waif standing there before him. The image transfixed in his mind's eye was so powerful that it wiped away the present and sent him back, ten years and more, to a different time and place.

The woman who stood before him now was tall and stately, with warm brown hair that cascaded softly to her girdled waist. Her face was round and soft, and her sad eyes the colour of the quiet ocean. She stood apart from him, and with venom in her voice she spoke, but it was a faint echo to his ears.

*'Love you? My lord of the isle, surely you cannot pretend to trust in the hollowness of such a fiction. I might have loved a different man, but I could never love you. Let us have this devil's farce over with, so that we may do our duty in the marriage bed afterwards. That is what we are here for, isn't it?'*

Will blinked. The vision of his wife on their own wedding day faded slowly, like a dream that he tried to hold back. Reality shifted around him, and he turned to see the silhouette of a man on horseback entering the village gates at a brisk trot. Sound around him died as the villagers crowded in upon him. The rider waved a banner of dyed silk above his head and spoke.

'Good people, freemen, I present to you the arrival of Thane Wulfric of Easterling, his wife and household, his loyal companions, and Wulfgar son of Wulfric, warrior-in-training and betrothed of the lady Gertruda of Leabury.'

With that introduction, and the thunder of dozens of iron-shod hooves on the turf, the thane's party entered the village.

Wulfric was easy to pick out at the head of the party; he seemed the timeless and classical illustration of thanedom. His sand-coloured beard and ringed moustaches flowed in silken rivers down his burly neck. His ceremonial iron-banded helm was decorated with the long horns of an aurochs. His shield was studded with spikes of iron and criss-crossed with pale slash-marks where foemen had swiped at him in battles past.

The rather weedy-looking lad at his right hand did not bear much resemblance to him. Nevertheless, he was attired as befit a noble warrior. Wulfgar thundered into the village square beside his lordly father, and Will turned with a start to see that

Brother Francine was trembling just behind him.

The thane and his son brought their horses to a halt, and the whole village cheered as the thane raised a single fist. Clearly, this Wulfric was a man of some military reputation. Bemused, Will watched as he dismounted from his horse and greeted Francine with grudging courtesy.

His eyes swept over Will, who was difficult to overlook in any crowd. 'And who is this?'

Will inclined his head. 'Thane Wilhelm, sir, come here by chance upon my travels. Honoured to make your noble acquaintance.'

Wulfric nodded stiffly, impatiently. He turned to the priest again.

'Something appears to be missing in this gathering, Father,' he said, respectfully but with an unspoken threat in the undertone of his voice. 'Where are the bride and her family?'

'My lord—' Father Francine quavered. The entire village, Will realized, was listening intently. He opened his own mouth and stepped forward—

'My lords,' spoke a young man from the midst of the crowd.

Everyone turned to look at the lad, who was dressed as a common farmer. 'There will be no wedding today,' he continued, and his voice was steady.

A wave of incredulity swept over the massed spectators. Maidens hustled together and whispered ferociously from beneath bowed heads. Children wailed and tugged at the skirts of their mothers, who in turn clutched at the arms of their husbands. The thane's face registered honest surprise beneath his sandy moustache. Wulfgar's expression, however, was that of a dog sent to bait the badger.

Will closed his eyes, and groaned inwardly. The lad stood before his betters, bold as silver, ignorant as dirt. Given half the chance, Will thought, Badger-baiter would tear him to bits.

Wulfgar started forward angrily. '*What* did you just say, churl?'

The lad swallowed but did not back down. 'Gertruda has changed her mind,' he spat. Will guessed that anger was fuelling the lad's idiot bravado. Fair enough, except for the moment when it all ran out and turned to fear. 'I love Gertruda, and I'll not let *you* take her from me.' A mad light came into his eyes. 'I'll fight you fair for her hand, one-on-one combat, in sight of the gods. She'll not marry you.'

Wulfgar began to frame a retort, but his father held up a hand. Excited titters ran through the crowd. They had come for a wedding, but now it looked as though they might get to see a slaying as well. The prospect thrilled them beyond telling.

'Stand down, lad,' Wulfric said, in as kindly a tone as any hornèd thane could cultivate. 'Don't be foolish. What you are suggesting is madness. Why, we have not even heard from—'

'*Let them fight.*'

A sudden hush fell over the assembled crowd as the lone figure of the bride herself came forward. Gertruda looked very small as she stood there, Will thought. Not much of a figure to die for. But her jaw was squared in determination. 'Let them fight,' she repeated. 'What Doric said is true. I no longer wish to marry Wulfgar. Let them fight.'

Will moved forward.

'Aye,' he said loudly, transposing himself next to Doric. 'Allow this fray, my lord, and allow my friend Doric to name me as his champion.'

Doric stared at him. 'Who the hell are you?'

Will clapped him on the back. 'Why, do you not know your friend in need?' he said with a wide grin. He looked towards the thane for support.

'Why should you want to help this fool?' Wulfgar burst out.

Will shrugged. 'Because I agree with the lady; no freewoman should be forced to marry someone she does not want. Because the lad here'—he gestured to Doric—'is clearly no warrior, and cannot hope to win against an experienced swordsman. And furthermore, if the lad *were* somehow to win this match, some no doubt might think he cheated by using pagan magic, which no-one could accuse me of, for I am a good Christian.' Behind him, Brother Francine, ever dependable, made the sign of the Catholic cross. Will continued, 'Thane Wulfric, I implore you. You know that this is the only reasonable course of action, given the words that have already been said.'

Wulfric looked from the young farmer's boy to his son, who was practically quivering with rage. 'I'll admit,' he growled, 'my son would do better to fight a true warrior.' He looked at Will. 'I expect you not to go easy on him.'

Will bowed in acquiescence.

'My lords,' Brother Francine piped up, 'am I to understand that this is to be a duel to the death, as per common law?'

'No,' said Will and Wulfric almost simultaneously.

Will grinned dangerously. 'Let the victor be the first to draw blood. I have no hunger to kill anybody today.' Young Wulfgar bristled indignantly.

It was not long before the dusty village square was transformed into a duelling ring. With much excitement, the villagers moved the feasting benches into a crude circle, behind which the crowd gathered. Chairs were brought for the thane, his wife, and his principal companions, and set atop the wedding platform for a view over the crowd. The combatants were taken into the church by Father Francine and required to surrender up their arms and armour. Wulfric had apparently decreed a fray by the sword, and had given Francine two identical Saxon shortswords, which the friar set gingerly upon the altar. Will struggled out of his rusted chainmail, which Wulfgar smirked at disdainfully, and put his belt and knife in the hands of the friar. The thane's minstrel made an entrance.

'My lord,' he said, addressing Will, 'I have been instructed to obtain your name and titles for the announcement of the combat.'

'Will.'

The minstrel pursed his lips as though he had just swallowed a sour currant. 'Will . . . who?' he urged.

'Just Will,' Will said. 'I was a noble, it's true, but now I am merely nobody.'

The minstrel puffed up like a bullfrog. 'A warrior like yourself cannot be merely nobody!'

Will shrugged indifferently.

The minstrel stalked off, inflated with indignation. He brushed past the lad Doric, who was coming in, without a word.

Doric wasted no time in niceties, but looked accusingly at Will, his brown eyes flashing. 'What exactly is it you're playing at? I demand to know what you intend after you have won this match.'

Will smiled grimly. 'What can I do,' he said, rolling up the sleeves of his stained tunic, 'to convince you that all I intend is to ensure that you win the hand of your fair lady?'

The boy glared at him. *'Why?'*

'Honestly? I'm not sure.' Will laced his sleeves around his elbows, exposing several of his minor scars. 'All I can say is, it looks like God meant me to intervene in this affair. Are you ungrateful?'

'No.' The boy folded his arms. 'Unless you lose.'

'Lose?' Will winked at him. 'Against this green boy Wulfgar?'

THE COMBATANTS MADE THEIR ENTRANCE to the ring, the friar shuffling along behind them. Wulfgar kept giving Will strange looks, his eyes narrowed into slits and half-turning his head. No doubt this was intended to be an intimidating glare; Will thought he looked constipated. He gave Wulfgar a cheerful smile and a wave. The boy looked ready to burst.

A cheer went up from the crowd as the thane's minstrel leapt into the ring to announce the match. 'Good people of Leabury,' he began, stretching out both his arms, 'honoured Thane Wulfric,'—he bowed—'Lady of Easterling, my lady of Leabury, I present a duel between warriors for the purpose of winning a lady's hand. On my left, Wulfgar of Easterling,'—the crowd gave a ragged cheer—'on my right,'—he hesitated only the tiniest bit—'Will Nobody.'

Chuckles coursed through the crowd, led by Will himself. *Will Nobody? Well, I suppose it sounds better than Will with No Memory.* He bowed theatrically, and the villagers erupted into laughter.

'May the best man win,' the minstrel concluded, thin-lipped.

Father Francine approached. 'I hereby declare this match

between warriors to be carried out in the sight of the Lord our God, in the understanding that He will bring to victory he whose cause is the most righteous.' He held forth the wooden cross around his neck, which both combatants in turn bent to kiss. 'I declare the winner of this duel to be he who first draws blood from his adversary. God is watching,' he warned. 'Fight with honour.'

The combatants hefted their swords as the priest ambled away.

Wulfgar started forward, scuffing up dust in front of him.

*How predictable.* Will moved languidly backwards, forcing Wulfgar to go through his own dust cloud to get back on the attack, rendering his move obsolete.

Wulfgar came on through the dust, his eyes watering, and their swords crossed twice, once low, once high. Will parried easily, moving along the perimeter of the ring. Wulfgar was forced onto the defensive, slashing wildly as he tried to press forward. His form was good, but he was tragically slow. As Will quickly paced towards his right, he slashed wildly, still aiming for an opponent that was already gone. Will stuck out a foot in front of him.

Wulfgar fell heavily to his knees, dropping his sword, and scrabbled wildly in the dirt to retrieve it. Hoots of laughter came from those in the crowd who had seen the action take place. Will leaned his sword airily against his shoulder, waiting for him. When he saw precisely how long it was going to take for the boy to retrieve his sword and fumble back into a fighting stance, he turned around, taking a deep bow for the enjoyment of the crowd. Then he turned back, timing it perfectly to meet the thrust of Wulfgar's sword. The villagers gasped in admiration.

Will moved exactly three steps backwards, parrying his opponent's blade perfectly with each step. At the end of the third step, he slid his sword against Wulfgar's, coming in close as he forced the boy back, brought the crossguards of the two swords together, and flicked. Wulfgar's blade spun out of his hand.

This time he dove for it, making the villagers crow with amusement. Will lazily moved towards him, and the lad scrambled to his feet, thrusting the blade out in front of him and fumbling the guard position. Will twisted to his left, bringing his blade into the wide opening left by Wulfgar, but instead of cutting him, he brought the flat of the sword down hard on the boy's buttocks. Wulfgar howled with pain and indignation, and the crowd howled with laughter.

Red-faced, Wulfgar ran at Will, abandoning every last vestige of discipline in his frenzy to get at his opponent. Will easily parried his wild thrusts, tripped him up again, and as he hit the ground, Will deftly brought his sword down, point first, to hover over the back of his neck.

The crowd went suddenly silent. The friar had decreed 'first blood,' but they knew that it could be blood drawn from a mortal wound as well as a scratch, and even a death wound if the fight came to that. Will sensed the thane, on the edge of his vision, jumping to his feet. The fight so far had been comical; he'd enjoyed putting the arrogant boy in his place, but this swift stroke had reminded everybody that warriors normally duelled to kill. They gaped in suspense.

Carefully and deliberately, Will drew the point of his sword down the boy's exposed vertebrae. The lad shuddered on his knees.

'Let me give you three good lessons today, Wulfgar,' Will

said vehemently, low enough so that only the boy could hear him. A trickle of blood blossomed at the tip of his blade. 'Never underestimate the ability of an unknown opponent. Never mock your adversary before you have even begun. And *never* try to intimidate your elders and betters.' He drew up his sword, reversed the blade in his hand, and held out his other hand to help the boy to his feet. 'You will only anger them, and get yourself killed.'

The boy stared at his outstretched hand. Will stood quietly. For a long moment Wulfgar seemed to be duelling inside, between his anger and his common sense.

Then he reached out and took Will's hand, getting heavily to his feet. The crowd started cheering, and Will handed Wulfgar his sword, allowing him to join in the glory of the applause. He bowed again to his audience.

Slowly, Thane Wulfric descended from his platform. All fell silent once more when they saw him walk solemnly over to Will, his hard jaw set, his moustache bristling. Acting on an instinct for survival, Will went to his knees as the thane approached, only rising when he was motioned to do so, when Wulfric was close enough to stare at him eyeball to eyeball. He was exactly the same height as Will, but wider, a huge man and frightening potential adversary. His left hand clenched on the hilt of his own sword, slung by his side. Finally, he spoke.

'You've got some nerve on you, Will Nobody,' he growled.

Will did not look down. 'I am sorry if I have offended, my lord.'

'*If!*' The thane laughed harshly. 'Do not be coy with me, Will Nobody.' He wielded every word like a whip, as though he were chastising a dog. 'Every move you made here today was calculated to offend. Every humiliation.'

Wulfgar began to speak, but his father silenced him with a gesture of his hand. 'Have you anything to say for yourself?' he demanded, looking straight at Will.

'Yes.' Looking into the man's eyes, Will thought he knew what to do. 'Your son needs a better master-at-arms, my lord.'

There was silence for a long, heart-stopping moment. Then it was broken by the harsh sound of Wulfric bursting into sudden, explosive laughter. He laughed until he was bent double and there were tears coming out of his eyes. Will didn't pretend to see the joke.

The thane clapped him on the back. 'Well said!' he boomed. 'Indeed, Will Nobody, it is not every day we see a man of your calibre in these parts.' He held up a hand to silence the noise that had broken out amongst the crowd. Will found the faces of Doric and Gertruda, stricken in the front row.

'Come,' said Wulfric, and motioned them forward. He gave Doric a long, appraising look, then turned to Gertruda. 'This is the man you would choose, girl? This is the one you want?'

'Yes, my lord.' Gertruda's voice was barely above a whisper.

The thane threw out his arms expansively. 'Then you shall marry him today!' he proclaimed. 'Come, I have commanded it. We'll ally our families some other way, perhaps foster your brother with my daughters. We have come to see a wedding, and so I decree we shall have one.' He glared around at the villagers, who scattered. 'Prepare the feast! Festoon the church! And someone, for the love of God Almighty, get the bridegroom baptized!'

THE DAY ERUPTED INTO EXCITEMENT twice as great as before. Will and Goldie, the hero and heroine of the hour, were press-ganged into major roles in the preparations. Wulfric settled himself in the village square and entertained Gertruda's petrified family with vivid tales of the hunt, wherein people were invariably injured by wild boars and raging aurochs, at the top of his considerable voice. A group of five men, Will included, dragged Doric to his homestead, put him in a nightshirt, and with much ribbing and bawdy jesting, accompanied him to the village pond. There they looked on as Brother Francine dunked the bridegroom soundly in the water and proclaimed him to be reborn in the spirit of the Christ, saviour of all men's souls. To the friar's gratified astonishment, at least a dozen more youngsters came forward afterwards, begging to be baptized as well. Doric's escort took him home to be washed, combed, and dressed, and Will was given the unenviable task of explaining what it meant to be a Christian to Doric's disapproving family.

As they marched young Doric to the altar, Will thought that he had probably never been to a party quite as rowdy as this. Fully half the participants were already roaring drunk, and evening had not even arrived yet. The Saxon warriors from Easterling were playing at some obscure game of chance with a pair of villagers, with much howling and cursing every time the tricksters swindled another shilling from them. There were a full dozen musicians now, and the honeyed mead was flowing like water. Even the thane looked tipsy, and Wulfgar, to Will's amusement, had fallen asleep in the seat next to his father.

The appearance of the bride, at last, caused everyone to briefly sober up. They assembled into a solemn gathering so fast that Will thought someone must have worked a spell. The bride was radiant, her blue dress bringing out the colour of her eyes, and her tresses falling in soft ringlets beneath the flowers her handmaidens had woven into her hair.

But then Will caught sight of Goldie, at the bride's right hand, her hair shining like liquid gold in the setting sun, and he lost sight of the other girls. There was something otherworldly about the waif, and he couldn't tell what it was. Though she stood next to them, in a way she was also very far away. Like a Welsh slave girl who had been the daughter of a king, perhaps. Or a Frankish destrier that had been put into a field with the common herd, who ran with them but still remained more than what they would ever be.

Were it not for Goldie, none of this would have taken place. She had saved the day, even though he had been the one hold-ing the sword. Some strange feeling tugged at Will's heart, the memory of the urgency in her voice when she had asked him to intervene, the kindness in her wide blue eyes and the way she had taken his hand gently in her own that morning. She was his to protect now, and Will suddenly knew that he would never fail her.

As he stood in the assembled audience, listening to a young couple exchange their wedding vows, it was to Will as though his own wife appeared by his side, clad in the raiment of their own wedding day.

'You don't remember much about our own marriage, do you?' she teased, looking wistfully at the bridal couple.

'No,' Will admitted. 'Now I get the idea that, perhaps, I'm better off that way.'

She turned and looked at him. 'Do you really think so?'

'You know,' Will said, 'when they told me I had a wife, I

thought—foolishly, I suppose—that we loved each other very much. I tried to form a picture of you in my mind.' His voice saddened. 'I thought about how happy we should have been together, and how devastating your death. I imagined our sadness in never having a child.' He heaved a deep sigh. 'Seems like the only thing I got right is how beautiful you were.' He gestured meaninglessly. 'But we must have been married for more than a decade, because I recall being even younger than Doric at our wedding. And now, I can't even remember your name.'

She smiled at him. 'It's Aedfrith.'

Will was stunned. He gazed off into the distance, wondering that his own mind had recovered this dearly-sought-for snippet. But he knew that it was true. Somehow, he knew.

'Aedfrith,' he whispered.

Someone was tugging at his sleeve. He looked down, and the spell broke as he saw Goldie beside him. The ceremony was over, the bride and groom settled at the banquet table, and a group nearby were starting to sing a spontaneous song about, he realized, his victory against Wulfgar. Goldie gestured towards them. 'You're famous now,' she said with a smile.

Will listened. 'I have a new name.'

Goldie cocked her head to the tune. 'Will Who Spanked Wulfgar?'

Will ran a hand theatrically over his moustache. 'That's me,' he said.

Goldie laughed. Will looked down in surprise at the sound.

'Come on, Will Who Spanked Wulfgar,' she said. 'We have seats at the high table.'

# Chapter Three

# The Sea-Demon

*I remember the night I left Fort Horsa with vivid clarity. How could I not? After all, those are my first living memories.*

*I camped in the dark forest out of sight of any potential observer, and there beneath the trees I strove to make sense of what I was.*

*My horse looked curiously on as I poked and prodded my own flesh in the light of my fire, stripped myself of the clothes I was wearing, clawed and pummelled my own head trying to remember . . . what? Anything. Anything! I could speak and ride and build a fire in the woods, but of myself I knew nothing. I could recall no family, no childhood, no human experiences of any sort . . . yet I knew I must have had them, else how could Thane Wilhelm, his lands and his soldiers, his* dead wife and waiting peasants, ever have come to be?

When my head began to ache with the weight of these questions, I finally let myself take refuge in despair. I would never remember. I need only know myself from this point forward, and Thane Wilhelm, for better or worse, was gone.

In the long hours of that first night, I examined myself.

My skin was pale as milk, but wherever I touched, my body was hard and lean, little flesh to spare. It seemed that I had spent most of my life on campaign, dressed in armour from head to toe, living off the land rather than enjoying my wealth. There were old scars on my arms and shoulders, and the palms of my hands were callused, as tough and supple as the leather of my sword's scabbard.

I felt for the aching gash along the top of my forehead, an inch-long cut that might have been where I hit my head and lost my memory. This invited me to find all the other marks of injury upon my body, too many to count. In addition to my smaller scars, I had five old wounds that ached at a touch in the damp. One, a long swordstroke, stretched all the way from my left shoulder to the small of my back. Another on my upper right arm seemed to have been the result of the mauling of some animal, for it showed the marks of fangs. There was a gash at the bottom of my ribcage that was clearly an arrow wound; I recalled that, and savoured the remembrance. There was another like it on the outer muscle of my right thigh. The last was a slash across my collarbone, which looked to be more recent than the others.

I realized that I was quite tall; I towered over most of the people I had met thus far. My body was covered in brown hair, thick across my chest and my manhood, like the pelt of some wild animal. Correspondingly, the hair on my head and face grew thick and luxuriant. When I cut off some of it to examine in my hand, I saw that it was darker than the common shade I had seen amongst others. Though all over my body *it grew coarse, it had not yet started to turn grey. I realized then that I was a young man still. Might my features be comely? That I could not know, though I glimpsed hazily in the fog of my memories certain encounters . . .*

*The body I grew acquainted with that night was tough and hard, and I felt little compunction about driving it to its limits. It is different with Goldie.*

*She is still too thin, still eats like a horse, but she has begun to look healthier. She will always be small of stature, but one can now imagine her taking up the role of a churl's wife, holding a babe at her breast, dressed in warm wool with her shining hair cascading over her shoulders. With that hair shining like molten gold in the light of our campfire, one can imagine how it might look were she to lounge on a rug before a roaring hearth, how it would feel to lie beside her, to stroke her hair and hold her close—*

*This is the truth of it: the half-starved waif is beautiful, desirable to me, and I cannot help but feel shamed by these malformed yearnings. I long to take Goldie in my arms and proclaim my undying devotion to her. I want to feel her warm the blanket beside me. I want to know what it's like to love carelessly, to lose myself in pure hedonism . . . as did Thane Wilhelm, all too often, as those ever-strengthening glimpses of my past have shown me.*

*It is no fault of Goldie's that she is beautiful. Men use this as an excuse for their actions, when they succumb to their own unforgivable flaws. She can be nothing other than the way God made her, with her shining hair and innocent smile. Yet men who look upon such beauty will not rest until they have corrupted it.*

*I will not stoop to these desires, not ever reveal the face of my depravity to her. She keeps her charms to herself; shows no interest in*

LIGHTNING FLASHED, TEARING THE SKY in two. The sea raged and roared, echoing the growling of the thunder. The wind shrieked across the moor, whipping up wet sand from the beach and harrying the waves into a frenzy.

'We've got to find shelter!' Will shouted above the noise of the storm.

Goldie didn't answer. It was pointless. She could hardly hear Will, and his voice was louder than hers. She stumbled on, gripping her cloak tightly against the wind. She wondered if she should suggest that they seek lower ground, but that was pointless, too. The only lower ground from here was the beach, where the sea surged angrily up and down, throwing spray fifteen feet into the air as it crashed against the cliffs.

*The cliffs . . .*

She grabbed at Will's arm as she saw the cave, only a short walk ahead beneath a rocky mound where the cliffs began. She pointed.

'Too dangerous!' Will shouted. He cupped his hands around his mouth. 'What about the sea?'

Goldie drew herself closer and shouted in his ear, 'It's above the tide line! Look! The bushes grow *below*!'

The wind blew at them with force, whipping Goldie's long hair over both their faces. Will yelled back, 'But the storm!' The wild waves surged far up the beach, and it could not be certain where the water would end.

'We stay here, we perish!' Goldie shouted with finality.

Will looked ahead, doubt in his dark brown eyes. A squall of rain whipped across them, water carried horizontally with the wind. Will turned back to her, and nodded. He seized her arm. 'Come on!' He broke into a run, half-supporting her at the same time, shielding her from the worst of the rain with his bulk.

*One more thing he's useful for,* Goldie found herself thinking. *I shall miss him, one day when we part at last.*

THE STORM RAGED OVER THE SEA and across the barren moor. Will hadn't wanted to turn east—it was the exact opposite of the direction he should be going—but there was plague in the kingdom of Deira, and rumours of war all along the north-western hills. So he had taken a detour, heading towards the sea. There was supposed to be a hamlet near the coast some-where close by, but the storm had come upon them before they could find it.

Will and Goldie no longer looked much like the bedraggled travellers that had arrived at the wedding in Leabury. Their new friends had delayed them solicitously, even the thane, who seemed to have taken a liking to the man who had humiliated his son.

'What is a warrior of your calibre doing without a host?' he had asked, draining mug after mug of sweet mead.

'Returning home,' Will had replied.

Wulfric had offered him the position of master-at-arms for his nobles at Easterling, but Will had politely declined. The thane had insisted he retire his old chainmail, and that Will could not refuse. As replacement, Wulfric had presented Will with a sleeveless shirt of leather armour, held in place with straps over the shoulders and split at the sides below the waist for mobility. It was an old-fashioned garment, something a Roman soldier might have spent silver for. Landed thanes like Wulfric tended to be traditionalists, but Will had to admit that the boiled leather was probably as tough as his old rusted mail anyway. Plus, leather was lighter and easier to care for on the road.

Gertruda had wanted to give Goldie an embroidered apron with the dress to match, but Goldie had refused on the grounds that it would never survive the journey to the north. So now she was wearing a practical brown travelling tunic, white breeches and garters, soft boots and a sheepskin cloak. Gertruda had been very generous and immensely hospitable. Will suspected that he had gained weight whilst sojourning there, and Goldie had lost her pinched, hungry aspect.

She certainly felt quite solid as he helped her up the cliff in the dark. Will tried his best to be careful, but the impulse to reach cover got the best of him, and he nearly slipped headlong down the wet rocks more than once. When they finally reached the welcoming cover of the cave mouth, he was bent double, out of breath from the climb. Goldie, who had happily leaned most of her weight on him for the ascent, examined the rocky retreat and declared that it was well above the reach of the sea.

There was nothing to start a fire with. Will squatted down on a rock in the darkness and watched the storm rage, shivering to the touch of the icy wind that snaked through the cave.

He turned as he felt Goldie crouch down next to him, putting a hand on his shoulder to steady herself. She unlaced the cloak from her shoulders and turned it inside out, exposing the dry inner lining. Will's own cloak was soaked through, and he undid the clasp that held it at his shoulder. Goldie began to dry his hair with her cloak, none too gently.

'Are you trying to strangle me?' Will took the cloak from her. Goldie looked briefly embarrassed, then stood up and found Will's pack, ferreting inside it for something to eat.

'It won't be a very comfortable night,' Will remarked.

'Better than staying out there.' Goldie turned towards him just as another bolt of lightning flashed across the black sky. 'This storm is full of portents. The faeries are riding across the heath, I could feel it in my blood. Better for mortals tonight to stay within walls.'

'Your superstitions are ridiculous, girl.' Will turned to look at her, resting his back against the rock. 'The storm could have killed us on its own, no help needed from pixies or sprites or little river-men.'

'Oh, you would not be killed if you were taken by the faeries.' Goldie tilted his pack. 'Why is it suddenly so dark?'

Will blinked. She was right; he had been able to see the glint of her hair in the reflected witch-light of the clouds just a moment ago, and now there was only her outline in the darkness. Goldie sat up impatiently and tried to drag his pack into the light, and then found that every corner of the cave was as dark as the next. She frowned and looked out of the mouth of the cave.

'I can't even see the ocean waves,' she said, and got to her feet.

A horrible premonition suddenly overcame Will, and he jumped up and forestalled her.

'What?' Goldie whispered as he seized her arm.

Will's heart was hammering in his chest. There seemed far too little air in the cave, though it had been draughty before. The cave was actually growing darker, and Goldie was fading from view, though he kept his grip on her hand. Will felt as though he might scream. The darkness seemed alive, as though some poison had poured itself into the cave to join them. Goldie's breath was coming faster than usual, catching in her throat.

Will closed his eyes, forcing himself to calm down, overcome the panic that gripped him.

He opened his eyes again. He could see nothing.

With a sudden squelching sound, something struck him out of the blackness.

Goldie screamed in his ear, and Will lunged, losing his grip on her hand. He had almost lost his footing. His grasping hands closed around something slippery. With an oath he released it, feeling a long, thick, damp shape slip serpentinely through his fingers. He stepped backwards, and tripped. Unseen appendages writhed beneath his feet. One of the slimy things closed over his wrist, dragging him towards the mouth of the cave. Pulling back for all he was worth, he resisted, won free for a moment—and then felt more seething tentacles close around his ankles, around his waist, around his neck.

Frantically Will reached for his sword, which was gone—it was attached to his pack, too ostentatious to carry on the road, and he had only his knife on him. Whilst his hands were still free, he writhed to locate it. With divine providence he felt his hand close over its hilt. Pulling it free, he stabbed at the thing slowly closing around his neck.

The knife's blade bounced harmlessly off the slippery surface of the tentacle.

Furiously, Will tried again, and again, stabbing, cutting, clawing with his fingernails when nothing else availed him. The screams that bubbled up in his constricting throat never came free.

He looked up, and realized, without any doubt, that he had been the idiot to pay no heed to Goldie's superstitions.

The creature that had him in its grasp was limned with a silver light, the kind of ghost-light that sailors talked of seeing in the furthest parts of the ocean. It illuminated the horrible sight of a thousand writhing coils closing in, ready to wrap securely around and squeeze the life out of him. He imagined what it was going to be like to die in that cold, slimy embrace. Vaguely, he hoped that he would lose consciousness before his bones were crushed inside his skin.

Out of nowhere, a silvery flash seared his vision, and a terrible wail was heard over his own struggles for breath. The tentacles retracted their grip, and Will gathered failing strength and fought himself free.

Goldie's shadow filled his vision. With his sword in hand, her movements were amateurish—but deadly efficient. Tentacles thudded to the floor around her, streaking her with black blood. The sword in her hand was pure silver against the blackness of the beast she fought.

Even as she chopped and swiped at tentacle after tentacle, the beast pressed its advantage and surrounded her with thousands of appendages. At the mouth of the cave, Will thought that he could see the outline of the monster now, silhouetted against the storm. It resembled a gigantic human shape from the waist up; below, its tentacles slithered in all directions over the roiling surface of the sea.

Had he been a weaker man, Will might have fallen to his knees and begged for mercy, entreating this dark god to spare him. But then and there, setting aside all rational arguments against the existence of such things, he decided that they would not die crushed in the maw of this evil creature.

'Goldie!' Will ran towards her, dodging the squirming severed tentacles that fell everywhere, and caught hold of her, dragging her backwards as the monster reached for them. 'We've got to find another way out here!' Giving her a meaningful push towards the back of the cave, he took the sword from her hand and faced the monster in her place, moving backwards as he did so, dodging its slimy grasp, waiting for it to overstep its advantage.


GOLDIE MOVED CAUTIOUSLY INTO THE DARKNESS, holding on to the cave wall. It turned her suddenly to the left, and she followed it to the other side. Sickeningly, she realized that she had reached the true back wall of the cave. They were trapped. Desperately her hands scrabbled in the dark for any hole—she could find none. But as hope started to fail, she felt a whisper of fresh air on the top of her head.

Hoisting herself up by a protruding rock, Goldie felt along the roof of the cave. Yes—there was a skylight here, a tunnel through rock and earth, and beyond her head she could feel moisture from the rain outside, and breathe fresh air. She didn't know if the tunnel would be wide enough to admit her, let alone Will. Did that really matter? They could force themselves out if needs be.

She jumped back to the ground, and for a moment was awestruck by the tableau before her—the figure of the warrior fighting for all he was worth against a gigantic monster that had arisen from the salty sea. There was lightning in the background, lending the scene a cold, violent light.

'Will!' she shouted, and he turned towards her voice. Surmising quickly what she had found, he started towards her.

'There's a tunnel to the outside at the roof,' Goldie quickly explained, pushing him towards the draught. Tentacles snaked into the cave after them, slithering along the walls, seeking to find them and block all escape. Everything was covered in its blood now; it did not seem to deter the monster one bit.

Will shoved her behind him as he raised his sword again. '*You* go first.'

'No!' she protested.

'Goldie, if I don't get through, we'll both be stuck,' Will said urgently. 'You're smaller than me. It makes better sense.' He gripped his sword, and scowled at her. 'Go! I'll hold the monster off, then I'll follow you.'

Goldie stood for a moment, irresolute, but then realized there was no point to arguing. Will was fighting again, but his movements were slower than before, his brow glistening with sweat and his breath coming in gasps. She had to move, if there was any chance of getting away.

She turned towards the cave wall and hoisted herself up into the darkness, feeling around until she found the tunnel and clung to the walls. It was perfectly wide enough. She could make it—but Will needed to come after her.

'Will!' she called into the darkness below. 'Come on!'

There was no answer but an oath. Goldie's heart constricted inside her. Impulse told her to return, that Will was in trouble.

Goldie took a deep breath. Her limbs trembled with the effort of holding herself aloft.

What would she do if she went back? Face down a centuries-old immortal monster and ask her nicely to return her protector to her? It would never happen. Goldie shook with helpless anger.

*She won't kill him,* she told herself. She could feel tears pricking at her eyes. *When those of the other world strike, they do not kill outright.*

But sometimes, those who had been taken into the faery realm faced a fate worse than death—

She had to leave. She couldn't risk the sea-monster noticing that she had escaped.

Crying both with concern for Will and at the pain of keeping herself aloft, Goldie dragged herself up the walls of the tunnel, using her feet as a hoist. The tunnel grew steadily wider, and the rock gave way to earth, which slipped beneath her grip. Soon she was supporting herself, it felt, by a feather. She stretched further, clawing and scrabbling at the shifting dirt, knowing only that she could not fall back. If she did, darkness would take her.

She finally felt the tunnel take a horizontal turn. Throwing herself along it with relief, she crawled the last few feet to the surface.

She emerged into the storm. She was on a hill covered with bracken and gorse, overlooking the ocean and the formidable monster that had risen out of it. Keeping low in the furze, she watched silently as the tentacled giant-woman drew a convalescent figure triumphantly forth from the cave.

Tears ran down Goldie's face as she recognized Will swinging helplessly from the tentacles. She couldn't tell whether he was dead or only unconscious.

The storm had blown out most of its strength. The wind dropped, giving way to a penetrating, icy rain.

A whirlpool formed in the dark sea, and the tentacled woman slithered over the surface of the ocean towards it, her prey dangling in her clutches. They sank into the whirlpool, vanished beneath the surface, and the sea became still, washing steadily up and down the beach, swirling away dark gluts of blood left by the battle.

'Will,' Goldie whispered.

Was the creature gone? Goldie steeled herself. Some instinct told her that the monster would not return, not anytime soon, and so she crept back into the cave via the tunnel.

The cave was slimy with blood. Goldie stepped on severed tentacles, which squished wetly underneath her feet. Revulsion overcame her and she threw up. The smell of blood was everywhere, underwritten by a nasty, fishy stench. She gave up on finding anything useful, and decided to leave, but then spotted something glinting coldly in the darkness.

It was Will's sword. Goldie gingerly recovered it from the gore. Looking further, she found a knife, too, from which she surmised that Will was now completely unarmed, wherever he was.

Goldie remembered how Will had stabbed fruitlessly with his knife at the tentacles of the creature, and again she looked at the sword in her hand. The steel felt curiously alive, as it had when she had drawn it from its scabbard, and something in her fancied that it was thirsty for more blood.

'Is it the blood of monsters you seek?' she whispered. 'You shall have it, I promise you.'

Goldie left the cave and stood upon the little hill, gazing around. Now that the storm had calmed, she could see an isolated homestead close by, with animal enclosures and a large wooden longhouse. Perhaps the people there could tell her where Will had been taken. She had to find him, and find him soon, find him before—

She set off down the hill.

GOLDIE RAPPED LOUDLY AT THE DOOR of the house. It opened smoothly after a few moments, revealing the countenance of a stout woman in a long underdress. Goldie became conscious of the fact that she was covered in blood, though none of it was hers. The goodwife went quite pale, and made the sign of the Christian cross over her breast.

'Be you a demon, or something of the ilk of monsters?' she breathed.

Before Goldie could answer to that, a tall man with brown whiskers appeared behind the woman. 'Stand aside, wife, it's just a girl!' he cried with a hint of the same accent Will had, and led Goldie inside. 'Are you hurt? Whose blood is that?'

'I'm not hurt. This is the blood of—' Goldie hesitated. 'Of the monster that dwells in the sea off this coast.'

The goodwife's complexion paled, and her husband furrowed his bushy brows. 'You've escaped the clutches of the sea-demon?' he demanded.

'I did—but my companion was not so lucky,' Goldie said.

The husband shook his head, and the woman put her arm around Goldie. 'Pray for your friend's soul then, girl,' she said. 'For it's gone to judgment now. None ever return from the sea-demon's lair, nought but bare bones.'

As the woman spoke, a host of fair-haired children appeared from the recesses of the house and crowded around, asking questions. 'Why is she covered in blood?' 'Did the sea-demon get her?' 'Why isn't she dead?'

Goldie pulled away from the goodwife, gripping Will's sword in her hands. 'Will is *not* dead!' she cried. 'Not yet! Not if I can get to him first!' She turned to the woman's husband. 'Tell me where the demon makes her lair.'

The woman put a hand on her heart. 'The demon's lair? No-one knows where that is. None but—'

'I know where it is,' one of the children said.

His parents turned as though to shush him, but the lad—all of thirteen, by Goldie's estimation—stood before her with a defiant look in his eyes. 'I'll show you where it is.'

'Ulbert, for the love of God Almighty—!' his mother began.

He turned to face her. 'Mother, look at this stranger,' he said. 'Have none of you seen that she carries a sword dark with blood and rank with the smell of the demon that has terrorized our village for so long? The blood of that monster has been shed by her with that blade—something not even the best warriors sent by our thane have been able to do!' The lad stood aloft like the speaker at a public meeting. 'I will show you her lair if you promise to rid us of the demon forever.'

'Nothing would give me greater joy tonight,' Goldie said grimly.

'Wait,' Ulbert's father interjected, taking his son by the arm.

He faced Goldie. 'Is the monster wounded?'

She nodded.

'Then she will not be killing your friend just yet,' the farmer said. 'She will rest, heal her wounds, and most likely aim to enjoy her meal later, when she has recovered from the fight. Not to mention,' he gestured at the bloodstained sword, 'that she will be after you, too, for offering her such injury. I suggest you wait until dawn, when the sea has subsided and the sky is clear, before accosting her in her lair.'

'You'll need be a strong swimmer to cross to her cave,' Ulbert said. 'She dwells underwater at the bottom of the seabed.'

Raindrops pattered against the roof of the longhouse. Goldie could still hear the rumbling of the sea far away, the tide rising though the force of the storm had gone. She was wet through, and registered that fact for the first time since she had lost Will. And she was cold. If she sat down, she might not be able to move again until morning.

'At the break of day,' she finally agreed, taking the place on a bench that was offered to her. 'No later. I will never forgive myself if I let him die.' She hesitated. 'May I have food and shelter for the night?'

'If you rid us of that monster,' the goodwife replied without hesitation, 'you are welcome to help yourself to anything we own.'


WILL REGAINED HIS CONSCIOUSNESS in a most unpleasant fashion.

He awoke to stifling darkness and a sense of slimy, moist walls all about him. The floor beneath him was squishy to the touch and moved when he prodded it. There was a rancid smell all around him, as of rotting meat.

To his horror, the walls around him suddenly opened to the sky and a forceful wind shot him out of the damp cave to a floor of rock.

Dripping with slime and stinking of rotten fish, Will looked up to see the monster of the thousand tentacles squatting over him. With a sense of disgust he realized that he had just been spat out of its mouth. With loathing he examined the sticky residue all over him and wished, fervently, that he had been dropped in the ocean instead.

Will realized almost immediately that he was in a cell. This cave was closed on all sides except for a narrow barred exit that he could see beyond the creature's bulk.

Will moved. The giantess seemed to be watching him, though it was difficult to tell. Her head was a good twenty feet up in the air, and the gloom of the cave rendered everything to dreary tones of grey and sickly green. Seeking to steady himself, he groped around on the floor and laid his hand on something hard and brittle. Retrieving it, he realized he was holding a fragment of skull, undoubtedly human. He decided to keep his hands close to his body until he shook off the disorientation.

In his blurry vision, the ogress appeared to be shrinking. It was some time before Will realized that his eyes weren't as faulty as he thought: the monster indeed *was* shrinking, and becoming human, in appearance at least. She shrunk and her tentacles retracted until she was the size and shape of a woman.

Will tried to blink away the fogginess in his head. It was difficult to find the form of the hideous monster in this lovely, silvery-glowing young woman. She walked towards him on two perfectly proportioned feet, completely naked. Her long hair coiled around her slim body like seaweed, a greenish glow hidden in damp tresses of raven black. Her eyes were the colour of molten silver, gleaming in a face that recalled the smooth surface of a precious marine pearl. Yet despite her beauty, there was a savagery about her that made him recoil even as he admired the shape of her breasts, the perfect curve of her hips. Congealed blood streaked her skin, dripping to the rocky floor from the many wounds lacerating her glossy limbs.

Will stared wordlessly up at her, half admiring, half abhorring. She was so different from the monster he had fought that he felt half-inclined to believe she was here to help him. Yet common sense whispered to him; half-remembered stories fought their way to the surface of his mind, cautionary tales of beautiful water-monsters who devoured the unfortunate men whom they ensnared, their beauty nothing more than a silken lure meant to entrap and enslave the proud heroes who were found weak against their charms.

The men in the stories never escaped alive.

The woman ran a hand down her forearm, flicking blood towards the ground. 'Well, what have I snatched?' she asked coyly, showing sharp teeth as she approached Will, who shrank away.

'I'm so lucky to have picked the male, when that little chit of a maid was escaping. Men,' she crouched down before him, 'are more useful to me. I would have been decidedly unhappy if I'd seized the maid. Woman's flesh is so insipid, so soft, so fatty, but one does what one must to survive, I suppose.

'I wonder . . . would you have come to rescue her?'

'Are you—are you going to eat me?' Will whispered in revulsion.

She smiled wider, the fanged points of her teeth glinting when she cocked her head. 'Perhaps.' She put out a hand.

Will flinched as she touched his cheek. Her hands were as cold as death. She smiled, moving her face closer to his, and a putrid chill emanated from her breath. 'Yes . . . I can feel it.' She shuddered in pleasure. 'You are still full of power, full of life.' She brought her hand down his face, caressing the hollow of his neck, and Will felt a confusing stab of arousal. Was he trembling now from desire, or from fear?

She brought her hand downwards, settling it somewhere between his legs as she leaned over him. Her silver eyes caught his gaze, and she fixed her other hand in his hair, holding him so that he could not pull away. Will wasn't sure whether he wanted to recoil any more. He was being drawn into those deep silver eyes, sinking away beneath the surface.

'Do you know,' she purred against his lips, 'what the desire of every faery maiden is?'

He shook his head, mesmerized.

'To have something of our own,' she whispered. 'To cradle it against us, to sing it to sleep at night.' She smiled again as his eyes widened, comprehension dawning. 'Yes . . . I may have the life eternal, but I have been waiting so long to find a man strong enough to give me a child.'

Will could hear his own heart pounding in the silence as she paused.

'Are you man enough, ferocious warrior? Or will your prick shrivel in fear like all the rest?'

'N-now?' Will's voice was husky.

She lowered her eyelids almost modestly. Her hands left him so fast that he fell to the ground in surprise, and within a moment she was on her feet, standing over him as he lay prone on the cold stone floor.

'I must rest,' she said. A drop of blood fell from one of her wounds, landing on his cheek. 'At dawn tomorrow, I will return. If you desire, you will be mine forever, the father of my first child. But if not . . .' She licked her lips. 'I will make use of you another way.'

She slithered out through the shadows, disappearing unseen and silent. Rubbing his aching head, Will groaned and rolled over onto his side. The barred gate of his cage came into sharp focus. Beyond, there was only darkness.

Moving slowly, he got to his feet and began to explore his surroundings. He walked the length of the rocky cavern along the wall. The rock was slightly moist and icy cold, and a kind of witch-light danced off its surface, providing just enough light to see by. There was a constant pressure from above, a muffled roaring that had to be the ocean.

So they were somewhere below the seabed. Will shivered as he walked, and decided to remove his sodden clothes in an effort to squeeze the water out of them.

Against the other wall, a spring of fresh water welled from an opening in the rock, flowing back into a drain on the other side after travelling the length of the cavern. Will stuck his foot into the spring to test its depth, and reached the rocky bottom about two feet down. He nearly leapt straight into the air when he felt something in the water brush his leg.

Shivering, he peered into the stream to see, astonished, a blur of light moving in the water. Narrowing his eyes, he discerned the shapes of several long eels weaving their way in and out of the cave, their hides glowing eerily in the black water. Will briefly wondered what the eels lived on, glanced around at the fragments of human bone strewing the floor of the cave, and decided to put the question in abeyance.

The openings by which the stream and the eels entered and departed the cave were too narrow for Will even to fit his hand into. Conserving his strength, he donned his damp clothes again, huddled up in a corner that seemed drier than the others, and tried to think his situation through.

The only sure way out was to kill his captor, but for some reason Will shrank from that thought. There might be more tunnels in the darkness, perhaps leading out of her lair to safety. If he could somehow get through the barred gate—

He wanted to laugh madly at his hopeless situation. He was a captive of an ogress who changed her shape at will, whose goal was either to have a child by him or to eat him. It was as ridiculous as any heathen superstition he had ever heard. *The immortal ones exist, whether you believe they do or not,* Goldie had told him, ages ago.

*The monsters do, at least.*

*Goldie.* What would she do without him? If she'd any sense, Will supposed, she would have made her way to the nearby village by now. From there, he wasn't sure. Would she attempt to rescue him, or would she give him up for dead? If she chose the latter, he would never see her again, and the thought left a queer feeling in his gut.

*But if she chooses the former, if she tries to rescue me, she might well get herself killed.* That would be worse. He didn't know how he would be able to go on, if he were responsible for the death of someone he cared about. The thought disturbed him, but he continued to worry at it until sleep finally crept upon him and carried him off.


WILL OPENED HIS EYES. The rocks were singing.

The rocks of the seabed were older than anything else in the world, and they remembered everything. They remembered songs that people had forgotten long ago, ages of heroes and bards that had long since slipped beneath the waves.

The rocks sang. They sang of a sword, and the brave man who would wield it.

They sang of the old gods, and of the kingdoms that would fall with the coming of the Christ.

They sang of the immortals, a sweet wistful melody of the river-maidens of the north. Beautiful and wild, they could never be held by any man.

Will listened to the song as he walked barefoot beside the babbling river. Reflections of the sunlight glinted silver and gold off the marbled surface of the water. The grass was soft beneath his feet, and the sky was as blue as the eyes of the maiden he loved.

He would sooner listen to this song than any other. He would rather hear of gentle beauty than of the exploits of heroes, or the rise and fall of empires.

But the sky was darkening above, and Will reached for his sword as the winds buffeted him.

The sword was not there. Of course; he had dropped it in the cave. It had drunk the blood of the monster, gorged its fill, but he could not satisfy it.

A young man ran towards him as the sky lowered. His long auburn hair streamed in the wind. Tattoos of bright blue adorned his face and his bare chest.

'You have to protect us!' he shouted at Will.

Will shook his head. 'I can't. I've lost my sword.'

'What are you talking about?' The youth grinned widely. The outline of his form blurred, shifted into a slim, silver-armoured figure. 'I'm right here.'

His sword was in his hand. Will reached up into the sky and set the lightning free. The sky cleft in two; the sword did not break.

There was a lake, a vast expanse of reflected blue, cushioned by grassy hills and caressed by a gentle breeze.

Will raised his arm to throw his sword into the lake, but the youth caught his wrist.

'What are you doing? Don't give me back to the river-queen.'

He was atop a black hill, with black rain falling on the tombstone of his father. The sword was buried in the stone at the top of the hill, and its roots twisted deep into the bowels of the earth. Will laid his right hand on the hilt of the sword, and the earth haemorrhaged as he tore the sword from her body.

The auburn-haired youth was back, and changed into the armoured man, who knelt before him. Then he transformed back into the grinning youth, who laughed as he fled the scene.

'Stop!' Will yelled in desperation.

The youth looked over his shoulder. 'You'll have to do better than that, Will Nobody,' he called, 'if you want to master me!' This time, he turned into a dappled grey mare and galloped away, leaving Will stranded on the desolate mound.

The stones sang a song of fire, of ash blowing in the breeze, of burned towns and black mud, and of the man who would be emperor of the dead.

Sinking into the mud, Will closed his eyes and let himself go. One day, he would sleep forever . . .

WILL'S EYES FLEW OPEN. The witch-light from the cave walls glinted off the fangs of the sea-demon.

He flinched back, cracking his head on the rock he had been sleeping against. He folded sideways in pain, groaning. For a moment, he thought he must still be dreaming, but this was his reality now. A dank cave with no escape, and the sinister mistress who was staring at him hungrily.

She waited until he had recovered himself, never moving from the squatting position she had adopted as soon as he had opened his eyes. Her pearly skin was smooth and unscarred, with no suggestion of the terrible wounds that had been there just the previous evening. She had covered her body with wisps of translucent green silk, and similarly coloured gems winked in the folds of her shining black hair.

Will had no way of knowing if it really was daybreak or not, since there was no sun shining in the depths of this slimy hole, and the sea pounded above just the same as it had during the night. The pain where he had hit his head was only momentary. Will gathered his limbs together and stood, trying to keep a good distance away from the sea-demon. She mirrored his movements as he got up, her eyes fixed upon his face all the while.

'Is it dawn?' Will muttered.

'Yes.' The sea-demon's tongue flicked briefly over her lips. 'I am hungry this morning, warrior. For one desire, or the other. Do not keep me waiting long.' She cocked her head to one side as the heat crept into Will's cheeks. 'What is the matter?'

'I—' Will licked his lips, trying vainly to moisten them. 'I feel weak.' It was only half a lie. 'I have not eaten.'

There was a flicker in her metallic eyes of something like anger, and she moved very close to him. She was tall enough that she could match his gaze if she were to stand on tiptoe.

She laid her hands on either side of his head, and he did his best not to flinch. Her mouth quirked slightly as he shivered in her grasp.

'You have not eaten?' Her eyes regarded him up and down, and she showed her pointed teeth. 'Neither have I.' Her grip slackened, and she ran her hands down into his neck again, eliciting the same confused response from his body. 'Take off your clothes,' she commanded in a low, silky voice.

Will could see no choice but to comply. He began with his leather armour, which thudded to the floor. As he struggled out of his still-damp shirt, he thought he saw a glint of admiration in her eyes. Unbuckling his sword belt, he saw the corners of her mouth part into a smile.

*If this is to be,* Will thought as his mouth went dry and his heart hammered in his chest, *it may as well be on my terms.* Letting the belt clink down beside the armour, he reached for the woman's hand with his own and let his fingers slide across the smooth skin of her wrist.

Her reaction was instantaneous, and painful. She seized his wrist with her hand, and with inhuman strength she twisted it, causing such pain that he cried out, certain that the bones would break in her grasp. There was no way to struggle free; he could feel the imprint of each of her fingers against his forearm, and knew that with just a flick of her wrist, she could snap his arm in two. She bore him down to his knees as the pain twisted in him. Out of the corner of his eye, he thought he could see her shadow on the cave wall twist and writhe.

'Please!' he managed to cry out. 'I meant no harm!'

'What did you intend?' she hissed, her voice close at his ear.

'I only . . .' Will sought desperately for inspiration. 'Your skin—you healed so quickly. You were all cut up last night—'

She let out a hiss from between her teeth. 'Even your faery-forged blades cannot harm me for long.'

*Faery-forged?* In his mind's eye, Will saw the blue-tattooed youth grin at him. But this was no time to dwell on strange visions he had seen in dreams.

Roughly, the sea-demon pushed him to the floor, releasing the grip on his arm as she did so. Will felt the impact of the rocky floor against his bare back, felt his shoulder blades bruise and bleed, but she was crouching over him now and he did not dare to move. She bared her teeth as she raked her hands across his chest, but Will felt no desire for her now. At that moment, he had no doubt that she would hurt him without hesitation, tear him apart and take every enjoyment in doing so, if he did not react as she pleased.

Will closed his eyes tightly, clenching his fists against the cold floor.

*Think of Goldie,* he told himself desperately.

A terrible roar resounded through the cave. Will felt the sea-demon's weight lift from him. The roar went on and on, as though the sea had encroached the caves somewhere and was rushing in. Will cracked open his eyes. The sea-demon was on her feet, head turned towards the exit. Her lips parted in an angry hiss.

She turned towards Will, her long hair flicking about her. 'Stay here, or you will regret it,' she commanded, and ran out of the cave, leaving the barred gate open behind her.

Will came to his feet, breathing heavily. He felt sick to his stomach, and if there had been anything in it, he might have retched. His immediate instinct was to retrieve his clothes, which he hastily pulled on again, even the armour. He felt safer under the leather. Shame swirled through him, settling like lead in his gut. *Perhaps I should have died before I let it get that far*, he thought, trembling from cold and pain and the terror which still had him in its grasp. But his life had suddenly seemed like too much to give up without hope; the future which had once been bleak now seemed a better prospect than a violent and lingering death.

There was no way he could go through with it now, he knew. He had to get away. He stepped out of the cell and peered to both directions. To the left, a distant light cast an eerie glow over the tunnel walls. To the right, there was nothing but blackness. Will took a few paces along the tunnel to the right. It stretched out for some distance in front of him, but there was no knowing where he might end up.

He turned to the left, realizing that the roar had stopped. The cave was silent.

It dawned on Will that someone had come to rescue him. That noise had probably been them breaching the gates of the sea-demon's lair.

And who would be rescuing him? Who else knew what had

happened to him, besides Goldie?

*I pray she has brought my sword with her.*

Steeling himself, Will set off down the left-hand tunnel.


THE TUNNEL LED INTO AN OVAL CHAMBER which Will could just make out by cautiously peering around a bend. Voices from the chamber drifted up to him as he flattened himself against the tunnel wall, praying for luck.

'He is leaving with me.' Goldie's clear, sweet voice travelled towards him, and Will could not help but feel a rush of affection towards her. But it was mingled with fear, for he was not at all sure that his sword would guarantee victory. It hadn't, last night.

'And you will take him from me?' came the sea-demon's unmistakable hiss. There was a pause. 'You think that toy will ensure your safety?' She gave a low growl. 'Do you think I don't know what you are, little girl? Do you think that gives you any protection? I care nothing for the writ of the River Queen, and she has no power here.'

*The River Queen?* Will had no time to wonder who that was.

'This has nothing to do with her,' Goldie was saying, her voice pitched higher than usual.

It was now or never. Will could almost sense the sea-demon coiling up, ready to spring. He moved from the wall, and came out full in Goldie's sight, behind the sea-demon's back.

Goldie made no indication that she had seen Will, but continued to talk. She was holding Will's sword straight in front of her, not relaxing her posture one bit, her eyes never leaving the sea-demon's face. 'This has nothing to do with the River

Queen.' She took a deep breath. 'You are vile,' she began, and continued to rant loudly. 'You waste your immortal life on this game—this toying with your victims, this fear and horror. Aren't you ashamed of yourself? You are a stain upon the entire faery race.'

The sea-demon bristled perceptibly as Will stealthily crept up behind her. He made a motion with his right hand and, God be thanked, Goldie understood.

She threw the sword overarm, and Will, rejoicing, leapt to catch it.

With a smooth unhurried motion, as though she had been expecting this all along, the sea-demon stretched out, caught Will's sword by its hilt, and pivoted neatly, catching him with the tip of the blade to his neck. Will froze in place, terror turning his blood to ice. Goldie made as if to leap forward, but held herself where she was upon seeing the sword hover just under his chin.

The sea-demon smiled, her eyes going from Goldie to Will and back again.

'I see how it is,' she said softly, her voice taking on the texture of silk once more. 'Love. Between the two of you.' She turned to Goldie. 'You know this will never end well.' She whipped her head around, mesmerizing Will with her silvery eyes once again. 'Don't you know what she is, warrior?' She began suddenly to laugh. 'I've almost a mind to let you both live, just to see what tragedy tears you apart in the end.'

Will found his voice. 'Please,' he whispered, 'let the girl go.' *Goldie shouldn't have to give her life, just to save mine. It makes no sense. I should be the one sacrificing myself for her. Instead, she saves me. She comes to my rescue. I cannot watch her die. Not for my sake.*

'Why should I listen to you?' the sea-demon hissed. 'You broke our bargain.'

'I'll keep it this time,' Will promised, his stomach cold with fear. 'I'll do whatever you want. Kill me or keep me, whatever you please. Only let her go.'

For a moment, the sea-demon stared disbelievingly at him, and Goldie leapt.

She moved with a flash of speed that Will could hardly believe, easily as fast as the sea-demon had caught his sword, and the monster was taken by surprise. The sword nicked Will's chin as Goldie barrelled into her. She lost her footing, falling, and lost her grasp on the sword.

Some instinct told Will where to lunge, and the hilt of the sword practically fell into his hand. As the sea-demon hit the floor, Goldie, still moving with unbelievable speed, rolled clear. As Will stood by, hefting the blade in his hand, she shouted, 'Will! Kill her!'

The sea-demon turned to look up the length of Will's sword.

There was an incredible anger in him now, and he planned to ram the blade down her throat. She deserved to die, didn't she? How many men had she killed, over how many thousands of years? He deserved to take his revenge.

The sword rose in his hand, but never fell. One half of him was screaming at the other half, but it had met something immovable. The sea-demon's silvery eyes locked with his. He thought he saw pleading and fear in them.

'Will!' Goldie shouted. He heard her as if from a long way away.

'Yield,' Will whispered to the prone, beautiful woman.

'Will, kill her!' Goldie screamed. 'Kill her now!'

'Yield,' Will repeated, mesmerized by the molten silver in her eyes.

The eyes changed from silver to steel. Pleading turned to contempt. There was a great rustling, and the sea-demon shook all over. Horrified, Will saw tentacles start to sprout from her limbs, her upper body contorting to demonic proportions. A groping tentacle snatched the sword from his hand and chucked it in the direction of the rocky passageway, where it slammed point first into the wall. Will gaped at it for a moment, and the sea-demon gave a roar that more than half deafened him.

With a loud and surprisingly crude curse, Goldie seized Will by the arm and dragged him towards the passageway. Bits of the roof were falling with the violence of the sea-demon's transformation, and the floor shook.

'I'm sorry!' Will began. 'I couldn't—' Guilt, terror and shame twisted in him all together. 'I've doomed us both.'

'Not quite,' Goldie breathed, laying a reassuring hand upon his shoulder.

'What do you mean?'

Goldie pointed. The very roof of the cave was shaking as the sea-demon writhed and contorted beneath it. Larger bits of rock were falling now, and cracks were spreading across the shaking floor.

'She'll rip her own lair apart,' Goldie said with satisfaction. 'It's uncertain whether the sword would actually kill her, but this cave-in will do the job.'

Will looked back at the scene. 'We have to keep her angry,' he said with determination. 'She might realize the damage she's doing otherwise.'

'How are you going to—' Goldie trailed off as Will stepped over to his sword. Half the blade was buried in the wall, but it seemed quite unhurt otherwise. He closed his fingers around the hilt. Yet another vision from his dream flashed before him.

Gently, Will pulled at the sword, and it slid free of the rock with a metallic scrape, leaving a sword-shaped hole. There was not a chip on the gleaming edge nor a scratch on the leaf-shaped blade; it shone as bright as ever it had.

AT THAT MOMENT, THE SEA-DEMON was in indescribable pain.

The weakness imparted by her injuries had not yet fully departed, and the toll of pain normally exacted by her transformation into her monstrous form was magnified tenfold. She writhed and screamed, unable to gain any control of her body, and thrashed at the walls of her own entrance chamber without realizing that she was doing so.

As she started to regain some restraint, she heard through the mists a voice calling, 'Hi! Here, you tentacled monstrosity!'

Ever sensitive to taunts and jibes, the sea-demon lunged in the direction of the voice. It was ineffectual, and the nasty jibing creature slashed at her exposed tentacle, eliciting a terrible screech. She regained herself through the pain and looked down. The warrior danced just a few feet out of her reach, just a swat away. She remembered the compassion in his eyes when he had refused to strike her. But she had never had any such obstacle as compassion to deter her, and she brought down a mass of her heavy black tentacles to crush him.

Somehow he danced out of her reach, and the only thing she accomplished was to rattle the seaward wall of her hideout.

Pieces of rock fell from the sides of the cave, and she roared indignantly at the defacing of her home. Curling up a tentacle, she aimed to grab the man by the ankle, but he saw her coming and the blade of that cruel sword sliced right through her leathery flesh. Abandoning all restraint in her pain and rage, she lunged headlong for him. He backed into the very corner of the cave, and she hit the seaward wall with her full bulk. The whole room shook, and a huge mass of sharp rocks fell from the roof and landed squarely on her outspread tentacles.

THE MONSTER WENT MAD. She thrashed and lunged, tore her own tentacles to get loose, hurled herself at everything within her reach. More and more rocks fell from the walls and ceiling, and Will ran for his life, dodging the raining debris, running and stumbling as the floor shook beneath him.

When he reached Goldie, they both fled headlong, leaving the cave behind them, making for the safety of the tunnel beyond. A great crash resounded, and from the roaring noise that followed, they realized that the sea had breached the gates. With eyes wide in horror, they waited for the water to surge in and take them with it—but the sound of falling debris continued, raised to a crescendo, then slowly ceased until nothing more than a soft dripping could be heard. A swirl of salt water rippled past their ankles, then subsided. They turned to look at each other, then simultaneously made their way back to what had once been the entrance chamber.

The far end of the chamber was obscured, blocked with rubble. A tiny spurt of seawater trickled to the floor; the rest was securely plugged by the great rocks that had fallen directly across the entrance-way. A few squashed tentacles protruded from beneath the rockfall. Nothing else remained of the sea-demon.

Goldie stared, transfixed, at their handiwork. 'I've just realized,' she said slowly, 'that was the only exit.'

Will took a deep breath. 'It's not. It can't be.'

'What do you mean?'

'Come with me.'

Will led her up the tunnel towards the cave where he had been kept, to where the witch-light ceased and the tunnel stretched on in darkness.

'That's our way out,' he said grimly. 'That's got to lead back to land somewhere.'

Goldie hesitated. 'But how are we to find our way in the dark?'

'I've an idea,' Will said. He strode into the cave, trying not to glance in the direction of the spot where the sea-demon had pushed him to the floor. There was still a throbbing pain in both his shoulders, and he was certain that he had been bleeding.

The glittering eels swam heedlessly in their shallow river. Hefting his sword, Will lunged at the first one he spotted. Caught on the blade, it thrashed its last and died almost instantly. Will breathed a sigh of relief when he saw that death did not cause whatever miraculous quantity that carried the light in its blood to wink out into darkness.

Goldie shivered as they set off down the dark passage, with only the eel's light to guide them. She was wet through, Will noticed for the first time; she had obviously swum to get to him. She was clad only in a thin under-tunic and her breeches, and they clung wetly to her skin.

*We need to get to the surface,* Will told himself, and did not dare to think anything further. His sword gleamed in the dark as he held up his eel lantern. He took hold of Goldie's hand, and felt her grasp his firmly back. Together, they walked into the pit of blackness beyond the cave.

# Chapter Four

# The Faery Sword

'What is Christianity?' Goldie asked as we left the happy village. 'I have seen people merry about it, happy to convert, and yet I have also seen them murderous, filled with all of life's worst impulses. Like the night you saved my life. You say that you are a Christian ... what does that mean?'

As I began to explain it to her, my memory drifted. My first certain memories, the most precious to me. Leaving the ruined fort. Travelling onward, ever unsure of which direction I should go. It was midsummer, and the sun blazed from its position of glory in the sky.

Flashes of another life came to me, but I could not even begin to put those fragmented memories in the proper order. And nothing in that land jogged my memory. People knelt before smouldering altars and prayed to the woods and the hills. I ignored their rituals as I ignored much else. I continued to exist, to survive, but there were days when I wondered whether survival was worth it.

One of those days, I was sitting quietly by the side of a river when Caedwic found me.

I had been there for hours, simply staring into the water. All of a sudden I became aware that someone had taken a seat upon the log next to me. I took my eyes from the water and looked at him. A serene grey man, clad in nondescript robes, leaning upon a knobbly stick.

'What do you see in the water?' he asked me.

I shrugged. 'Nothing of use.'

'You are a troubled man,' he said.

I laughed shortly, bitterly. 'Is that so?'

'Do you not wish to share your troubles with a friend?'

His welcoming face betrayed nought but good faith, but I reacted with suspicion. 'What are you?' I demanded.

'A follower of God,' he replied.

'God? Which god?'

'The only God,' he said. 'The Christ, our saviour.'

For the first time, some spark of recognition enlivened within me. I remembered a wooden cross upon a windy shore. People raised their eyes to a god who lay dying before them. A priest chanted in a strange tongue. Proud warriors bowed before him.

'Tell me more of this god of yours,' I demanded.

So Caedwic revealed to me the miracle of the holy faith. We travelled together for nearly a month, speaking every day of the god who made men's hearts kinder. To be a Christian, as it was revealed to me, was to live with empathy and goodwill towards my fellow men. Furthermore, when I lost myself in prayer, in silent contemplation, I found *that I could make more sense of the memories that haunted me. It was not easy—I suspect that it will never be easy—but I was able to see my old life, now interspersed with the wisdom of the new.*

*After journeying with Caedwic, I discovered that the world had changed. The people and places no longer pass me by; the grey fog is lifted from my weary eyes. I see God in everything, and far from inspiring me with a sense to restrain or impose order upon the world, I am filled with joy. I wish to live.*

*After I explained this to Goldie, a new sense of understanding entered her eyes. She accepts my faith—but I suspect that she will never convert herself. She is too wild for that; she belongs to the land, to the forests and fields. Not to a Christian lord in his high hall.*

'AND THEN ULBERT LED ME to a deserted promontory,' Goldie said. 'There was just the slightest suggestion of an undersea cave, a darkness in the water, a whirlpool rising to the surface . . . and he told me that the lair of the creature was somewhere at the bottom of that dark well.'

'And you swam down there?' Will asked incredulously.

Goldie shrugged. 'I'm a very strong swimmer. Always have been.' She glanced at the walls of the tunnel, which were starting to show an eerie light of their own, hardly less gloomy than the light that came from their solitary eel. 'I love the water, but not this undersea underground. I prefer rivers.' She shivered. 'Look at all the salt on the walls. Everything's salty. You can't drink a drop of it, and I'm thirsty.'

*Speaking of rivers.* Will had had just enough time to recover from the scene with the sea-demon, and to turn things over in his mind. 'Who is the River Queen?' he asked cautiously, hoping that he did not seem overly suspicious.

Goldie hesitated for a moment. 'Who?' she asked offhandedly. *Rather* too *offhand*, Will thought to himself.

'The River Queen,' he repeated. 'You mentioned her when you were talking to the sea-monster.'

'I truly don't remember,' Goldie quickly replied. 'Honestly, I don't know what she was saying half the time. It made no sense to me. I just played along to buy some time for you.'

For the first time, it sounded like Goldie was lying to him. She had spoken half-truths before, and still refused to talk about her family, but now she was actively trying to cover something up. But there was little point in pressing her, Will knew. He did not even know what he was hoping to uncover; he only knew that things were not as they seemed. Which things, or how he could begin to unravel them, he had no idea. But he had not finished picking at that encounter yet.

'What do you think she meant when she asked me if I knew what you were?' he asked, trying his best to keep his tone neutral.

There was a long pause.

'I suppose,' Goldie finally said, 'that she meant I was a pagan, and you a Christian.'

This answer did not make much sense. *How could the sea-demon know things like that?* Goldie was evidently not ready to give away any of her secrets just yet.

'She certainly thought that we were quite . . . close,' he remarked.

Goldie gave a high, musical laugh. 'For sure. She was raving.'

Will managed to fake a small chuckle, and they continued to walk as silence fell.

Goldie cleared her throat. 'I do consider you a friend, though,' she said.

'And I the same for you,' Will replied, even as he strove to hide his disappointment. There was some part of him that had been wondering why Goldie would have made such a perilous journey to find him if she thought of him as no more than a pleasant travelling companion, but she was the kind of person who always helped where she could, even when it came to interfering in a stranger's wedding. Part of him had hoped for more, but it was simply not to be.

They were silent for a while, and Will returned to thinking. They had been walking for what felt like half a day, and still the tunnel showed no signs of leading to the surface. They had passed several crevices in the rocky walls, none wide enough for a comfortable entry. Will had judged that their best course was to stick to the main passageway, which seemed like the most obvious way out. But they were still in darkness, with no glimpse of the world above, and no real assurance that they could escape. Will dared not voice his fear that they might have doomed themselves to death along with the sea-demon.

Abruptly, they were forced to a sudden halt.

The wall before them ended dead. Will shone his makeshift lantern upwards, towards the roof, but could not see beyond a couple of feet. Aghast, he stared at the blank wall of rock before them, unable to admit defeat when they had tried and hoped for so long. He balled his hand into a fist and punched it against the rock, feeling his knuckles bleed with the impact.

'Will!' Goldie restrained him, taking his hand in hers. 'Don't do that, please.' Her voice shook. She looked up into the darkness.

'We have to find some way to see what's up there,' she said.

Will sank to his haunches, exhausted. His sword clattered to the cave floor as he sank back against the wall. 'I can't even find the strength to carry on,' he muttered. 'Goldie, if you . . .'

'You need to rest,' Goldie interrupted him. 'If you sit down for a while, it'll help.' She smiled at him encouragingly. 'I'm here, it's all right.'

Will closed his eyes tightly and leaned his aching head in his hands. It did not work; when he opened them again, they were still trapped, and he was still feeling sick, and aching all over. Goldie had taken a seat next to him, wrapping her arms around herself in an attempt to conserve some warmth.

For a long time, there was no sound but the faraway dripping of water, magnified by the winding tunnelways they had followed down to this gloomy spot. Their eel torch was fading, and this particular chamber had very little of that peculiar cave-light that glowed in these dark underground places.

Will shook the carcass of the eel from his sword, and dipped the blade in a puddle of water to clean off the blood. The sword gleamed even in the uncertain light, regaining its lustre easily. It was a wonderful sword in more ways than one, truly. As he dried the blade on his shirtsleeve, he had the strange feeling that it was watching him somehow. A half-formed thought niggled in the back of his mind.

'Goldie,' he began softly, not wanting to disturb her. She turned her head to him, hugging her knees to her chest.

'Yes?'

'Do you know anything about . . . about visions sent in the

form of dreams?'

'It depends,' she answered cautiously. 'Are you sure they are not ordinary dreams?'

He shook his head. 'I have never had a dream like this before.'

'What did you dream of?'

'It's hard to explain . . . but I think it was all about this sword here.'

Goldie's eyes immediately went to the blade, and narrowed with a sort of suspicion. 'Did anything happen to the sword in your dream?'

'It turned into a man.' He hesitated. 'Not just anyone; a Pictish warrior. Those northern wildling people who tattoo themselves blue, and fight with axes. Then he turned into a few other things.' Will frowned, remembering. 'A horse. No—a mare. And into an armoured man like to the Frankish riders.'

'This . . .' Goldie hesitated. 'This does not sound like anything I know about. I only know how to deal with dreams that are sent by the gods.'

'And who do you suppose this dream was sent by?'

'Something else.' Goldie sounded almost apologetic. 'Will, where did you get this sword?'

'I don't remember. Probably from my father.' He turned to her when she did not reply immediately. 'Why?'

'It puts me in mind of a story.'

'Which story?'

'I could tell it. But it is very long,' Goldie cautioned.

Will chuckled mirthlessly. 'Need I remind you, we have nothing but time?'

'Very well. It begins centuries ago, before the men of the

north conquered this island, and before humans lived sepa-
rately from faeries. Back then, the sprites of the fields and the
nymphs of the rivers clustered around men who were valiant
and good of heart, and gave them many gifts.

'My mother told me this story,' she continued, 'as our people
have told it for many years. Now, of the faeries, you must know
that most of them are female. For every son that is born to them,
they have twenty or more daughters. When a son is born, there
is great rejoicing. The faery men are unlike any others, outshin-
ing all with their beauty, their charm, and their feats of bravery.
They are greatly prized by the faery mothers.

'In the time I speak of, there was such a son born on this island. We only know him now as the Faery Prince. In his youth,
the Prince was very close to a human king known as the Griffin,
and his son, the Young Griffin, who like the Prince was youth-
ful and courageous. These two young men were inseparable,
and did everything together. Either one was more valiant and
handsome than the other, and they loved each other like
brothers.'

Will scratched at his beard. 'I had a friend like that once,' he
mused.

'You remember him?' Goldie asked, surprise in her voice.

'A little of him.' Will ran his hand over his beard, having little mind to tell what he remembered. 'Go on.'

'To honour their prince, the water-sprites forged him a
sword the likes of which had never been seen before.' Goldie's
eyes seemed dark as stormy water in the gloom. 'This was a magical sword for him to use in battle, the blade unbreakable, the
balance perfectly fitted to his hand. It had a multitude of magical properties, all of which are not even known, and it forged

itself a mystical bond with the man who wielded it.'

'A mystical bond?' Will repeated.

'This sword was a sentient entity, possessing its own will, its own purpose,' Goldie explained. 'There was an ancient spirit that dwelled in the blade, making itself known through mind-pictures and feelings, and in this way it gave its wielder the opportunity to master its magical gifts. Anyone else would only have a good sword, but the master of the blade would be fighting alongside a trusted partner skilled in magic.

'Well, as time went by, and as the Prince won battle after battle and became renowned throughout both mundane and faery realms, his friend started to grow jealous of him.'

Will grunted in surprise.

'His jealousy festered and oozed until he could stand it no more. Whilst his friend slept in the tent beside him, the Young Griffin stole the sword and murdered the Prince in his sleep.'

Will huffed. *That escalated quickly.* 'That couldn't have been good,' he remarked.

'It most certainly was not. For the first time, the sword was used to kill one of the faery race, its own people by whom it was forged. Part of the sword twisted, its magic darkened, and it moulded itself to fit its new dark master. It became a blood-thirsty weapon . . . a demon sword. From that moment forth, the blade thirsted for bloodshed, and it found the spirit of a human much better suited to its bloodthirst than the immortal spirit of a faery.

'All this was completely lost on the Young Griffin, who took up the sword and fought many battles with it, steeping it in both faery and mortal blood. Disgusted, the water-sprites swore that never again would they have dealings with humans. Many humans and immortals died in the aftermath of that feud, which lasted for generations. Eventually, the gods intervened and irrevocably separated the mundane and faery realms. They decreed that the faeries would not trespass in the mortal world for longer than a day; any faery who stayed past nightfall would slowly start to lose their magic and eventually die, becoming no different from a human.'

Goldie had almost seemed to be saying these last few sentences to herself. She stopped for a moment, seeming to reach again for the thread of the story.

'And where was the sword during all this?' Will prodded her.

'In the hands of the royal house of the Griffin's tribe,' Goldie replied, shaking off whatever mood had suddenly taken her. 'The sword was passed from generation down to generation, and became renowned throughout these isles. Each wielder used it to gain the high kingship for himself and to win deeds of renown. Men forgot that the sword actually belonged to the water-sprites, and it turned itself to their weal.

'So it was for many years, until the Romans came, bringing their rules and laws, and their new religion. The Griffin's descendants held out, for a time. But they could not resist the scarlet serpent, the silver-fanged invader from the south. The druids, keepers of holy knowledge and legend, were massacred, and with them went the traditions that had been handed down by word of mouth, from generation to generation. When the last Griffin lost his lands and life to the invaders, with his dying breath he thrust the sword into a rock. None were able to draw it out.'

'This story suddenly seems familiar to me,' Will remarked.

'I'm sure I've heard of children's tales with a similar line.'

'Many legends are told of this magic sword,' Goldie answered enigmatically. 'In truth, the story ends there and does not pick up until centuries later, when a young war-leader allied with the Romans drew it from the stone.' Goldie paused. 'This man was valiant, if stern, and had the respect of all his underlings. He was also a Christian.'

Will raised his eyebrows. Goldie continued.

'Though he had drawn it from the stone, the young warrior didn't claim ownership of the sword, not at first,' Goldie said. 'He knew that this sword was a weapon of the pagans who despised the invaders. Also, he could sense the evil spirit in the blade thirsting for blood, which he held to be against his faith. But he kept it by his side nevertheless, not to wield, but to safeguard.'

Goldie took a deep breath, and went on, 'But this warrior had a secret lover: a female water-sprite who visited him in human form, although she never stayed the night. Some say that one day, she told him of the sword's true history and persuaded him to give it to her.'

'I've heard it told differently,' Will said softly.

'Other versions of the legend say that the Roman soldier befriended a mystic who possessed druidic knowledge from ancient times. He asked for advice, and was told that the evil spirit that dwelt inside the sword could only be put to rest if it was restored to its makers.'

'That also sounds different from what I've heard.'

'*And* there's a version that says the sword was broken in his service,' Goldie said.

'No,' Will interrupted her. 'The sword did not break.'

Goldie raised an eyebrow. 'In truth, the hilt of the sword was damaged, and split badly in a battle,' she said. 'But the blade could never be broken; it was forged by faery magic.'

Will frowned. 'But if the Roman never wielded the sword, how was the hilt damaged?'

'At some point, he did start to use the sword,' Goldie said. 'We do not remember the reason why. He lived in dark times. His masters, the Romans, were preparing to leave the island, and he found himself fighting against warriors out of the north. He tried to protect his people, but his life consisted of war and little else; his kingdom was threatened without cease. Under those circumstances, he may have felt that he needed to use every weapon available to him.'

'We still find ourselves living in dark times,' Will remarked.

Goldie half smiled, and continued, 'When the hilt was broken, he handed it over to his own smiths, who had never seen such a design before. None of them could produce a satisfactory replacement; all their attempts felt foreign and uncomfortable in his hand. In desperation, he visited a Pictish mystic—either the friend and advisor that some stories tell of, or possibly a man he had hunted in former days, when he fought for the Romans.

'The mystic knew that the blade and hilt had been put together by the water-sprites, the true owners of the sword. He may have urged the warrior to give the sword back to them, but in other versions of the story, his faery lover stole the sword and took it back to her people.'

'A happy ending,' Will said. 'The blade returned at last to its people.'

'Hardly,' Goldie retorted grimly. 'If the mystic thought that returning the blade would heal it, he was wrong. The water-sprites were horrified to find that their long-desired sword, far from being the holy relic they imagined it to be, had become anathema to them, poisonous, forbidden. They detested the very sight of the blade, and none amongst them could master the will of the evil spirit that now inhabited it.'

'But they repaired the hilt?' Will asked.

'They did,' Goldie affirmed. 'But none of them had any use for it anymore, and it was decided at last that it should be given back to the mortal world.'

Goldie paused for a moment, allowing the soft dripping of water down the tunnel to add to the suspense of the next words she spoke.

'On the eve of his greatest battle, the Roman received a visit from the queen of the water-sprites, who delivered the sword back into his hands. He won the battle and brought a respite from the invaders, for a while. But when he finally threw down his last foe, he found himself changed.

'A warrior foremost, he had never bothered overmuch about what would happen to him once the kingdom was at peace. With no more foes to fight, he began to question his purpose, and vowed that he would become a different man, a better king.' Goldie paused, and brushed damp hair-strands from her face. 'The Welshmen tell of what he did after, of how he ruled and in what manner he met his end. But my people remember mainly how he gave the sword back to the faery queen, throwing it into the mountain lake where she resided. By that time, he was an old man, and ailing. The water-sprites gingerly took possession of the blade to find that it, too, had changed along with its master. It still would not allow a faery to wield it, but it was content to rest and no longer ardently desired bloodshed.

The queen placed the sword in a secret place, vowing that it would only return to the mortal world if a man worthy to wield it appeared again.'

'And that's the end of the story?' Will asked as Goldie's voice faded.

'No,' she replied. 'That is the history of the sword so far as I know it. There is a gap of two hundred years or so, and then—somehow—that sword turns up in the hands of a wandering Saxon thane found on a desolate battlefield in strange circumstances.'

Will blinked at her. 'What do you mean?'

'That monster of a sword—that sword that was wielded by the old king, that was liberated from the stone, that was used by generations of warlords to fight their bloody battles—is none other than this sword!'

Goldie pointed dramatically at the blade that lay innocently upon the ground between them.

Will started to laugh. 'Well, that was entertaining all right,' he said. 'What an ending! The next time I tell a tale about a sword, I'll remember that.'

'Will,' Goldie said incredulously, 'come on. Do you not remember how this sword sliced through the sea-demon's flesh like butter, when your knife never even left a mark?'

'Perhaps there is something magical about it,' Will conceded, 'but that hardly proves that it's some relic from a thousand years ago. I certainly haven't noticed it asking me for more blood.'

'Where did you get that sword?'

'I don't remember.' Will scowled as he realized he was repeating himself. 'It probably came from my father, from his father, who might have had it forged. Or possibly from further back, in the true north. I don't know.'

Goldie stood up and took the sword from the floor, levelling it in front of her. 'Will, do you remember your father's name?'

Will frowned for a moment. 'Wilmuth, as I recall. Why?'

'And your grandfather's?'

'Idda of the Isle—'

'Do they sound like Welshmen or Picts to you?'

'Of course not! They were Saxon—'

'Then why,' Goldie interrupted, 'do you fight with a sword forged by Briton smiths?'

'What?' Will actually leapt to his feet, his eyes fixed on the blade she held in her hand.

'How have you not noticed by now?' Goldie asked. 'Your own Saxon smiths could never have forged it. Look.' She held it up in the dim light. 'Fashioned leaf-wise, rather than pointed in design. The shape isn't straight and tapered for stabbing at an armoured opponent, but forged and balanced to slice and chop, like they used to do in the old days. And look—' She thrust the sword point down to the floor. 'Will, this sword is more than two-thirds my height; it's *the* longest blade I've ever seen.' She looked back at him with an air of triumph. 'This sword is ancient. Why would you have it? Where did you get it?'

Troubled, Will took the blade from her. 'It's true,' he said quietly, 'that I haven't used it very often, simply because I haven't needed to.' He turned it over in his hands, and studied the hilt. 'Now you mention it, this does look odd.' He inspected what he could in the gloom. 'Hilt of elk antler and silver . . . fairly standard, but . . . these rivets certainly aren't the ones that were originally used to fasten this.' He showed her. 'This hilt has been changed since the sword was forged.

'Not that that means anything much,' he continued, half to himself. 'Plenty of old swords have needed their hilts replaced . . . but there's no craftsman's mark on it, nor a smith's signature on the blade.'

'Last night,' Goldie said, 'when I used it, I felt immediately that there was something sinister. I didn't dwell on it, because I needed to get to you.' She glanced quickly down at the floor, then back to his face. 'There is something about this sword that puts one's own self in danger. Some kind of spirit lives inside it, imposing its will on whomever would wield it. Can't you feel that when you're holding it?' she asked, scrutinising his face. 'Its spirit is directly at war with the Christian ideals you claim to hold.'

Unbidden, Will shivered, though he told himself that it was due to the cold.

If the sword was indeed at war with him, it must be drawing up its battle plans now, for even when he deliberately brought up the image of the Pictish youth in his mind he felt nothing, no sinister emanation, no metallic voice needling at his back of his head.

*Wait, I have felt all these things. The dream, the wordless voice, the sudden anger and something needling at my state of mind.* He felt a chill run down his spine.

'What is that roaring?' Goldie suddenly asked.

'It's the sea,' Will replied automatically. 'You've been hearing it all day.'

She shook her head. 'Not that loudly.'

'The tide's probably coming in,' Will said despondently.

'Doesn't help us much either way.'

'You're wrong,' Goldie said. She turned her head up to the roof of the cave. 'There!'

'What?'

Just as Will spoke, a load of water sprayed from above down onto his head, drenching him.

As he cursed, Goldie's face transformed into an expression of pure joy.

'The tide's coming in!' she exclaimed.

'What are you so happy about?' Will demanded. 'We're trapped in a hole! If the tide's coming in, it's going to drown us like rats in a bucket!'

'Silly!' Goldie retorted, feeling all around the walls for a handhold. 'If the tide's coming in, it's coming *in* somewhere!' She hoisted herself up against the rocky cave wall. 'Which means that we can follow it *out*!'

Like a cat Goldie scaled the wall against which they had been sitting. She let out an exclamation.

'There's a tunnel up here that lets the water through!' She leaned inside. 'There's water here, and it's busily rising!' She turned and looked down at Will. 'Are you coming or not?'

Feeling Goldie's hope rise within him, Will tucked his sword in his belt and gathered the last of his strength. The way up for him was a lot more difficult than it had been for Goldie, and she helped him clamber through the crevice at the top to join her in a narrow tunnel that was rapidly submerging.

'Just follow me!' Goldie called, starting off into the tunnel, waist-deep in water and tripping on her feet as the current sucked at her knees. Stooping in the low tunnel, Will obeyed her without a word.

It was the hardest part of their entire journey. The cave remained low, narrowing in places so that Will could barely squeeze himself through, and the sea roared underfoot and sometimes all around them. They were submerged several times in the narrows, and in one place they had to crawl through a passage, heads just above the level of the water, ripping their palms and knees on sharp rocks as they went.

But at last, they squeezed through a crevice, falling to their knees upon the rock outside in relief. The sky seemed glorious, and the open ocean stretched before them, a short swim all that lay between them and the sandy beach.

Goldie really was an exceptionally good swimmer, much faster than Will, and she laughed with joy as she landed on the beach sand, warming in the late afternoon heat. Will followed, filled with just as much joy, and light-headed with relief. Seizing Goldie with exuberance, he enfolded her in a deep hug, burying his face in her thick, damp hair and wrapping his arms completely around her.

Goldie's voice was close by his ear, reticent in tone. 'Will, anyone can see us.'

'Oh. Oh, right.' Goldie pulled away from him as he released her, and Will felt some part of himself skulk away in shame. What had come over him? Of course Thane Wilhelm could do as he pleased, but Will had vowed never to hurt Goldie—and should she be seen to embrace him in public, she would be held as nothing more than his lover.

'We're going to live,' Goldie said in a voice as hopeful as the dawn. 'The gods be thanked!' She gazed at the cliffs above them. 'I know this hill, look. There's the cave where it all started last night.' She pointed. 'We'll be back under a rooftop, with decent food, in no time!' She started off down the beach. 'By rights, we're heroes to the village!' she gabbled excitedly. 'I can't wait for their reception!'

# Chapter Five

# The Burning Town

'What will you do after you have made it home?' Caedwic asked me one day.

We had been crossing a series of rolling hills, and for once the weather was pleasant. Golden sunlight glittered through the leaves of the young chestnut trees above us as we sat resting. Looking down upon the green of slope and meadow, feeling the sun on my face, I felt truly at peace. I answered with the truth: 'I don't know.'

We sat for a long time in silence and peace. Then he continued, 'I think that our road together will soon end. You must go north from here, but I shall continue east. Along with all the fellow travellers I have met upon this road, I will remember you and your mission.'

'Couldn't I accompany you?' I asked. 'I have no mission—not truly—only an obligation to uncover the life I once had. There is so much I could still learn from you.'

'Will,' he retorted, 'when you are running from something, then nothing will lead you to contentment until you stop. Instead of running away from your past life, you must learn to face it.'

So we parted, and I met Goldie.

I seek not my past home to explain who I am, but who I was. I must accept that I cannot change the past; I cannot bring Aedfrith back to life, nor be a better husband. This yearning that I feel to wander, to grow, to do good—I must turn it to the present and the future. Since I have met Goldie, I feel that I know how I must henceforth live my life: as a true Christian, doing good for the sake of others. She is like the summer sun, which shows the way to go. Her selfless desire to help others inspires me to do the same.

I know not what I may find waiting for me at my island home, but I know the way from there. If it is my destiny to remain there and be the thane of my lands once more, then I will be a thane, fair and just, and rule with all the wisdom I never had before. If it falls to me to wander again through the countryside, I shall dedicate my life to doing what is right, not fighting in wars of lost causes.

Whatever happens, I will leave Thane Wilhelm far behind. Does it even matter if his memories return to me?

THE SUMMER EVENING WAS SLOWLY falling. The wind-swept hills along the coast basked in ruddy light, the sun sinking over the fields like a drowning man consigning his last breath to the ocean.

They passed across fields and farm tracks, meeting no-one. This struck Will as passing strange, especially at this time of the year when the farmers were waiting upon the harvest. The homestead where Goldie had spent the night lay before them, lonely in the wide countryside around. Will shivered and wondered if it was merely the darkening sun that lent him this feeling of foreboding.

Goldie frowned. 'Why does everything look so—so empty?'

Will squinted ahead to the farmer's homestead. It glowed red in the light of the setting sun. There were noises on the wind, too faint to make out.

'Will—' Goldie's voice was faint. 'Is that . . .'

Simultaneously, they realized that the homestead and the wooden-walled town behind it were both on fire. The screams of terrified people could be heard on the wind. They both started to run instinctively ahead, making for the burning farmhouse.

Suddenly the earth beneath their feet shook, and a sound like striking thunder rent the air. Goldie stumbled and fell to her knees. Will managed to keep his footing, but his heart was pounding deep in his throat, threatening to suffocate him. *I should not be so afraid*, he admonished himself. All he wanted to do was to take Goldie's hand and drag her away, take them both far from here.

The town was obviously under attack. The fields, which had stood ready for harvest in the sun, were burning. The main road, which they could just make out from where they stood, was overrun by a glut of black figures, armoured warriors and mounted men standing guard over three great catapult-like machines. As they watched, one of the machines pivoted, flinging a burning load into the air. As the missile landed in the middle of the town, another concussive blast was felt beneath their feet. Will raised his hand as if to protect his face, even though the fire was too far away to do him any harm.

'Will.' Goldie turned towards him and took his arm. 'We have to help them.'

'How?' Will asked softly. His hand was shaking. As he lowered it from his face, it instinctively went towards his sword. Grasping the hilt, he suddenly felt calmer. Panic retreated, stealing away behind the curtain of rationality. It was as though the sword whispered calming words to him, helping him fight the fear that threatened to overwhelm his mind.

'I can help them,' Goldie was saying. She still held on to him. 'If you help me get there.'

Will clasped her hand tightly, drawing her to him. 'We can make it, I think. If I carry you on my back.' Goldie was still barefoot, and she would never make it across the burning ground by herself.

She nodded. Will gathered her up, and set off across the fields of smoke.

The run towards the town walls was a blur. Fast-moving fires threatened them from either side, and cinders smouldered sullenly underneath his boots as he ran. He dared not stop, not even when the smoke became worse and he struggled to breathe. By the time they reached the wooden walls, both of them were coughing and wheezing. Goldie scrambled to the top of the wall from her position on his back and anxiously held out her hand to him, even though she could never have summoned enough strength to boost him up. Instead, Will took a running jump to the wall, caught the top at his second attempt, and clung there with the last of his strength as Goldie grabbed him, toppling them both over to the other side. For a moment, he lay with his breath knocked out of him, then he helped Goldie to her feet and out of the smoke.

They emerged into pure chaos.

There didn't seem to be any kind of organized defence; the townsfolk had seemingly been taken completely by surprise, and the only fighters amongst them were holding the gate against an incursion of armoured warriors. Missiles of flame rushed overhead, landing in showers of sparks and flame. Some of them exploded into pieces, shedding bits of burning material all over the place. People screamed in pain as debris landed upon them, sticking to their clothes even as others tried to help them get rid of it. There did seem to be some sort of fire brigade in progress, but the well-water was too deep and the people too hysterical to make much difference.

Goldie immediately made for the knot of grim-faced workers at the well and started hauling buckets of water with a speed Will would not have believed possible. Within moments, it seemed, people were running hither and thither with purpose, dousing the flames with a will that had been absent before. None of them stopped to question the wild-looking girl streaked with salt and ash.

Will drew his sword. He had some sort of idea to join the fighters at the gate, and the sword was eager in his hand, anticipating the fray.

A ball of fire burst a few feet before him, spewing tongues of fire all around. The force of the explosion threw him backwards. He landed hard, losing his sword. His ears were ringing, and every injury he had suffered in the past day ignited in him once again. His heart sank down into his stomach and the taste of terror was in the back of his throat, threatening to overwhelm him. If he had eaten anything that day, he would have retched.

*Warriors burned to ash where they stood . . .*

He was trapped there, and he could not escape. And this time, the fire was coming for him. He had cheated it before, been saved by a quirk of fate, but now he was trapped, and there was no way out.

*They fell as they ran from a fiery weapon . . .*

The flames were waiting, ready to engulf him. Shadows flickered through the fire, shapes that tantalized his memory, familiar yet alien, images from another life. One of them was shaped like a woman, her form moving towards the tiny shadow of a child. Two stood together, looking down at him as though he were a child, dwarfing him in their magnificence. A line of shadows dressed in flowing robes of flame thronged around him, their shadow hands beckoning him into the fire. There was a weird beauty in their dance, an otherworldly force that called to him. His fear began to drain away, and he got to his feet.

It was then that he saw the black shadow—the dark priest.

*No,* was all he could think as his terror overwhelmed him. *No, no, go away. Go away. Haven't you harmed me enough? Not like this—I don't want to go like this . . .* He was crawling in the mud, the priest's black robes fluttering away from his grasp, and bits of burned men rained down all around him.

It seemed that he had just remembered Aedfrith, her face and her voice and her name, and now she was in his arms, dying. Around him, the walls of his childhood home were spattered with blood. As he sobbed over the blade buried in Aedfrith's breast, the dark priest stood over him, laughing.

'*Enjoy your last days, Thane Wilhelm. You will spend them in madness, trapped in nought but your own memory, unable to break free, my slave until death alone frees you—*'

As though from a very long way away, Will heard somebody screaming his name. He looked back with a strange, calm horror at his wife's bloodied, broken body.

The shadow of the priest was fading, though his laughter still echoed in Will's ears. The ground beneath him shuddered, rumbled, answering the call of a great and primal force. He felt it rush beneath him, sweep through him, carry him in its wake like water. The roaring drowned out everything else; he was alone in the maelstrom, swept away by the waters—

Will awoke with a gasp, drenched in water that was streaming over him and throughout the entire town. Goldie was holding his head above the water, calling to him as she cradled him in her arms. He wanted to stand, but he was trembling all over and could not be sure what was happening nor where he was.

'Will!' Goldie's voice was raw with relief. 'You're going to be all right. It's over. We're safe.'

'What . . . happened?'

'The well burst!' Will had not realized that there were others around, but now they made themselves heard. Their voices were filled with awe.

'It was a miracle sent from God himself . . .'

'Nay, 'twas the faeries of the river. They dwell in wells . . .'

'It saved us . . .'

'We all would have burned . . .'

'A miracle . . .'

'The well did burst,' Goldie whispered. 'It flooded the town, and put out most of the fires. And I think that whoever sent it, also . . . also saved you.'

Will's eyes burned with tears. 'Goldie . . .'

'Shh, now.' She helped him stand, letting him lean upon her shoulder. He was still shaking.

'My friend is hurt.' She looked around at the townspeople. 'Is there a healer amongst you?'

'I will help him,' said a voice from the crowd, 'as you have valiantly helped our fire brigade. I could almost believe that you caused the miracle that saved us all.' The voice was warm and friendly, and Goldie propelled him gently, but Will felt no sense of safety nor relief. The wound he had been dealt was too deep and too personal, though it might not show on the surface.


WHEN WILL FINALLY SURFACED FROM a smothering dream of despair, he found himself beneath a half-burnt roof, though he could not have said how he had gotten there. Someone had laid a damp cloth on his forehead, and he was lying on a carpet of straw. Automatically, he sat up, looking for Goldie. She lay asleep just a few inches from him.

They were not alone upon the straw, Will realized; the wounded of the battle surrounded them. There was a smell of cooked meat in the air, and he felt queasy just thinking about it.

*The priest. The dark priest.* Will pressed his hands to his head. *I should have known him, but I did not, though I've seen him in my dreams. So many things I've forgotten, that I don't know. Who is he? And how did he manage to reduce me to such a shivering wreck?* He looked down at his shaking hands. *Who saved me from him? And what would have happened if I had not been saved? Would I have had to relive that terrible vision forever?*

*Not a vision,* he realized. *A memory. I asked myself how Aedfrith died. Now I know. It was not the travail of childbirth nor wasting of disease. It was—murder.*

Clenching his hands into fists, Will hardened his resolve. It was time for a course of action.

Gently he shook Goldie awake. She opened her eyes slowly.

'Will? The Lady be thanked . . .'

'I need to speak with you,' he said. 'Outside, away from everybody else.'

She nodded, and rose to go with him. Outside, the choking ash permeated everything. The ruins of the town were soaked through, and blackish water was swirling everywhere. It looked as though some vindictive god had used the town as a funeral pyre, then doused it with a vengeful flood of water from the sky. Black mud and wet ash combined to colour the entire place in the greyish hues of a barren hell.

Will gestured around at the wreckage. 'Tell me again, *how* did this happen?'

'I was at the well when it exploded,' Goldie said quietly. 'It was as though something suddenly rushed up from underground, and the water just came spraying out. I only found you after the danger was over.' She looked uncertainly up at him. 'You were unconscious, only—not. You were whimpering, though I couldn't make out what you were saying. And then a wave of water came up and swirled all around you, dragging you with it, and you stopped twitching and woke up.'

'And the army that was at the gates?' Will asked softly, wearily.

'The flood of water hit their catapults, doused their fires, and threatened to wash them away.' Goldie frowned. 'They managed to haul them out before disappearing . . . then they vanished as if by magic. A sudden mist blanketed their passing, hiding them completely. Scouts have been sent to search for them . . . but there's no sign. Just like there was no sign of their presence before they turned up last night at the gates.' She hesitated before continuing, 'Will . . . it's not natural, whatever they did to you, how they seem to move, that fiery weapon of theirs . . . it's nothing that I could have thought even existed.'

Will managed to smile grimly. 'The best of us couldn't have thought of all that's happened in the past two days,' he said.

Goldie moved closer to him. 'What happened to you? It was like some kind of madness . . .'

Will tried to avoid her eyes. 'I don't know,' he muttered. 'It . . . it has something to do with Fort Horsa, though. It has to.'

'Fort Horsa?' repeated Goldie, lost.

'Where I came to after battle, without my memories,' he explained. 'My army there . . . was all burned to death. *Burned,* Goldie.' He shivered and glanced around at the once thriving town reduced to ashes. 'Like this place would have burned if not for the miracle.' He rubbed soot from his eyes. 'I . . . I can't go home,' he said, as much to himself as to her, a sudden realization that had come upon him.

Goldie looked puzzled. 'Why not?'

'It has something to do with *me.* I tried to convince myself otherwise, that it was but some southern feud that I had no stake in . . . but I cannot fool myself any longer. Whoever is behind this battle, I know him—I mean, I knew him . . . a dark priest who casts a shadow of evil . . . and he will not stop until he has destroyed me.' He felt oddly calm, now that it lay all in the open. Like he was discussing someone else's fate rather than his own.

'I was saved, again . . . but by whom?'

Goldie looked quickly away, and he caught her hand.

'You know,' he said quietly.

'I am not certain.' She shook her head. 'But I . . . I do suspect something . . . I've felt something like this power before, and it may have had a reason to save the townsfolk. But it would be too dangerous for mortals like y—like us to go and find it . . .'

'I can go wherever I need to on my own,' Will said. 'I can't ask you to put yourself in danger for me.'

She met his eyes defiantly. 'You wouldn't last long on your own. I am from the true north, at least, and I know something of the powers of the faeries. You're not going anywhere alone.'

'So where do we need to go?'

Goldie sighed. 'I'll show you,' she said reluctantly. 'It won't be far, but we need to head west, and soon.' Her eyes scanned the ruined town. 'If this dark priest is after you, we don't have much time.'

# Chapter Six

# The River Queen

*How is it that Thane Wilhelm has escaped me a second time?*

*Am I not the terror whom they name the Dark Priest, the fire that comes in the night, the sorcerer who wreaks his hatred upon the entire world? There is no-one in this land who can oppose me, and yet some-one has, and all to save Thane Wilhelm, my mortal enemy, the one I swore to destroy.*

*The generals celebrated the capture of Fort Horsa, but I cared only about one man who fought there. My happiness was genuine when they told me that not one had survived. Later, when I found out they lied, I reduced them to squalling infants before destroying their bodies.*

*A greater power moves in the land, opposing me, and I do not know its name, only that it protects Wilhelm from me, as if he is worthy of protection.*

*What I would give to see him suffer. He will know the pain he has caused me, at the end, and my revenge will be complete.*

*Now the general of my army vexes me with complaints about the men we lost. Does he think I care about these insignificant lives whilst Wilhelm is running free and unpunished? I am the sorcerer of the Church, you fool. I have burned this land to cinders, showing no mercy to lord or peasant. I have defeated great ones of my order, and it is only because I value your strategic expertise that I do not capture your mind right now and grant you the same madness as your subcommanders.*

*Justice cannot live whilst Wilhelm does. I would call it God's work, but I now know that He does not care about justice. How could he, when he allowed Aedfrith to be taken from me?*

*I remember when I believed in God. How comforting it was to think that a greater power watched over all of our lives, that everything could be good and pure if only we tried. When she and I were children, we never thought of sin. We never planned for lust and vice to come between us; we loved each other with a pure love, an innocent love, something the world could never understand. How could any earthly man comprehend the heavenly bond that existed between us? Her father belittled me—her mother thought I would corrupt her—corrupt her? I only ever wanted what was best for her!*

*Something in this land has unnatural power, and I must find out what it is. Who watches over the bloody thane? Who dares to protect the man who ravaged Aedfrith?*

*If only we could go back to innocent childhood, you and I, my love, my Aedfrith. I should have convinced you to run away with me, to marry me in secret, then they could never have touched you. When his father came looking for a bride for his cursed son, he would never have been able to take you away if you were already bound to me.*

*Instead, innocent as we were, we believed that our dreams would come true, that we could both serve God as we had promised each other we would. Two lives were destroyed, that day you left weeping, but you left, and there was nothing I could do to bring you back. No amount of praying moved God to make them let you go. When I begged the thane and his son to take you to the convent instead, they laughed and rode me down. I can still hear your screams . . .*

*I left for the monastery alone, with you forever gone from my side. That should have been a moment we shared together—I to serve God in wisdom, you to serve Him in innocence. It was the promise we made to each other, but you were not allowed to keep it, and that I will never forgive.*

*In truth, you died the day you left with him. What I found when I returned eight years later was not the innocent, pure girl I had known and loved. The woman who bore your name had become a hollow shell filled with man's corruption, and my love for you sickened and turned to contempt.*

*That hollow, meaningless shell is gone now from the world, but the man I hate still remains.*

*I will hunt him through all the hells that exist, if I must. I have the power now, and he is alone. I have the upper hand, as long as I can discover who is protecting him. And when I find out, I will destroy him, as he deserves to be destroyed. He will suffer for all the ways in which he enjoyed the girl he stole from me. He will suffer.*

THE VISION OF AEDFRITH'S MURDER haunted Will, and he could not sleep that night. Goldie found a sheltered nook in a nearby wood, a corner of undergrowth protected by a thicket of berries that had grown together, winding their branches through and around one another until they had produced a passable roof to keep off the rain. There was barely enough space for them both, and as soon as Goldie fell asleep, tired out with her exertions and worries, Will got up and went to sit upon a nearby root.

Foolishly, he had thought that he could make peace with himself and begin anew without the past of Thane Wilhelm to trouble him. But his past self's ghosts were still there, and as he had suspected all along, they were dark and terrible. He clung to the vision like a child to a beloved parent, yet at the same time, he wished that it would go away and that the questions it had stirred up would leave him.

*My wife was murdered.* The thought engendered a hollow pit in his stomach, and spread a deathly chill throughout his whole body. All this time, he had assumed that Thane Wilhelm had been motivated solely by the joy of fighting and the rewards he could gain, but now he wasn't so sure. *Did I seek revenge on her killer? Is this the quest my entire life was built to fulfil?* Perhaps he had not been the faithful and devoted husband Aedfrith no doubt wished for, but if she had been murdered, he would have been honour-bound to bring her killer to justice. And if he could not find the murderer, he would have to live his entire life with a stain upon not only his honour, but the honour of both their families . . .

*If I go home now, I will have failed.* Perhaps this was why he had never returned, even after five years had passed. *What other reason could there be?*

*Unless* . . . but he couldn't think about that. He had wept for her; it stood to reason that he would seek vengeance against the one who had caused her death.

*Unless I caused it. Unless I, somehow, was at fault, and she died because of me.*

Will shook himself. Why had that thought occurred to him?

A light rain had begun to fall, but he hardly even noticed. Goldie slept silently, safe in the thicket of bushes. There was a satchel at her feet; it contained some food that she had been able to beg off the villagers, but neither of them had had much appetite for supper.

*Dear God—what do I do with her? I cannot take her with me if I am to pursue revenge.*

Will passed his hands through his unkempt hair, feeling suddenly exhausted. Perhaps whoever was behind the miracle of the exploding well would also have a safe place for her to remain. Goldie deserved to be safe; she had gone through too much already. Caught by a mob, attacked by a monster straight out of a particularly vivid nightmare, and nearly burned to death tonight. And now he was up against an enemy who not only had a weapon that spewed fire to mutilate and destroy, but who could also somehow send the demons of his mind, Will's own dark memories, to incapacitate, trap, and torment him. Will shivered. *I was lucky to escape. As lucky as I was at Fort Horsa.*

He frowned. *Both times, I might have been saved. Something broke me out of the memory; something tossed me into the ditch to escape the fire. And I do not think that it was the providence of the divine, either.* He brushed his thumb over the pommel of his sword, which, lacking a scabbard, someone had wrapped up in rags for him. *If* that tale of Goldie's were true . . .

They looked a particularly sorry pair at this moment, himself and Goldie; they were both still covered in sweat and soot, she had been dressed in a tatty goodwife's frock by the villagers, and their provisions had been lost. Will couldn't imagine how they were going to survive, but that was a lesser worry at the moment. *A demon sword, she said. A sword I only remember carrying since my second life began.* More and more, it seemed as though someone had been *marking* him for vengeance. *But who? And what do they want of me?*

Will shivered in his damp clothes. He had had no chance to dry out, and his bruised shoulders were aching. His oldest scars were protesting at the damp and chill, and it was raining on him again.

*And in the rain, I remember.* He turned his face up to the sky, and resigned himself to a sleepless night.


THE MORNING WAS COLD AND CHEERLESS, the sky grey and drizzling. Unseasonable mist swirled ankle-deep above the bracken as they walked beneath the trees. Goldie led them deeper and deeper into the heart of the wood, following no path that could be discerned, her skirt catching on the thorns of the wild briars that twined along the ground. Yet she seemingly knew where they were going, for she did not misstep once nor hesitate in her progress.

The woods were silent save for the rushing of a far-off river, a sound that made Will think back to the stories Goldie told. *Water-sprites, the immortal ones, they who live in streams and lakes, wielding power over the destiny of man.*

On a day like this, tales of faeries could well be believed.

Will stumbled over a briar-root, put his hands out to break his fall, but managed to keep his balance after all. Disentangling his foot from the root that had somehow contrived to wrap itself around his ankle, he gazed around. It was hard to make out anything in the thickening mist, even the wavering form of Goldie somewhere in front of him.

Will blinked, but the rogue shapes hidden in the mist did not change nor resolve themselves. 'Goldie!' he called, and her name fell muffled into the folds of the swirling blanket that surrounded him.

He dared not move. Shadows were creeping through the woods at the edge of his vision, and strange noises half-heard whispered in the leaves above. Will's hand tightened on the hilt of his sword, which he had been carrying against his shoulder. As he swept it out in front of him, the rags fell away from the blade. The naked steel shone coldly in the gloom.

Twisting around, he could see no shadows nor hear any sound over his own breathing. He shivered. The world was silent, as though lying in wait.

As he turned back, holding the point of his sword level with his eyes, the woman appeared before him.

Will started, his eyes staring. He could not see where she could possibly have come from, and though she wore no clothes, her nakedness appeared to be concealed beneath swirling clouds of blue . . . or was it blue and white? Or many colours all mixed together? The patterns moved and followed wherever he put his eyes, and yet they seemed contiguous with the eddying mist.

Seeking to avoid the dizziness they had lent him, he looked

back at her face, which was oddly devoid of emotion. It seemed a sculpture of a woman who stood there, regal in her bearing despite her lack of rich clothes and adornments. Her heart-shaped, ageless face was the deep brown of a young oak tree, her coarse curly hair the dark golden leaves of autumn.

'Who are you?' Will demanded. 'What is this place? Where is Goldie?'

As her name escaped him, the mists parted and Will saw that he stood upon a high ridge of rock overlooking a vast marshland. Below, where fog hung heavily over the putrid mudflats, a young maiden with golden hair made her way towards the distant water.

'Goldie!' Will shouted, but she did not turn. She stood on the edge of the marshland, gazing out towards the deeper pools of clear water.

He wanted to run towards her, but some instinct made him remain. Her clothes had changed, he suddenly realized: she wore an apron of soft blue cloth and there were amber beads twined around her wrist. Her hair was braided into a tight crown around her head.

As he watched, she raised her arms over the water and let her body fall forwards. The silent waters closed over her, and Will's scream caught in his throat, his feet still rooted to the spot.

'No!' he said loudly, and closed his eyes. When he opened them, the marshland was gone. 'It's not real,' he whispered.

'You are wrong,' the strange woman said, her voice an eerie echo in the silent woods. 'It is what has been, and what she needs to return to.' Her grey eyes shone as cold as the steel of his sword. 'She does not belong to you, Wilhelm. She can never be yours.'

'You know my name,' he challenged. 'Who are you?'

'You may call me Helya,' she said. A faint breeze stirred her curly hair. With the sound of her name, impressions of a larger vision flashed by in the corner of his eye, too fast for Will to make any sense of them. *A grey-eyed king with a long yellow beard, perched atop a throne of rotting fish. Death-lights burning in the marshland, and a raven-haired maiden dragged beneath the surface of the water.*

'What is this place?' he demanded once more. 'What are these visions?' There were partings in the mist all around him, and each opened to a different world. Before him Aedfrith stood praying, her veil drawn over her face, darkness gathering around her in the gloom of a chapel. When Will turned his head, he looked down upon a very different scene: a green-eyed woman stretched out in a sunlit glade, her underdress hanging loosely over her body, and beckoned towards him. Close enough to touch her yet separated by a swirling wall of mist, a curly-haired young man strode beneath the forest canopy, looking back with a laugh of merriment.

Even as Will turned away from this happy scene, renouncing his curiosity and the pull of attraction he felt, another vision unfolded before his eyes. A laughing girl no more than eight years old was playing in a soft rainfall. In the background, peasants' hovels stretched up a rocky hillside.

Will's heart jolted in sudden recognition. This was the laughing child who haunted his memories, always joyful, yet she brought with her a sadness that froze his very heart in his chest. He could see her face now, though he still did not know her name, and he felt the pull towards her and the hold she had over him, prompting him to take a step forward. She had soft brown hair, almost the same shade as Aedfrith's, and her eyes were as dark as his . . .

Something nagged at the edge of Will's mind, pulling his gaze away from her. He looked down at his sword, the only solid thing in this shifting world of mist and memory. His own face was reflected upon the blade.

'I came to you for a purpose,' Will said softly, half to himself. He glanced up, and his eyes met Helya's. 'Quit tormenting me with these visions!' he spat. 'From you, all I desire are answers.' He brandished his sword. 'What is this weapon, and how did I come by it?'

A faint smile quirked Helya's impassive lips. 'What kind of champion would you be if I did not test you a little?' she asked coyly, then became serious again. 'You cannot change the past, Wilhelm. Remember that. What matters now is the adversary, the battle to come. You must let go of those you could not save.'

'You speak in riddles,' Will said. 'I am no-one's champion.'

'You are mine.' Helya held out her hand. 'The champion of the faeries, the hero I chose to save all of us. It is why you wield our sword.'

Will hesitated, looking down at her outstretched hand.

'Come with me,' she said, 'and I will answer your questions. I will show you what happened that day.'

*What day?* he wanted to ask, but the world around them both was disappearing. Helya sank into the mist, dragging him with her. Darkness closed over his eyes, smothering him, then released him just as abruptly. When his eyes opened, he found himself in an entirely new place.

The faery woman stood beside him upon a low hill, gazing

downwards. Baking sun blazed down upon a field of armoured soldiers beneath a wooden keep. The soldiers marched towards the pair of them, mailed footsteps resounding upon the ground.

'Come with me,' Helya said, and somehow Will heard her above the din. She led him down towards the foot of the hill, from where they could see the foe the soldiers faced.

Will went rigid, and he whipped around to face Helya. 'I *remember* this! Those catapults—or at least they looked like catapults—that unnatural mist, the ash hanging in the air—'

'And there you are,' Helya said, pointing.

Will gaped. The man in command of the army, egging his men on at the top of his voice, showing no fear in the face of such a foe, was himself.

'This—this is what lies in the past! I am going to see what truly happened on that day?'

She nodded, drawing back. Will turned his eyes back towards the foe. The same that had brought fire and death to the town by the sea. Of that he had no doubt . . .

Why was there ash floating in the air? Nothing was on fire, not yet. He looked towards himself, a rough, scarred man who had seen many a battle, a warrior who feared nothing. *You fool,* he thought, *can't you see? Can't you feel there's something wrong?*

Within the enemy army on the other side of the ridge, Will could make out a black-clad figure standing apart from the fighting men. *The dark priest.* He tried to move forward for a better look, but he could not move beyond where he stood in the past. Frustrated, he fell back. His past self ran back amongst his soldiers, yelling at them to hurry, and Will was compelled to follow. As he turned back to go down the ridge, from the corner of his eye he saw the priest raise both arms high above his head.

The catapults remained stationary, but the ash floating in the air caught fire.

Both the past and present versions of Thane Wilhelm watched in horror as the very air turned to flame, devouring every man it touched.

The soldiers within that fiery blast collapsed without even screaming, the flames searing them from the inside out, yet there was noise aplenty from those who had seen it happen. The entire vanguard went down, and Thane Wilhelm was left scrabbling in confusion, half his host fallen instantly, the other half fleeing in terror. When the first fiery missile flew from the catapults, he was already stumbling backwards, consumed with fear, towards the ditch that encircled Fort Horsa . . .

Wilhelm lost his footing spectacularly, tripping at the top of the earthwork and losing his sword and shield as he fell towards the bottom of the ditch. As fate would have it, there was a protruding rock waiting to hit his head against. Will winced as he watched from the top of the ditch. His past self slumped unconscious, disarmed, a deep cut on his forehead where he had hit the rock on his way down.

'Is that all?' Will asked as Helya appeared beside him again. His heart was pounding and his breath shallow, as though he were truly reliving the entire ordeal once again.

She took his arm. 'Wait.'

Moments passed as they watched the completion of the slaughter. It did not last long. Fires raged all over the plain, and roiling black smoke waited to smother those who somehow escaped the burning. But here upon the earthwork, Will realized, there was comparative safety. The wind blew away from the fort, chasing the smoke towards the poor souls trapped between their lord's walls and the foe.

Will's eye was caught by a lone soldier furtively sneaking towards the earthwork. Where had he come from? He held his round shield protectively in front of him; his face was hidden by his helm. He padded along the top of the ditch, glancing around as if to make certain no-one had seen him.

The young soldier spotted Will lying prone at the bottom of the ditch. Setting his shield aside, he removed his helmet, revealing himself to be none other than the faery woman who now stood beside him.

Helya leapt into the ditch and knelt beside Will, laying her hand on his bloodstained forehead. After a long moment, she reached for her belt and unbuckled the sword that hung there. It was instantly recognizable, and he clasped his hand once more around the hilt as he watched. Helya fastened the sword to his belt, donned her helm once more, and made her way from the field of battle. As Will watched her go, she presently turned towards him.

'You were here,' Will said in surprise. 'But what—what did you do to me?' A sudden suspicion shot into his mind, but he dared not give voice to it. This woman was powerful—as powerful as the sea-demon had been, or perhaps even more so. Will had learned, in that dank cave just two nights ago, to recognize the appearance of the sea-demon's magical strength, and the same seeming practically emanated from the woman who stood beside him. Knowing this, he dared not voice the idea that she might have stolen his memories and his entire life from him.

'I gave you a great gift,' Helya replied. Will could make out nothing in her inflection or expression that told him whether she was telling the truth or not. 'The sword of a champion, forged by faeries and handled by heroes. The means by which you will defeat the Dark Priest and his sinister army.'

Her voice was caressing, seductive. Will had the impression that she was trying to wheedle him into something, but he was not yet entirely sure of what she wanted. 'Why me?' he asked curtly, hoping to gain some time to think.

'Why not you?' She folded her arms, and Will could almost feel her words bearing down upon him. 'You were a great warrior—you still are. You dedicated your life to fighting—why not use it to fight against evil?'

Will looked down at his feet. 'You don't know,' he said softly. 'That injury did me great harm. My memories—'

'—have been lost. I do know.'

She was unreadable, but it was clear what she wanted of him. *Get rid of the Dark Priest.* Like a pagan goddess in the old stories laying a quest upon a courageous hero. And it was something he would even do willingly—gladly—if he could be assured of success. But the question remained: why had Helya had chosen *him* for the job, as broken and confused as he was? Will did not believe a word of her vague explanation.

'Have hope,' Helya was saying. 'Perhaps your memories will return yet, in time. You must focus on the task at hand. You must destroy this evil man, and all his creations with him.'

Will gave a harsh laugh. 'Destroy him? How? How do you expect me to fight a foe who can penetrate my mind and make me into nothing more than a crazed thing?' He looked directly into the woman's eyes, which still held nothing he could read. 'How can I defeat his armies on my own, even with a magic sword?'

'The Dark Priest will not be able to enter your mind again,'

Helya promised, holding his gaze. When the light shifted, her eyes were almost the same colour as Goldie's. 'I will protect you from this power of his, as long as you persist in destroying him.' She waved a hand. The battlefield scene began to recede into grey, and they stood back in the mist where they had started. 'This weapon—the ash that burns—it threatens both the mortal and faery realms. It does not belong here, and you must be the one who stops its advance. You must defeat the Dark Priest.'

Will's belligerence, which had carried him thus far through the confrontation, was draining away against the strength of her will. He had no real answers, and it was clear that Helya did not intend to give him any. The weariness from last night settled heavy upon him, and he did not argue further.

The mist receded softly to reveal a sunny meadow very different from the gloomy forest that Goldie had led him into. When it cleared to reveal her again beside him, he wanted to hug her in relief. But he remembered what had happened the last time, and restrained himself.

Helya had vanished just as abruptly as she had appeared, and Will could almost believe that it all had been a particularly vivid dream. There was an undercurrent of anger running through him. Possibly, he realized, fuelled by the sword which was still in his hand.

*She showed me nothing, in the end, nothing that I did not already know or guess. My only consolation is that he cannot reach into my mind now. Or so she says.*

He turned to Goldie, who looked drawn and exhausted. 'Is it always like this? With the—the faeries?'

Goldie managed a tight-lipped smile. 'We should rest,' she

said, evading the question. 'Helya has given us fresh provisions and directions. We are to turn westwards towards the forest, and find the outlaw hideout named Rob's Nest. There we will find allies in the battle against the Dark Priest.' She lowered her gaze, and twined the fingers of both her hands together. 'If you choose to fight him, that is. Helya has already plotted your course for you, but she has forgotten that the choice is not hers to make.'

'What other choice do I have?' Will asked. *My wife was murdered.* 'I cannot go home.'

Goldie's eyes widened as though in pain, but she blinked and looked calmly at him. 'Well, I have a choice, too,' she said flatly, 'and I am going to show you the way to the Nest. This hideout belongs to Rob Lightfingers; I've been there before.' She added defiantly, 'And I am *not* leaving you. I won't.'

Will could not recall having asked her to leave him. What had happened to Goldie, whilst the faery woman had been with him? Will remembered the vision of the marshland, Goldie dropping under the water. She would probably not tell him if he asked. She seemed suddenly incredibly distant from him, different from the headstrong girl he had come to know during their journey together, holding secret depths of her own that Will could never plumb. Her secrecy, however, was nothing compared to the barrier of his own dark past, which had just been dropped squarely between them. Will did not know how to share such things with her, yet he dreaded bearing the burden of his secrets alone.

He caught her hand. 'Why not?'

Unexpectedly, Goldie grinned, deflecting the tone of the question even as she deftly freed her hand from his grip. 'What

kind of hero would *I* be, if I were to let you wander off alone?'
she teased. 'You owe your life to me, Will Nobody, don't you
forget.'

'There are too many women to whom I owe my life,' Will
groused. There was no choice but to accept it all. They did not
truly belong to each other, him and Goldie, and had no obligation to share secrets. 'Rob's Nest it is, then. We'll leave in the
morning.'

# Chapter Seven

# The Deserters

Water heals. I was born under the water, and it has always been around me.

Water cleanses the past. Water clears our eyes to see through falsehood, and it washes the deception of the world away so that we can see true.

I now see that I have never been content. Always restless, always longing for something more—this is who I am. Going from one world to another, finding peace in neither. I longed to leave my mother's people, and got myself lost so I could do it. To be sure, I didn't consciously run away. But I wanted to live with the others, with folk who were happy and showed it. I wanted to be part of their world, and in the end

*I spent longer with my foster family than I did with my mother. I thought they cared for me as one of their own. But the moment I went against their wishes, they no longer wanted to keep me. They threw me out to fend for myself. And I might have died if I hadn't met Will.*

*Or I might have consigned myself to the world of water. Even now, it calls to me. The other world promises everything that I do not have in this one: immortality, power, authority. But no love, no warmth, no smiling faces around me, no company to hold my hand when I am lonely.*

*Like the element they live in, the water-sprites are never constant; they can never stop moving. They cannot stand still and care for you, they cannot understand pain as mortals experience it. Eternities pass in the water, and it is changeful and yet never changes. In this world beneath the surface, far away from the sun, time does not exist and history passes with barely a whisper. Empires rise and fall in the world above, and the water-sprites see none of it. Babies are born, grow into children and parents and grandparents, and all that the water-sprites see are the reflections of their own beautiful faces in the water.*

*They use humans, the same way Helya plots to use Will. Their beautiful little world below the waves is everything, and they only pretend to have any interest in earthly affairs when they feel threatened. And if one hero dies, there's nothing stopping them from choosing a new champion.*

WILL AWOKE TO GOLDIE shaking him vigorously. She drew away when he sat up stretching and yawning. The previous day seemed no more than a bad dream, and he rubbed the sleep out of his eyes as he took in their surroundings. The sun shone brightly from the east, glittering off the surface of a deep pond that lay before them. A single oak tree rose behind him, shading the back of his head from the sunlight. Several yards beyond, the ancient forest brooded; an overgrown path wound between the trees into the distance.

'We need to get moving,' Goldie said matter-of-factly. Will looked up to see her holding her pack, her hair pulled back in a long braid. 'It's a long way to Rob's Nest, and it'll take us several days.'

Will was filled with lassitude, suddenly determined to enjoy his pleasant surroundings after the discomfort of the last two days, and it seemed to him that the troubles of the world could wait upon the demands of his stomach. 'Can't we at least stop for breakfast?' he protested. Rubbing soot and salt out of his beard, he continued, 'And there's a clean pond *right there* to get our clothes—and ourselves—washed in. Shouldn't questing heroes be clean, at least?'

As he spoke, he was opening his pack, and suddenly he realized that their original provisions from Leabury had miraculously been restored and more. His pack was stuffed full of food—basic stuff, oatcakes and dried fruit and dried salt pork, but more of it than they had had to start with.

He whistled happily. 'Many benefits to knowing some faery woman, I guess. We can make a decent meal every day on the road.'

'She's not just some faery woman, she's the leader of all the water-sprites of the north, and she styles herself the River Queen and the Daughter of the Marsh King,' Goldie snapped. She looked put out and impatient, but Will could not fathom why.

Will lifted an eyebrow. 'Oho, so *that's* the River Queen,' he said.

Goldie had at least the common decency to look contrite. She folded her arms in front of her, and said nothing.

'What was that other title you gave her?' Will continued. 'Daughter of the Marsh King?' He furrowed his brow, recalling the deep brown visage of the strange faery woman. 'I would have assumed she came from the south, from the lands around the middle-sea.'

'She is the daughter of both the sinister Marsh King and an Egyptian princess,' Goldie explained grudgingly.

Will looked up at her. 'I suppose these are more stories from your mother's people?'

Goldie coloured slightly. 'Where my foster family lived,' she explained haltingly, 'there is a great marshland. To venture too far therein is to trespass into the faery realm. The lines between the worlds are blurred there, and the people of this land remember many things that others have forgotten.' She shivered. 'Helya is an immortal of great power, and she is well-known even amongst the humans who dwell there. This place belongs to *her*.' She gestured around at the pleasant pond. 'I do not feel right here.'

Will scrutinized her stricken expression. 'All right,' he finally agreed. 'Let's pack up and get going. We can stop somewhere else for breakfast.'

Goldie sighed in relief. 'As we go west,' she said, 'the river will cut our path somewhere through the woods. We can stop there.' She hesitated. 'Thank you.'

'You know I never could refuse you,' Will teased, trying to lighten the mood. Giving a final wide yawn, he picked up his pack, steadied it on his back, and turned regretfully away from the sparkling pond. 'Lead the way, my lady.'


FOR THE FIRST TIME, Will saw Goldie brood.

It seemed that their visit to the faery woman Helya had turned Goldie's normally carefree nature to something far more private. Will knew that she was unlikely to confide her troubles to him, since she never had before, so he decided that he would try to distract and comfort rather than wheedle the whole matter out of her. He picked blue and white flowers—her favourites—from the hedges as they passed, and helped her weave them into her hair. He cleaned her clothes when she bathed and searched for fragrant herbs to add to their meals. And as they walked, he spoke of stories—all the old tales he could remember. How the three-leaved clover, symbol of God's hand in nature, inspired the first of the native saints to bring the Faith to his people. How a lowly monk sailed across the ocean and found lands full of monsters and demons and fire-breathing mountains in the west. How his own ancestors left the north and sailed the sea looking for adventure and renown.

Recollections of his past life continued to return to him, memories far too private to share: a girl with Roman features and hazel-green eyes that cast a mesmerizing spell over him; the energetic highborn ladies in the court of the Bernician underking, where his father had taken him as a young man; a buxom serving-woman whose hands plucked eagerly at his belt even as he undressed her; the face of his wife when she caught him gazing covetously at a visiting thane's daughter. Thane Wilhelm had been no stranger to the charms of women, but Will found it hard to imagine himself as an experienced rake now. In the end, most of his affairs had meant nothing, and the one woman with whom he could have built a stable home was dead. Though they had clearly been badly matched at their wedding, Will found himself wondering if he could have learned to love Aedfrith by now. Had he known of the fragility of life and sanity, how much difference it made to be able to have a home and woman to call one's own, perhaps he would have treated her better; perhaps he would have been faithful and content.

He found more memories, of his brothers-in-arms, the men he had known in his youth and those who had later fought beside him. How he had drunk and laughed together with his companions; the reassurance as he gripped a familiar hand before his first fray. There was one companion in particular whom he had held dear in the days before his marriage. Like many of the other figures in his past, Will could not recall his name, but remembered what he looked like. Curly red-brown hair that he wore long, green-blue eyes that sparkled with laughter, and a toothy mouth that was always ready to grin. Some nights, Will lay awake wondering what had become of him, just as he wondered about the little girl who laughed in the rain, the girl who had the same brown eyes as him.

They journeyed through the woods for nearly a week, seeing little evidence of human habitation. There was the occasional woodcutter's station, and sometimes the far-off sound of falling axes. They were never bothered by night nor on the road, which was really an uneven, overgrown path that would have been difficult to navigate on horseback. All around them, the woods luxuriated in the last green flush of summer, drinking the light rain that fell nearly every day and putting forth all their beauty in return. They passed profusions of late flowers, blue and pink and white. Merry streams bubbled from mossy rocks beneath fronds of ferns that grew close to the soil. Ivy twined up the trunks of tall trees, covering them in a glossy coat of glowing green. Large brown slugs nestled in the damp bark, and richly plumaged birds warbled in the branches above.

They walked for several days, and every day the woods about them grew yet more alive and wild, yet they came not upon another human soul. On the fifth day, the path disappeared into the brush, and Goldie cast around until she found a narrow woods trail to follow. By the looks of it, only foxes and badgers had used it for years. But Will found himself glancing to the branches above them, fancying that dark forms moved there, flitting from tree to tree. The oak giants that towered to the sky had surely never known the hand of man.

They stopped to make a lunch, sitting amongst the bushes. The woods here were so dense that a skilled woodsman could have passed unseen a handsbreadth away. There was no telling what lay ahead of them.

'Are you sure this is the right way?' Will asked Goldie. She had started to look more cheerful today; her unbound hair caught the sun and gave back the light like beaten gold.

'As long as we keep going west.' Goldie glanced up at the branches. 'Actually, I'm surprised we haven't come across them yet. Rob's men patrol the surrounding woods; that's how I met them before.' She glanced around, as if to make sure they were alone, and then looked at Will. 'There's something I want to say. To ask you, really.' She leaned forwards, and her eyes were grave. 'What happens after you have defeated the dark priest?'

Will avoided her eyes. 'To be honest,' he mumbled, 'I

haven't thought about after.'

'You'd sacrifice your life for a cause someone else wants you to fight?' Will looked up at the tone of distress in her voice. To his surprise, there were tears in her bright blue eyes, and she was staring at him with a sort of defiant desperation. He couldn't think when he had done anything to deserve such ardent emotion from her.

'Goldie . . . you couldn't understand,' he began. 'I have lived one life . . . I have made grievous mistakes, done things for which I must atone . . .' He took a deep breath. 'This is my fight as much as it is Helya's.'

Goldie reached for his unresisting hand, and held onto it tightly. 'What have you done?' she asked softly.

'I . . . I'm not sure,' Will forced himself to reply. 'Goldie, I am a broken man. At the very least . . .' He steeled himself, preparing to tell her about Aedfrith. He turned his eyes away again, and a sudden movement caught them in the branches above.

Will's hand went to the sword at his side. Following his gaze, Goldie looked up, and she tensed, her face transforming into a neutral expression. Will rose slowly to his feet as the trees about them came alive.

Clothed in green and brown so thoroughly that they could have melted away into the forest foliage, the archers were everywhere, at least a dozen of them. A few perched upon the branches of stout oak trees, whilst others rose from the bushes and ferns. Not all of them were men; Will's eyes were drawn to a short girl with a Roman cast to her dark features, alongside a brawny blonde woman with the hard eyes of a northern mercenary.

Goldie got to her feet. As Will faced the archers wordlessly, she stood before their leader, a young man of average height and straw-blond hair, who frowned and relaxed slightly.

'Goldwine?'

'Eofric,' she gave back. 'You remember me?'

The archer shrugged. 'Now you return alongside a rough man with the look of a bandit about him.'

Goldie smiled crookedly. 'Then he should fit right in alongside you lot, don't you think?'

Will saw the two women snicker, but Eofric had not relaxed the slightest bit, and was gazing suspiciously at him.

'What is your name, and where did you get that sword?' he demanded.

'Wilhelm,' Will replied. 'And my sword is no-one's business but mine.'

Eofric bristled. 'The bloody thane,' he whispered.

'What?'

'I *thought* I recognized you.' Eofric's right hand dropped from his drawn bow; he scrabbled at his belt and yanked a battered shortsword from its sheath. 'You don't remember me, do you? You never were one to spend much time with the common soldiers.'

'You—' Will paused. 'We fought together?'

'I fought for you since childhood,' the warrior said coldly. 'Not that you'd remember my face. Us peasants and churls weren't worthy of your notice, were we?'

'Did I do you some wrong?' Will demanded.

The warrior's mouth twisted. 'I deserted your army, Wilhelm. And I'm not ashamed to say I did.'

'You didn't answer my question.'

Another man, a tall fellow with brown hair, lowered his own

bow and stepped precipitously towards them. 'Wilhelm!' he exclaimed expansively. 'You survived the slaughter at Fort Horsa? My name is Ed, a mercenary who joined your company in the south. I walked away with Eofric; I mourned for those we had left behind when news of the battle reached us. And for the ears of all'—his gaze travelled from Will to Eofric—'I am not so ready to believe whatever rumour was told of you.'

'No rumour,' Eofric cut in. 'Everyone from his damned island knows the truth.'

It was time for humility, Will decided as he watched two strangers debate the truth of his own life. He released his grip on his sword.

'I did not survive Fort Horsa without injury,' he said softly. Two pairs of eyes turned to him, one curious, the other hostile. 'I—took a blow to the head and lost most of my memory.' He turned to the accusing eyes of the young warrior. 'I don't know what crimes you believe I have done, but believe me when I say that you remember more about them than I do.' He hesitated. 'I am not the man you remember as your commander. The battle that day changed me forever.'

Eofric glared at him, and spat at his feet. 'That's what I think of your excuses, *my lord.*' His eyes flickered towards Goldie. 'Where did you find this one?'

Goldie hesitated, her eyes going from one man to the other. 'Wait, what is Will supposed to have done?'

'The unthinkable!' Eofric burst out at long last. 'Five years ago, he brutally murdered his own wife and daughter in his fort!'

There was a moment of dense silence. Will could not move, speak, or think.

*I murdered my wife? And my daughter?*

With no resistance, tears pricked at his eyes and began to flow down his cheeks.

*I didn't even know I had a daughter. I forgot her.*

*How could I forget my own child?*

*How could I kill my own child?*

He was unaware of his surroundings, only that he was sinking to the ground. *It can't be true. It can't be. I don't remember any of it.*

All he could remember was sobbing as he held his wife, his hand grasping the hilt of the blade buried in her chest. Sobbing, that he had done this—that the berserk anger had made him do this—

Will was dimly aware of men dragging him to his feet, of Goldie's voice, confused and hurt, demanding an explanation, insisting that none of it was true. Other voices spoke over hers; there was talk of justice, talk of judgment for his crime.

Will finally found his voice.

'It's true,' he whispered. 'God help me.'

Eofric sneered at him. 'There are no gods who would help you.'


WILL SAT ALONE INSIDE THE THATCHED HALL, staring at the empty fireplace. The fire had gone out a long time ago, and only ash remained.

It was a mark of respect amongst the deserters who had once been his men, that they had not dragged him down to the stocks and left him in the mud to be pelted with refuse by every passerby. Will supposed that was more than he really deserved—

certainly much more than a good chunk of people here thought he deserved. As it was, his entrance into the little hideaway village, dragged along by two of their guards, had attracted quite a lot of attention.

Will shivered. It was raining outside again, and no-one had lit any lamps nor attended to the huge empty fireplace. He got up and paced to warm himself. The hall was draughty, a building used for law and justice rather than drinking and relaxation. Here the village gathering sat regularly in judgment, deciding upon the fates of those who violated the laws of gods and men. Those like him.

Despite the fact that some were literally calling for his blood, Will felt no fear. It had all evaporated from him now. What great thing was there to fear, if all that was evil had already come to pass? When his worst nightmares had all come true?

The lost vision, the picture of the girl in the rain, was now complete. She laughed up at him, her eyes brown like his, smiling wide as he had never seen her mother smile. *Wilge.* He could remember her now. The way she rode with him, sat upon his knee, played with his sword as he laughed and her mother frowned. The way she loved the summer rain and the garden with the apple trees.

He should try to remember how she died, he knew, but the thought was too painful even to contemplate. All the memories of her and her mother were snarled up, tangled into a tight knot that he could not unwind. The thought of Aedfrith brought him so much pain that he could not dwell for long upon her, and he could not seem to sort through the flashes that came before her death. All he could recall was her dying in his arms, by his own sword, and the terrible anger he had felt. There was no possible motive he could recall, no series of events leading up to the fell deed, no memory of what had happened to his daughter.

*Why should I pain myself, anyhow?* He sat down again, burying his head in his hands. It was far sweeter to dwell upon these newly rediscovered memories of his little daughter. He knew that the last thing he wanted was to have seen her dead; perhaps God had finally answered one of his prayers.

If Wilge had lived, she would be thirteen now, almost a maiden. Would she still love playing at swordfights with her father, or would she have grown out of that? Would she have dreams of wedding some handsome young atheling, or would she still be too young for that?

He was about to get up and start pacing along the length of the hall once more when the door swung open. Will turned. The short grey-haired, grey-robed individual who faced him seemed familiar—

The monk moved closer towards him, and Will stifled a gasp of surprise. 'Caedwic!' The Welsh monk held out his arms, and Will collapsed into his embrace.

'We meet again in the most unlikely place,' he said in his softly accented voice.

Will had to stifle a laugh. 'This is the last place I would have expected to find you.'

'And the last accusation I would have expected to be laid before your feet,' the monk said, his face suddenly serious. 'You are miles and miles away from your home; when did you turn from your chosen path? And why did you decide to come here, of all places?'

Will ignored his questions. 'Caedwic, do you—do you know

where Goldwine is?' She had disappeared when they'd dragged him into the village, and Will felt a stab of sickness in his gut about what she was probably thinking of him.

'The pagan girl who came here with you?' Caedwic moved towards the fireplace and frowned down upon the ashes within. 'She went with some of the village women, who welcomed her as a friend.' He cast an eye around the room, found the logpile, and began to build up kindling for a fire. 'They are debating your fate in the mead-hall at this very moment,' he said as he worked. Will looked on with folded arms. 'Some urge for justice and would like to hear your side of the story. But Eofric is determined to have you executed, and he has gotten a substantial faction of the outlaws on his side.'

'And what of their leader—this Rob Lightfingers? Where is he throughout all this?'

'Sitting in the mead-hall, listening to one side and then the other, entertaining his warriors as he does every night,' Caedwic said. 'Knowing that he cannot leave without attracting far too many eyes, he has sent me to speak with you in his place. No-one comments if I drink no mead; as far as they are concerned, I am a small holy man with a small following. Their leader himself does not even deign to listen to my teachings.'

'He's a pagan, this Rob?'

Caedwic sat back with a sigh and struck the tinder, watching as the fire began to smoulder. He leaned forward again to feed it. 'This little outlaw village is in open rebellion,' he said at last. 'It is a safe haven for pagans rather than bandits, existing to flaunt the authority of the Northumbrian king, who has gone crazed with the idea of converting this wild land.'

'Then what is it *you* seek here?' Will asked.

'Peace,' came the answer. 'Wilhelm, I am a man of God, and I have been all my life. I have witnessed the fighting between our two peoples, the Saxons and the Welsh, from generation to generation. I saw the crowning of an archbishop in the south before he had convinced all the Saxon kings of God's grace, and before he had even bent my own church to his teachings. The divide between pagan and Christian deepens and fuels more war; "Christian" becomes a byword for tyranny.' Slowly, Caedwic got to his feet. The fire was burning brightly behind him now. 'Come, I have something to show you.' Ambling towards the bench before the fireplace, he drew a small bag from within his robes.

Will took a seat next to the old monk, who began to unwrap the bag. There was an unusual amount of wrapping involved: two layers of sackcloth, a scrap of oilcloth, all securely wound together with string. Caedwic carefully spread the last layer of the bag upon the bench.

Will frowned. 'A bag of ash.'

'Not ash,' Caedwic said sharply. 'Ash does not burn.'

Will raised his eyes to the monk's. His heart leapt into his mouth, and he swallowed heavily.

'Watch,' Caedwic said, taking a tiny pinch of the black powder. He stood up. 'You might want to stand back,' he cautioned.

Will edged away, his heart still beating in his throat. Leaning heavily to the side, Caedwic tossed the pinch of powder into the fire.

For an instant, the fire boiled out of the confines of the fireplace. Bright orange flames reached for Will, stretching out their arms with an unholy fizzing noise. Panicking, he threw his hands across his face and stepped heavily backwards, losing his footing. By the time he made contact with the floor, however, the flames had retreated, leaving nothing but a long scorchmark across the floorboards. Caedwic's mouth was drawn; he clasped his hands together before him, as if to stop them from shaking.

'As you can see,' he finally said as Will picked himself up off the floor, 'this is not ash.'

'I have seen this before,' Will said, his voice shaking. 'Listen, Caedwic: there is an army—'

'I know,' Caedwic interrupted gently. 'An army of darkness led by a wicked monk who taints the very robes he wears.' His normally serene voice was tainted with bitterness. 'The Dark Priest, they call him. Wherever he walks, darkness follows.'

'You mentioned the king of Northumbria,' Will said urgently. 'Something must be done to stop this priest.'

Caedwic shook his head. 'Why do you think the Dark Priest runs loose with such impunity?' he asked bitterly. 'King Edwin plots to use him—and his cursed weapon—as a means to bend the entire land to his will. This is why the pagans are going into hiding. Villages have been burned to the ground; men and women have been slaughtered with the basest cruelty. This is the worst sort of wickedness: those who do the devil's work under the guise of God. They call themselves Christian. Hah!' He began to wrap the rest of the black powder up again. 'They are as Christian as—as the goats that roam the village fields!'

Folding his arms again, Will began to pace up and down. 'I wish I knew how I—the man I was—am involved in this,' he said. Every syllable vibrated with the frustration he felt. 'I know it is all in here!' he burst out, gesturing towards his own head. 'I *know* the answer is somewhere in there.' He stopped and thumped his fist against the wall. 'Half of me wants to march to war,' he said in a low voice, to himself.

'And the other half?' Will had almost forgotten that Caedwic was there.

'The other half—doesn't know.' Will turned back to face the monk, his hand on the hilt of his sword. 'You said that Rob had sent you to speak with me in his place,' he said, determined to change the subject. 'What does Rob wish to say?'

'There is something that he needs done,' Caedwic said, leaning heavily on his walking-stick. 'A task that he feels he cannot ask of his companions. The dangers are too great.' He hesitated. 'But if you help him with this, he will grant you your life and freedom.'

'And if I refuse?'

'Then he will put you to trial for the murders of your wife and daughter.'

'Caedwic,' Will said, moving in front of the fire, 'do you think that I am guilty of killing my own child?'

The old monk stared at him for a long moment without speaking. 'I have met many men in my wanderings,' he finally said, speaking slowly as though he were carefully selecting every word. 'Many women, too. You do not seem like a dishonourable man, Wilhelm, and yet I have seen people resort to terrible acts in times of desperation.'

Will moved away, carefully arranging his face to betray no expression. 'Tell me what Rob wants, then.'

'The Dark Priest's army is encamped a day's ride away from here,' Caedwic said. Will turned in surprise. 'We know this,' Caedwic continued, 'because we have a spy from his host. A young woman, the daughter of the Dark Priest's chief alchemist.'

'Alchemist?' Will frowned at the unfamiliar word.

'The man who produces this black powder,' Caedwic clarified. 'Part sorcery it is, and part mundane mixture. The mission that Rob needs done is to kidnap this alchemist. With him gone, the Dark Priest will have a shortage of fire-power, and we will have a small advantage over him.'

'Are there any battle plans to attack him?' Will asked.

Caedwic shook his head. 'Rob does not have anywhere near the numbers required to stand against him. He hopes that the loss of this terrible weapon—enough of it, anyhow—will cripple the priest enough to cease his attacks against the villages.'

Will snorted softly, but allowed Caedwic to continue.

'Four of Rob's warriors have volunteered for this mission already, but they lack an experienced leader. If you go with them, you will find the Dark Priest's encampment, smuggle the alchemist's daughter back to find her father, and then return with him.'

'Do I have a choice?' Will said grimly, speaking half to himself. 'It sounds like a golden opportunity for all of us to die. But I will go. Tell Rob that.' He turned back to Caedwic. 'And pray for me. Pray for all of us.' Impulsively, he drew his sword. The steel seemed to stare back at him, mirroring his very soul.

Caedwic stirred. 'May I see your sword?' he asked.

Shrugging, Will handed the blade over. Caedwic took it into his lap. The steel shone red in the light of the now-blazing fire; the old monk's gnarled hands held it reverently.

'Your sword was made by my people,' he remarked, wonderingly. He flipped the blade over, tested its weight. 'By God, what a balance! I could almost believe that this was our legendary Hardcleft come again!'

For a moment, Will considered asking Caedwic whether he believed in faeries. Just then, however, the old monk got to his feet, handing Will his sword back.

'Do take care of this blade,' Caedwic admonished. 'You will need it when you leave tomorrow. As for your comfort tonight, I am afraid that you will not be able to leave this hall. Your enemies want you someplace they can guard you.'

Will nodded, hardly hearing the monk. His sword was in his right hand; somehow, it felt as though it *belonged* there now.

*I haven't fought anyone since I spanked Wulfgar,* he thought as Caedwic finally said farewell and left him alone in the shadowy hall. *I was a warrior, once. Can I still boast the same?*

Will hefted the hilt in his hand and swung the sword in a wide arc through the air. The movement felt wrong somehow.

*Too low,* he told himself. *This sword is longer than the others.*

He tried again. Although he did not remember learning the movements, his body had performed them over and over, a thousand times or more. His feet picked up the pattern of movement and led him across the hall, then back again. Soon there was nothing but himself and the sword. It was a dance, the most beautiful dance there was.

Will slowed down his movements until he came to a standstill, panting. Leaning the sword against his shoulder, he wiped his brow. The fire was starting to burn low. The hall was utterly silent save for the occasional settling of the embers.

Dancing with the sword was much like prayer, Will realized. There was the same sense of peace and balance, in his body as well as his mind. Memories burned fresh in him, memories of countless hours practicing. On foot, then horseback; alone, then against an opponent, then in a mock melee. Himself a rangy, taciturn youth; his father, a heavyset man with a leg that could no longer march to war, supervising his training. Will remembered being taller, stronger, faster than any of the other boys he trained with. The sword-dance was what he had been born for. It was his greatest joy. It was a thrill comparable to nought else.

Will passed a hand before his eyes, and collapsed to sprawl beside the fire. He was no longer that boy, and he had come to view warfare with a jaded eye, seeing past the valour and glory of the battle to the horror it brought. How much of a warrior could he still be?

*At least I have a good sword*, he thought. *Hardcleft come again. If only Caedwic knew.*

# Chapter Eight

# The Dark Priest

*Below the reeking dungeons where the Persian alchemists practice their craft, hidden from the dread magi and their assassins, kept secret from an overambitious emperor, one man combined a set of simple ingredients to produce a deadly, empire-toppling weapon.*

*What journey did this recipe take from the far east, those lands of savage mystery, across mountain and sea to reach that teeming hub of empire, Ctesiphon, ancient city of riches and sorcery?*

*All forbidden things make their way to Ctesiphon in time, and so did I. From a fallen magus of Zoroaster, I learned to enter men's heads and coerce them into serving me. From a hideous desert witch, I learned to locate my enemy in a teeming sea of human minds, and to* use my hatred of him to my advantage. Everywhere, in fact, I learned to use my hatred. That is one thing the denizens of this dark empire do not lack. The poor hate the rich; the city people hate the nomads; the followers of the Prophet hate both Christians and pagans alike. Everyone has an enemy there.

But I knew that, strong as it was, my hatred of him would not suffice for my larger goal. I want all that has been denied me by the accident of birth. As poor as this miserable island may be compared to the riches of the distant East I have beheld, I want it. I needed a weapon to bring it to its knees.

The peaceful shire where I was born is but a faraway memory. The people I knew are less than strangers, my own parents buried in the earth since I was a boy. I shall watch it all burn, see them all bow to me. They may never love me, but I will see to it that they fear me, even as Aedfrith came to fear me after beholding my power. When she rejected me, when she told me she would rather stay with her unfaithful husband and the unmanageable child she had borne him, she sealed her fate. Though I once loved the girl who bore her name, this weary, dutiful woman was nothing to me. So I used her to my own end—to torment my true foe. To show Wilhelm that he never could have peace, not whilst I still roamed the land.

Like the fire-powder, my hatred is all-consuming. It has consumed the woman I once loved, and I revel in the power it brings me. But it is not only the thane of Mann I wish to break. Once he finally lies broken and stretched out at my feet, I will lay Aedfrith's memory down to abide with him, and burn and despoil this land until I reign supreme. Until bloodshed has filled my heart, and then I might love my people again.

Someday, I shall have it. When the last of Aedfrith's cursed, beloved memory leaves this earth, I will start to lay my hate to rest.

ONCE MORE, WILL AWOKE to someone shaking him. Coming to with a start, he restrained himself from lashing out when he saw that it was only Caedwic. The monk proffered a hot bowl of gruel, which Will gratefully accepted. There was a little light in the longhall, though the fire had long since turned to ash. Will tossed his thin blanket aside to start eating. Caedwic disappeared with a soft word, giving him some privacy.

*It's real, then.* Will chewed moodily at his gruel. *How do I prepare myself to die today?*

*I have no choice,* he told himself as he finished his morning ablutions. Lacing his boots up, he was struck by one thought. *I wish Goldie were here.* Whenever she was by his side, the situation, whatever it was, did not seem quite so grim.

Will stepped out of the hall, hoping to see her waiting for him in the rising sun. But there was only Caedwic again, walking towards him with three women.

Will folded his arms as he sized them up. The first two were not completely unfamiliar; they had been with the scouts yesterday. The blonde one was nearly as tall as him, whilst the dark-haired girl beside her was of a height with Goldie. Though she wore a skirt, Will glimpsed the sheen of metalwork beneath her cloak and guessed that she was armoured. The tall woman was dressed much the same as was Will, but her leather gleamed with recent polish and there was well-made ringmail beneath her vest. Her arm-rings had the soft sheen of true gold, and they were carved intricately.

The group halted before him, the third woman stepping forward. She was dark of complexion, dressed entirely in black, a shawl covering her hair.

'This is Aisha, the alchemist's daughter,' Caedwic said.

*It would be easy to feel protective of this girl,* Will thought. Aisha's smile was shy, her large brown eyes trusting.

'You must be Wilhelm,' she said. Her voice was halting, the accent strange, but she spoke precisely.

'Yes.' Will began to wonder at the girl's unthreatening, peaceful appearance. How had she escaped the Dark Priest? And made her way across a foreign country to find allies? *Perhaps that vulnerability is deceptive . . .*

'You two must be her protectors,' he said, turning towards the two armed women. The tiny dark one grinned broadly.

'I was under the impression that *you* were going to protect us all,' she said. Her golden-brown eyes glittered in amusement. 'You seem like the type of man who would. So tall and—bearded.'

'You are teasing me.' Will could not help but smile; he was reminded of Goldie on her most carefree days.

'No, I swear it.'

The tall blonde woman stifled a laugh, and patted her arm. 'Forgive her,' she said to Will. 'You may call me Elfhild. Lorica here means well, but she talks entirely too much.'

' "Talks too much?" When you are the one who keeps interrupting me?'

'When did I ever interrupt you?'

'Unbelievable! When everyone here has stood witness!'

Will got the impression that the two women would happily have argued the point all day, but they were interrupted by the arrival of two men. *Rob's warriors*, Will realized, noting their well-worn woodsman's leathers. They led five horses between them; one carried a sword, the other a bow with a quiver of arrows.

'Ed,' Will said, recognizing the man with the sword. 'You volunteered for this? To ride with me?'

'I have no quarrel with you,' Ed replied levelly. 'That is all Eofric's problem, not mine. I am loyal to Rob of the Nest, and I ride on his most perilous missions.'

'Very well.' Will turned towards the archer, a lanky boy no older than eighteen. 'And you, lad?'

'I care not.' The boy shrugged. 'And my name is Wilgerd, not "lad." '

'We call him Gerd the Archer,' Ed explained.

'You're good with that bow, then?' Will asked the boy.

'The *best*.'

There was not much more to be said; Will knew that it was time to get moving. The dawn had broken now. Ed handed him the reins of a horse.

This mare was much taller and more spirited than the tired-out old gelding he remembered riding out of Fort Horsa, but there was no choice but to mount up and hope for the best. She seemed level of temperament, at least.

Will turned back to call good-bye to Caedwic. The little grey man raised his hand in farewell. There was suddenly a lump in Will's throat. *What if I never see him again? What if I never see Goldie again?*

Will reached out a hand to touch the hilt of the sword that hung by his side. His resolve hardened, and he urged the mare forward, falling into pace beside Ed's horse.

As many times as he glanced back that morning, Will saw no sign of Goldie. When they left the forest to move along farm roads muddied with the tracks of labourers, he gave up at last and fixed his eyes on the road ahead.


HALF THE DAY PASSED before the road led out onto a wide sandy heath devoid of any sign of human habitation. The land was open to either side, and their riding formation loosened as they relaxed, knowing that they would see any trouble upon the heath long before it reached them.

Lorica soon became talkative; when she was not bickering with Elfhild, she rode up beside the men to tease them. Gerd seemed wary of her, watching her every movement as she rode, but Ed was at ease, settling his horse into a slow gait and sitting back in the saddle.

'Wouldn't it have been better to ride by night?' Will asked Ed, once Lorica had returned to Elfhild's side, the two of them flanking the alchemist's daughter.

The mercenary shook his head. 'The Dark Priest sends patrols more frequently at night, and this heathland is too uneven to navigate in the dark. It belongs to Rob now—or at least we have control of most of the land hereabouts—but occasionally the Dark Priest will send small parties to harry us. We judged it far better to go when we could see them coming.'

'You know where he is encamped?' Will asked. 'How long will it take us to get there?'

'We know where to expect him,' Ed replied. 'We should be in the right area by tomorrow night.'

Gerd rode up next to them, his face sullen.

'What's the matter, Gerd?' Ed asked. He glanced back, and Lorica flashed him one of her grins. 'Does she scare you?'

'Never,' the lad muttered. Ed laughed.

'She *should* scare you,' he said, looking at Will now. 'They should both scare you.'

'Why so?' Will asked mildly.

'They're not regular village women, as you've no doubt figured out,' Ed said. 'These two are real mercenaries, if not assassins. Steadfast killers. I don't know what Rob is offering them to work for him, but they're worth every coin.' He moved closer as he spoke. 'They are ferocious, in a way I've never seen a man be.'

'Have you heard the stories the men tell of them?' the boy asked, from Will's other side.

Ed snorted and rolled his eyes. 'I put little stock in rumours, Gerd. Neither should you. I repeat only what I've seen with my own two eyes.'

'The Spanish girl, Lorica,' the boy continued regardless, 'she's been trained as an assassin. Since she was a little child of eight years old.' He lowered his voice. 'By Theodoric himself.'

Ed guffawed, but the boy ignored him. 'He would bring her to the battlefield whenever he went to war. Not to fight. In the dead of night, he would let her loose and send her to the encampment of his foe, all in black and covered in soot so that no man could see a thing. She'd sneak past the guards all light of foot, till she found the tent of the rival king. Then, she'd take that little dagger hidden in her sleeve, and she'd use it to open his throat.'

Ed snorted again. 'Gerd,' he said, 'King Theodoric died a hundred years ago. Don't piss on a man's name unless he's around to answer you.'

'He had children, didn't he?' the lad said defensively. 'And grandchildren! What does it matter if it wasn't *him*, personally? The *king* it was—that's what matters most!'

'And where does Elfhild come in?' Will asked.

'She stole her from the king,' the boy said, his eyes suddenly somewhat misty. 'Went in and took her, like a man steals himself a wife, through all the guards and assassins and right under the king's nose.'

'Is that what you would do, Gerd?' Ed asked, grinning. 'Steal yourself a wife?'

'If she were my love,' the young archer answered defiantly. 'If she loved me. Then sure I would!'

'And how would you know if she loved you?'

'I'd know, wouldn't I?' A red-hot blush was starting to creep up the boy's neck. 'I'd see it in her eyes.'

Ed started to laugh so hard that he nearly fell off his horse. The boy's ears went beet red, followed by the rest of his face.

'I understand, lad,' Will said softly. 'I was once young too, and I also believed in love. But love cannot always be stolen.'

'Well, if I loved a girl, I would fight for her,' Gerd said haughtily. 'Even if it were against Theodoric himself.' With that, he kicked his horse into a trot and rode out in front of the group.


BY THE END OF THE DAY, they had begun to see a line of trees upon the horizon.

'We have made good time,' said Ed. 'We can make camp beneath those trees.'

Every one of the little group were exhausted. Nevertheless, they took care of the horses and managed to get a small fire going before the sun had truly set. They passed around hunks of bread, hard cheese, and sweet summer apples. Gerd drew the first watch and scaled a nearby tree for a better view.

'We'd better hope he doesn't fall asleep up there,' Elfhild remarked.

'Leave him be. The lover-boy's a good lad.' Ed winked at Will.

' "Lover-boy?" ' Lorica laughed. 'Is that what you three were speaking of so earnestly?'

Ed shrugged. 'We spoke of many things. Love. Seduction.'

'Oh, really?' Lorica lifted an eyebrow. 'Is anyone around this fire truly experienced in seduction? How about you, Will Nobody?'

Will shifted his position, not sure what to say. 'I would rather not discuss my wife,' he finally said in a low voice.

Lorica rolled her eyes. 'I was not wanting to speak of your wife, Will,' she said.

Will was nonplussed. 'Then what is it you would know of me?'

The Spanish girl reached for her sleeve and withdrew a stiletto knife. As she started to trim her fingernails, she said: 'We are women, Will Nobody. We know love when we see it, and we saw it in the forest. You are madly in love with that girl who travelled with you. What was her name?'

'Goldwine,' Elfhild supplied, talking right over Will.

'A tragic love,' Lorica sighed. 'She is pagan, wild and free like the forest. Never one to be chained down. You should not tell her that you love her. She deserves to be free, not bound to

an uptight Christian like yourself for all her life. You should
not let her give up her freedom for her love.'

Before Will could retort, Elfhild snorted. 'This only happens
in your southern lands, where a man cannot love a woman
without owning her. I think they could well be happy together.
The men where *you* come from only have two uses for a
woman.'

'Two uses?' asked Ed.

'Bread and babies,' Elfhild replied promptly. It was clear
from Lorica's smirk that she had heard the saying many a time
before. She nudged the warrior woman.

'But *you* have many more uses for a woman, don't you?'

Elfhild blushed pink, but ignored her. 'Follow your forefa-
thers, not your god, and she will have no reason to feel dishon-
oured by you,' she said to Will.

Will shook his head. 'It is easy for you two to talk. You don't
know the things I have seen, and done.'

Lorica raised an eyebrow. 'Because we are young, we have
not seen or done many terrible things? Or because we are
women?'

'I only meant—that at least you know who you are. You are
secure in what you do.'

Brow still raised, Lorica exchanged a glance with Elfhild. Ed
cleared his throat.

'You truly do not remember your wife and daughter, do
you?' he asked, leaning forward.

'Some things. Not everything,' Will replied guardedly.

'You will forgive me,' Ed began, 'but I heard from Eofric
that, as the years of your married life went by, you and your wife
liked each other less and less. People speculated that you did

not even share a bed as man and wife. He thinks that, one day, you simply had enough and killed her so that you could be free of her, and your daughter as well.'

'Does he?' Will replied emotionlessly.

'Another man I have met says that you killed her for cuckolding you with another man.'

'Another man? Who?' Will asked, momentarily distracted.

'The isle's priest. Who suddenly vanished after your wife's death, and has never been seen again, apparently.'

'The priest?' Will repeated to himself. 'That can't be right. Aedfrith was—she was deeply religious; she would never have defiled the station of the priest. I remember . . .' The words came to him from a great distance. 'She raised our daughter to say prayers every morning and at mealtimes. The two of them together. I was always busy.' His brow creased. 'The priest?' He felt discomfited, and could not truly say why. 'Something is not right. Who was this priest?'

Ed shrugged. 'Some boy who grew up in the household of your wife's father. He was called Albert, they say, but he took something different as a name for himself after he entered the priesthood and was sent to Rome.'

'A priest,' Will repeated softly.

Aisha stirred from her shadowy corner. 'The same priest, perhaps?'

'Sure,' Lorica said. 'He could have gone from seducing highborn wives to slaughtering peasants. That makes perfect sense.'

Aisha looked at Will. 'What do you think?'

'I don't know what I think,' Will replied testily. He stared into the fire. If only he could see truth there—but he might as well look to the water for that. Neither would help him.

An awkward silence fell. Ed announced his intention to bed down for the night, and stretched himself out next to his horse. Lorica and Elfhild leaned wordlessly against each other, whilst Aisha moved as close to the fire as she could.

Will sat back and gazed up at the stars. They seemed dim in comparison to the moon, which shone golden tonight, rivalling the sun in her beauty. Pagans believed that the sun and the moon were sister and brother, travelling in chariots around the earth. It was Goldie who had told Will this, and he remembered remarking that it seemed fitting for the sun to be a girl: a girl like her, merry and bright with golden hair. The kind of girl who could warm the soul.

'I miss the fires of home,' Aisha suddenly said, so quietly that Will could barely hear her. 'And the streets. Here there are no city streets, only muddy roads.' She held both her hands, palms outwards, to the little campfire, warming them. 'You have never seen the like of the fires in the great temple, where the priests keep watch at night. When I was a child, I would feel safe there, in the temple. I knew that God was watching over me.' She looked around at the others. 'Tomorrow, I can only hope that God is watching over all of us.' She stood up. 'I can only pray.' She bowed her head. 'Good night to all of you.'

'Life is short, Will Nobody,' Lorica said after she had left, and Will wondered suddenly where she had heard that nickname. 'Go to sleep. You will still love your Goldwine in the morning.'

'Aye, and that's the problem,' Will muttered to himself as he watched the fire burn low.

THEY RODE FOR ANOTHER HALF-DAY before coming to a wood with a great river that parted it in two. There were no settlements in sight, and the sun hid behind brooding clouds. They travelled along the river until the forest turned to field upon the opposite bank, and they knew that they had found the Dark Priest's hideout at last.

The army was encamped upon the meadow, surrounded by trees on all sides. Myriad paths led through the woods, rutted by the wheels of heavy carts and the hooves of many horses. Evidence of the army's patrols was everywhere: flattened undergrowth, trimmed bushes, and trees marked with crosses to show the way out of the woods.

They set the horses free to wander back to Rob's Nest and plunged into the depths of the forest on foot. From the cover of the trees, they could see the sprawling camp across the river. Ed and Gerd followed the river to the north and reported that they could cross it and swing back southwards to approach the camp through the densest part of the woods.

Before they left, they spent some hours watching the bustling camp. Close to the river, the camp followers had erected temporary shelters that looked as though they had been standing for longer than originally anticipated. Trees had been felled from the edges of the clearing, and campfires burned all over. A large band of soldiers rode in from the southeast, carrying several deer carcasses on wooden frames between their horses. A patrol moved through the woods, passing less than ten feet away from the little group, but they were laughing and distracted and never noticed the armed warriors hiding in the brush.

'It looks as though they have been here for much longer than they expected,' Ed observed.

'Good for us,' Will said. 'They have grown lax. See how close the hovels of the camp followers are to the trees? Anyone could sneak into the camp without the sentries noticing.'

Lorica grinned. 'And so will we, right?'

Will nodded. 'We'll intercept a patrol,' he said. 'Outfit ourselves in their gear so that we don't look too out of place. Lorica and Aisha, you two will pretend to be washerwomen.'

'Or camp followers,' Lorica said. 'That would be more believable.'

Will nodded. 'We'll approach from the north and move through the outskirts of the camp. If anyone stops us, we'll have to pretend that we're looking for whores, and you two, behave as if you're with us.' He glanced at Elfhild.

'I'll just keep my helmet on and hope they don't glance too closely at my face,' the big warrior woman said dryly.

'I'll have to alter your clothes,' Lorica said to Aisha. 'You don't look the part at all.'

'The next patrol that comes,' Will said quietly, 'we kill them, and take their clothes. Aisha, you stay here. Lie down; make yourself as hidden as possible.'

The others nodded. There were only five men to a patrol and five fighters in their group. The odds were good.

Lorica shimmied into a tree and waited upon a branch that extended over the path. The other four hunkered down in the underbrush. A thought nagged at the back of Will's mind.

*This will be the first time you kill a man as Will Nobody. It's your first slaughter.*

Mailed footsteps disrupted the peace of the forest. Will tensed, and threw a glance at Elfhild, who returned it with steadfastness. Gerd made a signal from where he and Ed waited, further down the path, then withdrew into the undergrowth again.

Will placed his hand upon the hilt of his sword. A thrill of excitement shot through him. Excitement and . . . something else. He could almost have thought that two wills appeared in his mind at once.

They waited until the five men were between them, Will and Elfhild in front, Gerd and Ed ready to attack to the rear. Lorica crouched on her branch without a sound.

Will signalled Elfhild with a nudge.

The two warriors erupted from the undergrowth, sword in hand, and ran two of the soldiers through before they had time to even reach for their weapons. Lorica dropped straight down onto the back of a third man, and slit his throat from behind. The last two were quick enough to heft their battle-axes and engage.

Bloodlust roared inside Will's heart. It was as though the blood on his sword had ignited some sort of long-forgotten battle frenzy. As one of them swung his axe at Ed, Will waded into the fray and ran the sword right through his leather armour. He sprawled dead at their feet.

The last man was wearing ringmail and advanced upon Gerd without mercy. The boy drew a long knife from his belt and managed to stay the first blow of the foeman's axe, but as he fell back, his knife was struck from his hand and the backstroke of the axe hit him across the face. Ed and Will both dove in to help him. Whilst Ed distracted the enemy soldier by swiping at his armour, Will found the chink between helm and mail and drove the sword into the side of his neck.

Spattered with blood from the last kill, Will drew a deep breath. He was still alive, and the taste of battle-rage was thick in his mouth. 'Is everyone all right?' he demanded.

'Right as anything.' Lorica grinned. She was beside Gerd, who was bleeding from the chin but not very badly. Ed gave a grim nod.

Will's head was reeling. The others were wiping their blades clean; he looked down at his own sword. A growling rage emanated from the red blade.

Will shook himself. It was not the time to give himself over to fancy.

They dragged the corpses away from the path and stripped them for disguises. Ed donned the loose tunic and pointed helm of a man from Aisha's desert tribe. Elfhild and Gerd became Visigoths with spiked helms. Will stripped the wool and steel from the tall lad whom Lorica had killed. His wide blue eyes reflected nothing but surprise, and his blond hair flopped over his forehead. Will left him there, beside the corpses of his brothers-in-arms.

Decked out in their disguises, they set off to ford the river. Aisha rejoined them, wearing a figure-hugging dress that was such a change from her regular clothing that she looked visibly uncomfortable.

They passed through the forest and crossed the river without event. Once the camp came into view through the trees, Will called a halt, and Aisha came forward to examine the layout.

'Your father is in the tent with the Dark Priest?' Will asked.

She nodded. 'The black tent. I can just about see it from here.'

Will squinted to see it, and nodded.

'What about the priest?' she asked soberly. 'He will not let us go without a fight.'

'We need a distraction,' Will said slowly. 'Something he cannot ignore. Something to draw him out.'

The six adventurers contemplated the camp before them.

'What's that wooden barn in the middle of camp?' asked Gerd at last.

'Store for the fire-powder,' Aisha said.

Rain began to drip through the leaves and onto their heads. Will looked up. It had been cloudy all day, he realized. A soft rain was starting to fall.

'This powder likes to burn, yes?' Gerd continued.

Aisha nodded, and the boy held up an arrow, grinning.

'I could set one of these on fire.'

'The fire-powder will be in barrels,' Aisha said. 'And it is guarded day and night. It would take far too long for the fire from a single arrow to reach the powder.'

Elfhild stepped forward. 'How many guards?'

'One, maybe two.'

Elfhild glanced at Gerd. 'Not too many for both of us.'

'All right,' Will interrupted. 'We will split into three pairs. Elfhild and Gerd, your job is to create the distraction. You'll go ahead of us and burn that barn to the ground. Ed, you and I will find the Dark Priest and keep him away from Aisha's father. If necessary, we may have to fight him.' Ed nodded grimly. 'Lorica, you and Aisha go find her father. Does he ever leave his tent, Aisha?'

She shook her head. 'Last time I saw him, he was sunken in despair. He does not go anywhere outside, not even to the latrines. I think the Dark Priest prefers it that way.'

'Without a doubt.' Will looked around at the five solemn faces and did not voice his final thought: *This is madness. There's a good chance none of us are going to survive this.* He gripped the hilt of his sword. Again he felt the excitement, the bloodlust. He would not die without leaving a mark upon the field of battle.

'May all our gods be with us,' he said in a low voice.

'They will be,' Aisha returned softly. 'I have prayed for a miracle.'

The others exchanged uneasy glances. They were an odd mix, Will realized. Ed and Gerd were pagans, followers of Rob. Lorica must have been raised in Christian lands, but her partner was almost certainly a pagan as well, hailing from the true north.

*And yet we are united in purpose,* Will thought. He gripped his sword. 'Let's go.'


BY THE TIME THEY REACHED the straggling hovels of the camp followers, the rain was coming down in earnest. Lorica and Aisha had the worst of it, with only their shawls to protect their heads; Will was glad for the cover of his stolen helmet. Their boots sunk ankle-deep in the black mud. Not a soul was about. Smoke poured from holes in shelter roofs. Here and there a fire flickered in a doorway, tended by a bedraggled woman holding a small child. Most of them did not even look up as the group passed; some drew back inside their hovels.

They were within sight of the great black tent and the wooden barn, almost at the end of the domain of the camp-followers, when a tall soldier staggered half-dressed out of a particularly slovenly hovel, cursing. A burly man with one eye was pushing him from behind, and he fell in the mud as they passed. The woman who emerged from the hovel on the heels of this spectacle was obviously a whore. With a sneer, she flung a handful of copper coins into the mud, and the soldier scrabbled after them as the one-eyed man looked on, chortling.

The group of six started to make their way around the unfortunate soldier, but at that moment he stood up, plastered with the sticky black mud, and levelled his gaze at Will, who was right in front of him.

*He is not drunk*, Will realized with trepidation as the soldier looked him up and down with sharp eyes.

'Who are you?' he demanded, his gaze flicking around the entire group. 'All of you. None of you look familiar.'

Ed draped an arm around Aisha, who did her best not to cringe back. 'We're just getting company, same as you. No harm in that, is there?'

The soldier's eyes lingered on Aisha, and Will became uncomfortably aware that neither of the two girls really looked like whores. *They should have played it as washerwomen*, he cursed to himself.

'Is that so?' The soldier folded his arms. 'Give me today's password, then.'

There was a moment of anticipatory silence in which no-one moved nor spoke. Then Will stepped forward and punched the soldier full in the face. He reeled, taken aback but not too surprised to retaliate, and dove for Will's legs, pulling him down into the mud. But he had no weapon. As Will fell, he managed to pull his knife from his belt. He lunged for the soldier, slashing the knife across his belly. As he fell writhing in pain, Will ended it by cutting his throat.

Will got shakily to his feet. The entire fight had been resolved in a few short moments.

He glanced towards the hovel, where the whore and her doorkeeper were watching open-mouthed, but neither of them had made a sound. Will signalled his group, and they moved away across the mud, leaving the dead man where he was. Aisha was trembling, but there was a resolve in her eyes that Will did not doubt.

'We have to move quickly now,' he said urgently, aware of the watching eyes upon their retreating backs. 'Elfhild and Gerd, you get to that barn. The other four of us will wait—here.' He ducked between two tents, the other three following close behind him.

Gerd and Elfhild moved away, and the other four fell to waiting.

It was an uncomfortable wait. The rain dripped down the back of Will's neck, and he was covered in sticky mud. Aisha was very pale, looking as though she might vomit. Lorica was biting her fingernails.

Long moments passed, and Will began to wonder if something had gone wrong. But there was no hue and cry, and the camp followers who had seen him knife the soldier had not stirred up a fuss.

Suddenly, Lorica moved. 'I see fire,' she said in a low voice.

The other three peered out. Smoke rose from the barn, pluming out into the air. Fire flickered inside, but no-one appeared to have noticed yet.

'They did it!' Will muttered, one burden falling from his mind.

As they watched, shouts went up from the camp. Lorica and Aisha stood ready to move. The barn burned brighter for a brief moment.

The noise that ripped through the air was louder than the biggest crack of thunder Will had ever heard, and much more ominous. Bright flame seared his eyes; a ball of red, yellow and black rose up into the sullen heavens as though to challenge God himself. The very air seemed to be moving before the inferno; clouds of dust and splinters of wood flew skywards only to rain back down upon the camp like the fires of hell unleashed. Pieces of the wooden barn, still aflame, black and twisted as though clawed by demons, fell all around as Will and the others did their best to shelter behind the tent. Aisha yelped as a piece hit her shoulder, but that was the worst damage any of them got. The same could not be said for the rest of the camp, though. The screams and groans that went up all around were proof positive that their distraction had succeeded beyond any of their wildest dreams.

When the flaming rain abated at last, Will stepped into the open to behold utter chaos. Men were fighting fires everywhere; though the rain still fell softly, the barn was burning with a fierce red heat, illuminating the entire camp with scarlet hellfire. Horses and men alike ran hither and thither, some afire, screaming in agony. Blackened corpses lay all around, and there was a strange metallic scent in the air.

Will's mouth was dry, and he had to rein in his fear with all his might. *How does it feel, priest?* he thought vindictively, ignoring the plaintive screams and burned corpses. *How does it*

Aloud he said, 'Time to go.' His heart was racing; visions of the burning village on the coast assaulted him, but he could not stop now. People were depending on him, and his conscience would have to wait along with his fear.

Lorica gave a stiff nod and disappeared into the chaos, leading Aisha by the hand. No-one noticed them; not with men taken by madness, some arming up as if thinking that an unknown enemy had suddenly assaulted them, others desperately trying to catch horses that were trying to get away from the terror at all cost.

Will turned towards Ed, steeling himself. 'This is it.'

The mercenary could have been made of stone; none of the turmoil that still raged in Will's mind registered on Ed's face. He gave a brief nod, and they plunged into the madness. Burning debris lay everywhere, but the black tent loomed in the centre of it all, untouched. Surely the Dark Priest would not leave his camp to this confusion, Will thought. He had to come out and face the distraction.

Smoke blew across the camp, obscuring his vision. They stumbled over scuffed-up mud and flaming pieces of wood, looking for the priest. They half-circled the tent and saw him not.

Will stopped and looked about him. He and Ed had become separated, through the flames and the smoke; he could not see the tall mercenary anywhere. The black tent was to his right. To his left, a small wooden building had caught fire, flames burning brightly even as the rain hissed down. In his path lay a large piece of the destroyed barn. Smoke billowed in front of him, stinging his eyes. He paused to wipe them upon his sleeve and looked up again. Through the smoke, he caught sight of a shadowy, black-robed figure.

Will stepped forward and drew his sword. He could not turn back now, if he even still wanted to. The smoke drifted away for a moment, and the two men made eye contact across the blasted camp.

He was much younger than Will had expected, thirty-two at most. Possibly younger than himself, he realized. There was nothing extraordinary about him: he was of average height and slight build. His black robe, the vestment of Christ's church, hung upon his spare shoulders like the plumage of a crow. But even across the distance which separated them, Will saw something in his eyes that nearly cowed him. There was no fear in those eyes; no humanity, either. They glistened with obsession, greed, darkness. There was something unhinged in his expression, as if he would break out in cackling laughter at any moment, but it was eerily balanced by the calm of the born priest.

'I know you,' Will shouted across the blasted ground between them.

A mad smile played over the priest's face. 'Then you remember.'

'Not all.' Will remembered the face, though the eyes had never been this mad before. In the little chapel on the isle, leading prayer. As a boy, in the fields . . . no, there was something else there. The boy's face, pleading, crying up to him . . .

'When did we first meet?' he yelled, desperate.

The priest laughed. 'You don't remember at all, do you? A broken man, Wilhelm, that's what you've become. Shattered. I could help you remember . . . if someone had not taken it upon themselves to defend you.'

'When?' Will repeated.

The smile vanished, and the eyes glittered with malice. 'When you collected your young bride.'

*Aedfrith?* Something nagged at the back of his mind, and he could not remember what. He was ready to throw his sword down in frustration.

'She was meant for the convent,' the priest was saying, as though he could read Will's every thought. 'Meant for God. And you—you defiled her.' The priest's eyes went to a point behind Will. He smiled.

Will whipped around and saw Aisha and Lorica, bearing a middle-aged man between them. When she recognized Will, Lorica ran towards him.

'No—' Will began, reaching out a hand to stop her as the priest focused on her and his smile widened.

Lorica screamed in agony and clutched her head. She fell to her knees, screams ripping from her throat, swaying from side to side. 'No, please!' she sobbed, and tears coursed down her cheeks. 'Don't hurt me!' she pleaded to something that only she could see, as the Dark Priest watched on, eyes glowing with sick enjoyment.

'Stop it!' Will yelled, moving forward. A river of hatred flowed from the sword in his hand. It wanted the priest's blood, and Will was in no mood to deny it. But the priest held up a hand.

'Come no closer, unless you want me to make her relive even worse things,' he said. 'Much more of this, and she will be rendered mad, a condition that will remain even if you slay me.' His eyes lingered almost lovingly upon the Spanish girl as she knelt shivering in the mud. 'It would not take too long; she has the most disturbing memories of anyone I have ever met.'

Will lowered his sword, his heart burning in hatred, and the Dark Priest's glance fell upon Aisha.

'Aisha,' he said mildly. 'Welcome back.'

Aisha suddenly turned, letting her father fall into the mud unsupported. All expression left her face; she became as blank and still as a doll. As Will watched in horror, she knelt in the mud beside her father, who was groaning in pain, clutching at his right leg. She clasped her hands about his neck, and squeezed.

'Aisha!' Will seized her and pulled her from her father, but she struggled in his arms, her fists flailing, her eyes like blank slates of pitch in her pale face.

'Stop this!' Will yelled at the priest.

'See my power!' the priest gloated, ignoring him. 'A beloved child can be made to kill her own father!'

Aisha seized the knife from Will's belt, squirmed loose from his grasp, and attempted to drive it into her father's breast. Will caught her arm just in time. She struggled wildly against him; the knife nicked his forearm as she tried to twist her hand out of his grasp.

'Aisha!' Will pleaded. 'Remember who you are!' He tried to touch her, to look into her eyes, but she was wild with madness, her eyes unfocused and empty. 'Remember your God! Remember—' He was desperate, trying to think of what to say to her. 'Remember the fires in the temple—the priests—the presence of God!'

A look of terrible pain came over Aisha's face. Her eyes closed, her face contorted. She began to sob.

The Dark Priest let out an angry cry.

Aisha dropped the knife and turned a tear-streaked face to her father. She threw herself upon him, talking rapidly in her language, and raised him out of the mud.

Will sat stunned for a moment, then he remembered Lorica. She was shaking, and he could not get her to stand. As he raised his head, he realized that the Dark Priest was no longer alone.

The host of the Dark Priest was made up of mercenaries from almost every land under the sun. But under the thumb of the priest, they all behaved alike. The horde of soldiers massed before him, dead-eyed, and Will knew that they had to get out of here. But there was no means of escape.

His sword was steady in his hand. *At least if I die, I'll take some of them with me.* It was no comfort. It was no match for the dream of seeing Goldie again, of holding her in his arms, looking into her eyes . . .

Hoofbeats sounded behind him, and Will turned to see salvation, arriving on horseback. There was Ed, Elfhild and Gerd riding close behind him, mounted on three of the horses that had fled the camp in the confusion. As Will watched in disbelief, Elfhild vaulted from her horse and took Lorica in her arms. The Spanish girl began to sob, and Elfhild carried her to a horse whilst Ed helped Aisha lift her father.

They turned to shout for Will, but the Dark Priest's horde had advanced, and formed a half-circle around him. Swinging his sword through them, driving them back, Will was able to gain the time for the others to arrange themselves. Ed came up beside him, slashing right at left at the enemy soldiers, clearing a hole for Will to escape. The horde fell back, and they both ran for the horses, which were already moving. They were forced to mount on the run; there was a terrifying moment when Will clung to the horse's saddle without any support for his feet, but he managed to pull himself astride the beast somehow as it broke into a full-on gallop.

Will turned to look behind. The Dark Priest was still where he had left him, curiously calm amidst the ruins of his camp. *We will meet again*, Will promised silently. *But only once.*


THEY GALLOPED UNTIL THE HORSES were useless, then turned them loose and snatched a short rest before continuing on foot. Though shaky on her feet, Lorica was able to walk. She stayed very close to Elfhild and did not speak, looking away when anyone else tried to catch her eye.

Aisha's father, Hakim, was a bigger problem. His leg was weak, and he could only hobble along. Gerd cut a willow branch for him to lean on, but he could still manage only a very slow walk. In the end it was faster for Will and Ed to carry him along in turns with Gerd and Elfhild, one of his arms slung over each of their shoulders.

Will pressed them for speed, fearing that, even now, a patrol from the stricken camp must have been sent after them. They came to the edge of the heathland by nightfall, and Will goaded them further. Only when the moon was high in the sky did he allow a rest and sleep. They stood watch by turns, Will staying awake longer than anyone else. In the stillness of the night, he lost himself in memory and prayer. Slowly, things were becoming clearer.

In the morning, they set off anew, even more slowly than before. Despite the frustrating pace, progress was made, and as evening fell they finally saw the green meadows that heralded

Rob's forest on the horizon. They quickened their pace, encouraged, but at the same moment heard hoofbeats coming up from behind.

They turned all in unison, hoping against hope not to see what they feared, but their fate was inexorable. A group of thirty men or more approached across the heath on horseback. Hope faded as they watched. Only four of them were in fighting condition, and they were all exhausted.

Still, Will did not want to give up hope.

'Aisha, Hakim, Lorica—run,' he said. 'Perhaps we can hold them off for long enough for you to make it. We will have succeeded, even if some of us are dead.'

Lorica and Elfhild did not say farewell. They clasped each other, they looked long into each other's eyes, but neither of them spoke. Lorica, it seemed, knew better than to protest that she could fight. She seemed weaker than before, and Will knew that Elfhild had supported her through the long march as much as what any of them had supported Hakim.

The four warriors turned to face the approaching horde. Will's sword screamed bloodthirst in his hand.

Amongst the many things that had come to Will in the darkness, there was the full realization that it was just as Goldie had tried to tell him, in the gloom of that cave that seemed so long ago. He held a demon sword in his hand, a second fighter who wholeheartedly supported every bloodthirsty urge he'd ever had, egging him to greater violence. There was a power to this entity that frightened him, in part because he recognized that some aspect of his own nature agreed with it. Now that he had killed men with it, he felt a new kinship with the blade, a bond as though between two brothers-in-arms, the same kind of bond he felt with the young men he'd known in previous days, or with the three who now stood firm beside him. There was a reason why the memory of his friend, the companion of his youth, had needled him so much. The sword was like to him, just as strong and fierce, and three times as wild. For now, its purposes agreed with his. But he was not its master, not yet.

The horsemen were nearly upon them, and Will steeled himself for the fray.

From the meadows behind, a fierce battle-cry sounded. Horns blew, and men roared. The hooves of many horses drummed upon the turf.

Will half turned, fearing that he was hearing things, and a dozen Saxon horsemen streamed past him. They were arrayed in leather armour, their spears couched before them, and as they rode they shouted an unmistakable challenge to the Dark Priest's horde.

There were fewer of them, and yet they were better armed, better equipped, and deadly. They reached the lines of the foe, pivoted and cut a bloody swathe through their horde. The Dark Priest's men fell by the handful, yet most sprang from their horses and hefted their weapons, aiming for the legs of the Saxon riders.

At last Will found his voice. 'Let's go help them!' he yelled, and the other three cheered and ran with him into the fray.

The sword sang in tune with its wielder as Will abandoned himself to the bloodshed. He brought enemy riders down from their horses with savage blows to the knee, pounced upon them when they fell and wrote their lives upon his blade. He exulted in the deadly dance, the most beautiful dance there was. He became, briefly, battle-drunk.

When he finally raised his sword and met no resistance, he reeled and nearly fell. He was covered in blood, blending into the red meadow where thirty men or more lay slain.

He raised his eyes to the burly man now approaching him. Piercing blue eyes were set above a flowing sand-coloured moustache. Although well into middle age, he held his iron-studded shield aloft with pride.

The man did a double-take. 'Will Nobody?'

'Thane Wulfric!' Will could have broken out into merry laughter. He ran his eye round the thane's men, and recognized many of them from the wedding that seemed to have taken place years ago. Even young Wulfgar was there, his beardless face flushed and sweaty, with fresh blood on his blade.

Wulfric swept him into a bear hug. 'You are the last man I expected to see!' he exclaimed. He waved a hand at the three tired warriors now ranged behind Will. 'I thought that you four were bandits!'

'Well,' Will began, 'there is some truth in that . . .'

Wulfric's brow creased. 'What do you mean?'

'These bandits,' Will said, 'are the only men to stand against the dark army that has made its way into these parts. The horse-men you just slew—your true enemy is their master. They are led by one who knows no mercy.'

Wulfric's face darkened. 'I know all that, believe me,' he re-turned. 'The ealdormen of three shires have joined forces to de-feat him and protect the people of the Mark against his depre-dations. Who are these bandits you speak of?'

'They are led by one who names himself Rob Lightfingers.'

'Hah!' Wulfric stroked his moustache. 'A name known to many. Feared by many, too. There are those who would sooner see Lightfingers and his merry marauders wiped out . . . but luckily I am not one of them.' He clasped Will by the shoulder. 'Will Nobody, I know you for a man of honour, and so all for whom you speak must be honourable men themselves. Bring this Rob Lightfingers to meet me, and we will crush this enemy of darkness together.'

# Chapter Nine
# The Secret Pool

After our triumphant arrival back in Rob's village, I helped Elfhild take Lorica to the home of the cunning-woman. Nothing can be done for the scars the Dark Priest has left in her soul—only time will heal those, I suspect—but we were able to obtain herbs that would put her into a deep sleep, hopefully dreamless. She was still complaining of pain in her head when we brought her back to the hut she shares with Elfhild, but now she lies sleeping as quietly as a child.

Elfhild asked me to watch over her whilst she goes to speak with Rob. Our mission was a resounding success. The alchemist is reunited with his daughter, much of our enemy's weapon has been destroyed, and Rob seems to have gained a powerful ally. Wulfric took to him at first sight. These two men are a study in opposites—one a battle-hardened thane of noble forbears, leader of honest, honourable men; the other a bandit king seated in rustic grandeur, a churl become great only by the acclaim of his fellow thieves and deserters. Now they are drinking together like brothers.

A resounding success of a mission—the only setback being Lorica's current condition. What horrors did the Dark Priest dredge from the depths of her memory to leave her so helpless? Dare I imagine them? It is either that or face my own memories, which have swirled brightly in my mind since the moment I beheld his face.

I remember the boy now, though I was a boy then too. I remember the day I first met my wife. Only sixteen, she was half a woman already, veiled and solemn, casting her eyes downwards when she spoke to me, fingering the silver cross that lay upon her breast. All I was thinking at the time was that she would be chill and distant in the marriage bed. I took hardly any notice of the lovestruck boy who tried to stop her leaving. I was watching her face, and she did not weep for him. Nor show him any favour.

Now that boy wears the robes of a Roman priest. Now he sows bloodshed and chaos, spreading his vile sorcery across the land like a blight spreads across a field of corn. That slighted boy has accomplished his revenge, and more. He has succeeded in destroying my life. He has succeeded in punishing Aedfrith for slighting him. Her crime was nothing more than trying to fulfil her duties as a wife.

I remember that same boy returning to the isle after his pilgrimage to the East, and the way he was changed. People whispered that he had gained strange powers, but I dismissed such talk as the nonsense I believed it was.

I remember the day Aedfrith and Wilge died, the way the bright sun glittered through the clouds, casting a shadow upon the fort. The feeling of foreboding I felt when I entered my daughter's chamber. The way she did not move, even when I shook her and shouted her name. The red marks on her throat, and the gibberings of my wife, who cowered in the corner.

I did not know what the priest was, what he could do. How he could make a child kill a beloved parent—or a parent strangle their own child. Will God be able to forgive my ignorance? I thought that Aedfrith had gone mad, or else killed the child out of hate for me. We had never managed to understand each other—this pious, solemn woman paired with a hot-headed rake like me. The years had only widened the divide between us.

Knowing all this, can I forgive the blind rage that came over me at that moment? There was no sense in the ramblings she gave me, and she did not even beg for her life when I raised my sword. It was only after it was all over, and she lay dead upon the floor, that I came to my senses again . . .

The gift that the Dark Priest has given me is poisoned, as befits his nature. I remember, but I find no comfort in regaining this lost memory. How can I rest now, knowing that I killed my own wife for no good reason? He has given me the taint of the kinslayer, the wifeslayer. Thrown me from my isle of relative calm into a seething sea of fire below.

I must avenge them. Both of them. It was my hand that felled Aedfrith, but it was the priest who took possession of her soul, who wreaked his cruelty upon both of us. Whilst I still live, there is no choice. Otherwise her ghost would surely haunt me until the end of time.

My trusty sword is stalwartly at my side. My demon sword, as Goldie has named it. If it takes a demon to destroy evil, then so be it. I revelled in the slaughter when I had this sword in my hand. I was a *fierce fighter, a force of death. God grant I will be the force that brings death to the priest.*

*The armies amass, preparing for battle, but I stand alone, awaiting my foe. My path is finally clear. Here I will not yield. Here I plant my sword. Here I make an end to this war.*

ELFHILD RETURNED SHORTLY BEFORE the middle of the night, tired-eyed. 'You are wanted in the mead-hall,' she said to Will as she sprawled upon a chair, stretching out her long legs.

Will did not answer immediately, and Elfhild turned to look at him in the candlelight. Something in his face made her draw back again.

'What's wrong, Will?' she asked. 'You look as though someone has died.' She glanced quickly over at Lorica, but the girl was breathing very deeply and obviously.

'Someone has,' Will managed to say, speaking past the lump in his throat, 'but it is not a story I am willing to tell.'

'Fair enough.' Elfhild cocked her head. 'You should go. Rob is not fond of waiting.'

Will did not move. 'Why the mead-hall?' he asked softly.

Elfhild shrugged. 'Do not ask me to fathom the inner workings of men's minds,' she said dryly. She got up and fussed over Lorica's sleeping form, tucking her tighter under the blanket. 'By the way, your lady is there. Goldwine.' As Will's expression immediately changed, she smiled. 'That is a reason to go, is it not?'

Will stood up, but something in him held him back. He

hesitated just inside the doorway.

'You—you fought well,' he finally blurted. Elfhild looked up in surprise. 'Both of you. It was an honour to fight by your side.'

'Thank you for saying that,' Elfhild said softly. 'But the honour goes to us as well, Will Nobody.' A soft smile played around her lips. 'You helped Lorica when you could have left her, and you were there when I had need of someone. For that, you have my friendship. Whenever you need it.'

Will remained where he was, stunned. It was surprisingly validating to hear words like that from such a stern warrior.

'Now go,' Elfhild continued, placing her hand on Lorica's shoulder. 'She is mine to protect, and I am here now.'

Just as it was impossible to refuse Goldie's requests, it was also impossible to refuse a command given by Elfhild. No matter how little he wished to drink with Rob and his men, Will went.


AMIDST THE BUSTLE AND NOISE of the mead-hall, Goldie stood apart, lurking beside the ale-kegs. She alternated between folding her arms and fussing with her braids.

The village women had told her that she needed to earn her keep if she was to stay this time, and Goldie could not disagree. Not that the other girls considered carrying ale and mead to be much work. Most of them had abandoned their pitchers long ago and found company for the evening, whether talking amongst themselves or inviting eager young warriors into their circle. The men from Leabury were a most welcome novelty, and it did not seem to matter overmuch that they did not share the same faith.

A mortal woman needed a husband, and Goldie's eyes roved around the room as she stood alone. Apart from their liking for this strange Christianity, the men of the Angles and Saxons behaved much the same as did the men who inhabited the land near the marshes where Goldie had been born. They loved nothing better than drinking and fighting and telling stories as they drank about the fights they had been in. There was a season for war, and it was drawing to a close. Little time remained for them to collect those tales. Once the harvest-time arrived, the cold and rain would send them tramping back towards the cosy hearth-fires of home, where the wives and daughters they had left at the end of the spring would be waiting.

As she was pondering the likelihood of finding a man who would let his wife march to war with him, Goldie saw Rob Lightfingers arise from his high seat to welcome a newcomer. She kept her eyes on the high table, and it was as though her heart suddenly arose from a deep sleep and started to dance.

It was Will. Alive. Everyone in the Nest had been certain that he would perish, and though she had seen some of his compatriots return, she had not yet laid eyes upon him.

Despite all they had been through together, Goldie had never seen him look so weary and vulnerable, and she had no idea when her heart had started to react so strongly towards him. She wanted to run away before he caught sight of her; she wanted to storm over to the high table and smack the senses out of him, berating him for bringing them both into this bloody business and spoiling the dream she had concocted of them together.

*My dream?* she asked herself in surprise. *Mine? When did you begin to weave this dream? Was it when he tried to kiss you, after you saved his life? Or was it when he drew back, and you realized that he would respect your honour?*

Beside her stood the heavy pitcher of mead that she had been carrying earlier. Goldie picked it up, ascertaining by the weight that it was still full. She tossed back her braids and made her way through the noisy hall to the high table.

Reserved for his warriors and guests only, Rob's mead was served in horns rather than the mugs used for common ale. As Will took a seat at Rob's left hand, the bearded thane Wulfric leaned over and pressed a horn into his hand. Wulfric turned his head to shout for one of the girls, but Goldie was already standing in front of the table.

Will looked up, his eyes travelling from the horn to the pitcher to the girl who carried it, and their gazes locked. He nearly lost his grip on the mead-horn he was holding, and he mouthed her name.

Her heart was still dancing, drumming too fast and wild to stay in her chest. She could not follow it, however. Not here; not in front of these men.

Goldie took the mead-horn from his hands and filled it to the brim. There was the sweet smell of fermented honey, the slightest brush of her fingers against his as she handed it back. She retreated into the shadows, leaving him in the company of the other men, but Will did not take his eyes off her, not even as he drained half the horn in one gulp.

Part of the shadows now, Goldie waited. *If I know you, I know what is going to happen, Will,* she thought. *You're in no mood for revelry; all you want is to be on your own. Something is amiss, and you want to brood upon it in peace.*

It took two more refills of the mead-horn, two more times

that he gazed up at her with something that was almost accusation in his eyes. But sure enough, the moment Wulfric ceased to pay attention to him, Will drained the horn and left the table, slipping out through a side door. Abandoning her pitcher of mead, Goldie went after him.

The villagers had set lanterns in the trees around the hall, and the common glowed with a soft golden light by which one could discern little more than man-shaped silhouettes. In the mild weather at the close of summer, Goldie found it easy enough to imagine that most of the young couples had made their way into the woods tonight. The season for love and play in the fields was nearly over, the month of harvest giving way to the month of the gods. As there was a season for everything, it was now time for the war to be won in a final great battle, for heedless lovers to think of winter and choose a mate. The year would turn on the day of blood, and girls like Goldie would need to relinquish their freedom in exchange for warmth and safety.

Will was nowhere to be seen upon the deserted village common, but some instinct drew Goldie beyond the lantern-light into the waiting forest.

She wandered a little way down the path, letting her eyes adjust slowly to the lack of light. An ancient oak tree stretched overhead. She walked around it, turning to face towards the lanterns. Then, she stopped. She knew there was a presence behind her, yet she felt no fear.

'Will?' she whispered, the sound stirring the leaves on the lowest branches.

In reply, a pair of large hands grasped her shoulders, drawing her towards him. Goldie twisted round and stared up at his face.

The lantern-light made a hulking shadow of him, his usually expressive eyes unreadable.

'Goldie. You're here.' His grip upon her was not strong, and she was able to turn and face him. 'You followed me.'

'You needed me,' Goldie said.

Will made a noise that was something like a chuckle. His hands fidgeted as though he would have liked to draw her closer.

'What's the matter?' she urged him. *Something is wrong.* 'Did Rob keep the promise that he would pardon you?' Her heart was pounding again, and she swallowed to moisten a dry mouth.

'Rob has kept all his promises.' Will's voice was thick, indistinct. He closed his eyes for a moment, swallowed hard, and opened them again. 'I remember how they died,' he whispered, as though he could not say it aloud.

'Aedfrith and your—and your daughter?'

'Wilge,' Will whispered. 'My only child. She was killed by the Dark Priest.' He paused, and shook his head. 'But I thought that my wife was responsible.'

Goldie hesitated, not knowing what to say to something so horrible.

'So I killed her in my anger,' Will continued, still whispering, 'imagining that I was avenging the death of my child. But the guilt of that deed—I think it drove me mad in a way. Before I lost my memory, I was already a broken man.'

Will's hands fell from her shoulders, but Goldie caught them in her own. 'It was a mistake,' she said. She felt relieved that he had told her. 'It can be set right.'

'Can it?' Will shook his head. 'Even full vengeance cannot bring them back to life. The best I can hope for is that they are resting with God. It hurts as though it happened only yesterday, but at the same time, I feel that they are as distant as the stars. As though they belonged to another man, not to me.' He was silent for a long moment, and gazed down at his hands, which were entwined with hers. 'What's more, I feared that I had lost you as well. That you would never see me again.'

'I tried to see you,' Goldie said, indignation rising in her voice. 'The priest would not let me near you; he—he said that you needed to face your sins alone.' *Whatever he meant by that. I could not understand a word of his explanation.* 'I always knew there was more to the story, more that you could not remember. I told Rob everything I knew of you, hoping that it would help save your life. But all he would hear was that you had a weapon against the Dark Priest.' She was suddenly crying, and she paused to gasp for air. 'I didn't know where he'd sent you, or if—if you'd come back—'

'I understand, Goldie.' Will wrapped his arms around her and held her tightly against him. 'I'm sorry.'

In the sure heat of his embrace, Goldie's reservations melted into nothing and flowed away. Now that they were alone, the carefully circumscribed rules that governed their behaviour towards each other did not seem to matter anymore. Around them there was only the night, and the night was indifferent. It would hide anything.

'I'm sorry.' Lightly, Will placed a kiss upon her forehead. 'But I need to know why. Why have you saved me so many times over?' His face was close to hers, his breath disturbing the stray hairs that had pulled loose of her braids. 'I need you to tell me.'

'I chose you,' Goldie said breathlessly, losing control of her heart again. 'My heart chose you, many times over. Wherever you are, it always follows you, and I cannot help but obey it.'

'You are all heart,' Will whispered, and she could hear him laugh softly in the darkness. 'Heart and sunlight. Like dawn breaking after the darkness of night.'

'Who am I if I do not follow my heart?' Goldie returned. 'I love you.' She stood on the tips of her toes, and turned her face up towards him. Without hesitating, he leaned down, and their lips met.

He was soft at first, as if fearing that she might still pull away, but within moments the embrace deepened. Will clasped her tightly as though he would never let her go. His mouth and body were both hard against hers, his beard silky as she trailed her fingers through it. He was unarmoured, and the heat of his body radiated through his shirt. She could feel his quickened breathing, the wild beating of his heart. A sweet, deep aching awoke somewhere in the region below her stomach, and she could feel herself flushing. When he suddenly broke off, she was too dazed to do anything but hold his eyes with hers, breathless with the intense yearning she saw in them. He held her fast with a hand around her waist, the other caressing the length of her braids.

'Stay with me tonight,' he breathed, and his voice was rough. 'Too many nights have I lain alone, dreaming of what I would do if you were there beside me.'

'Stay with you? Where?' Although she knew very well that they were within sight of the village, some part of her wild mind had imagined that he would take her right there against the tree. *If he is to make me his woman tonight, it will not happen within walls.*

'Anywhere,' he whispered. 'In the deeps of the woods.

Wherever you wish.'

Her hands dropped to his belt, and she looked down. 'Where's your sword?'

'With Caedwic.' He shrugged. 'I don't need it. Not tonight.'

Goldie hesitated. *He should not go unarmed*, she thought to herself. But retrieving the sword would mean waking the priest; and when it came down to it, the presence of Will's sword was almost like having another person attached to his belt.

'I know a place,' she whispered, pulling him towards her. 'I found it yesterday, when I was hunting for mushrooms. No-one will know where we are, and the only light will come from the stars.' Her heart was racing, rejoicing.

Will caressed her face, smoothing stray hairs from her cheeks and forehead. 'There's nothing I want more than you.' His breath felt warm on her face, setting her heart aflutter again. 'I love you in a way I've never loved anyone before.' He hesitated. 'But I can't promise—'

'Then don't,' she whispered back.

Will smiled, and took her hand. He followed as she led him down onto the wooded path. It was a warm night for once, as the sun had spent the whole day shining from a cloudless sky. They met no-one along the way, coming at last to a lazy pond with a little meadow rising beside it, sheltered on three sides by bushes and trees. The bracken grew dense here, blanketing the ground, and willow trees wept by the side of the water.

Goldie wasted no time in stripping off her apron and under-dress, for it was not the first time she had been naked in the moonlight, yet never before with a man. When she turned to face him, Will's breath caught in his throat, and his eyes roved unbound over her, widening in admiration. But it was not her body that he touched first. His hands went to her braids, loosening the ribbons and carefully unbinding her hair, letting it fall softly over her shoulders. He buried both hands in it and kissed her fiercely on the mouth. She held onto him, half dizzy, afraid she would fall. She could still taste sweet honey from the mead on his lips.

And then, he was collapsing in the bracken, pulling her with him. She helped his shirt over his shoulders and ran her hands over him. There were many scars on his chest and arms, and what wasn't scar tissue, was covered in coarse hair. *A rough, hard man*, she thought, but there was nothing but gentleness in the hands that caressed her.

Together they removed the rest of the clothes between them, trousers and shoes and under-britches, until at last they lay naked in each other's arms. Still, Will seemed determined to draw out his pleasure. Where his hands caressed, his mouth followed, and she could not say which of the two drove her into a greater frenzy. He trailed kisses over her face and neck, cupped her breasts, slid his hands and his face between her thighs. She cried out in impatience; she longed to feel *all* of him, to have him closer than just feeling his skin on hers.

But at last he took her, and if there was any pain, she could not remember it afterwards. There was only completeness; the aching joy as slowly he entered her, the sweetness as they moved together and the pleasure that radiated from their connection into every inch of her body. For this one night, he was hers: nothing else existed, and the whole of the weary world fell away as they reached ecstasy in each other's arms.

She slept with complete contentedness as the stars turned overhead. None watched over their sleep but the moon.

IT WAS THE CHILL OF RAINDROPS striking his face that awoke him; elsewise, Will could easily have slept all day. Above him, the dawning sun was giving way to a sullen, cloudy morning. His head rested against the root of a tree, and his naked body was wrapped in his woollen cloak. Beneath, there was nothing but crushed bracken over the earth.

Wiping the crustiness from his eyes and wishing that there was some drinking-water nearby, he gathered himself together slowly. Goldie was nowhere to be seen. The night before was a whirlwind of sensations, things done only under the light of the stars, things said in the darkness that would not bear to have the harsh glare of daylight blaze down upon them.

He was lying upon a gradual rise in the ground, and when he sat up against the tree-trunk, he could see a clear pond below, several yards away. Willow trees and water-plants grew thickly around the edge, but he could see ripples in the water and a tell-tale glimpse of golden hair between the leaves.

The spot Goldie had chosen was as wild and secluded as any patch of the outlaw wood, with tall ferns sheltering the pond from view of the nearest pathway. It was the kind of place where Will could easily imagine the old gods ruled, waking wildness in the hearts of men.

Since the day Will lost his memory, he had thought himself a civilized and reserved man, one who thought things through before he did them. But when it came to Goldie, all his careful considerations had gone out the door. She had awoken a wildness in him, a longing to be free and to taste all the pleasures of life. To lose himself in hedonism and, for just one night, enter the wild pagan world she inhabited.

Now, in the cold light of the morning, it fell to him to ask himself the questions that both of them had ignored in the dark.

*What if we stayed together—married each other? What if I died in this desperate fight against the evil priest?* His heart went cold. *What if she were to become pregnant?* The thought had not occurred to him before, but suddenly his heart was filled with longing. How sweet it would be, to hold a child of his own in his arms once again!

*I dare not hope for this,* he reprimanded himself. *I dare not.* But his mind would not leave off the promise of that beckoning vision. What if he were to take her with him and walk away, leaving the war and the pain and all of the suffering behind? He could probably outwit Rob's scouts in subterfuge, now that he knew the ways in which they operated. They could disappear into the world together, he and Goldie, working to earn their bread or settling somewhere to farm their livelihood. They could have a dozen children and a peaceful house with corn in the fields and geese in the yard.

*And what then?* Will broke away from the daydream with tears in his eyes. *The ghosts of the dead would follow me everywhere, and poison the happiness I might share with her.* He blinked away the silken raindrops that fell upon his lashes. Pushing his thoughts aside, he got to his feet.

Their clothes were all muddled together in a heap, but they were dry enough where they lay beneath the bushes. Will made his way towards the edge of the pond for a wash. In the middle of the water, Goldie surfaced from a swim and turned her head, spotting him. Smiling, she dove again and swam in his direction. Will frowned. The water was cold enough to set him to shivering, but that did not seem to bother her in the least.

'You're awake!' Goldie remarked, reaching the shallows and wading towards him. 'I thought you were going to sleep forever,' she teased.

'I felt as though I could.' They were both doing their best not to stare at each other, Will realized. Despite the fact that they had each seen everything the other would show on the surface, they were still afraid to swim deeper. There was a lot that he wanted to say to her, but he could not seem to find the words. 'Aren't you cold?' he asked, instead.

'I'll survive.' Goldie pulled herself out of the water and shook out her wet hair, splashing him with droplets. Will's eyes were once again caught by the beauty of her naked body. He felt a stir of arousal in him, and a sudden urge to take her under the cloak a second time.

'We should get back to the Nest,' she said, squeezing water from her hair. Will shivered in an abrupt breeze that ran over the pond, and nodded regretfully. It was still raining softly, the leaden sky promising that it would not quit anytime soon. In the silence and the rain, the pond seemed very lonely.

There was a sudden uneasiness in him that had little to do with the cold. There was something wrong in the air, in the grim grey gloominess of the skies. They were alone in a distant, unfrequented part of the woods, and—he realized—completely unarmed. He'd had a wash and change of clothing in Caedwic's quarters last night, before he went to help Elfhild with Lorica, and he'd left both his sword and dagger there, thinking that there would be little need for them now.

Goldie brought his clothes to him as she came down the bank, now dressed again in the neat dress and apron she had been wearing the night before. She held them for him as he dressed himself, and Will noticed her eyes lingering over his scars, particularly the old sword-wounds on his upper body. For a moment she looked as though she was going to make some remark, but in the end she took his hand and kissed the back of it, then left him to sort out his shoes.

Will wanted to run after her and take her in his arms, lie with her again, touch her hair and promise her that he would always be by her side. He wanted to promise her that he would live forever. More than anything, he wanted her with him forever. He wanted to carry the mark of her hand on his heart, the way she carried her love in her beautiful eyes.

He thought he understood, now, how the heathens so ardently believed in their Lady, the golden-haired love-goddess who fascinated every man. For himself, he could imagine no better figure to worship than Goldwine.


GOLDIE REMAINED FOR A LAST MOMENT, mesmerized by the water. Will stopped to call to her, holding out his hand, and she turned towards him. He was tense, his eyes scanning the trees as though he expected something to come bursting forth from the deeps of the forest.

'What's wrong?' she asked him, and his hand strayed towards his belt. There was no sword there.

'I don't know.' He seemed to shake himself back to the world, and set off down the path with her in tow. But they had not gone far before they both stopped dead. A branch cracked somewhere nearby, and there was a sudden movement in the bushes.

'Get down!' Will yelled, and pushed her towards the ground. Skinning her hands as she fell, she lay frozen. The hissing of flying arrows filled the air, and she heard the distinctive twang of the bowstrings used by Rob's archers. Arrows fell around her; she shrank away as they zipped into the grass. There was a strangled yell from Will, and her heart went as cold as ice. There was the sound of someone running towards the trees.

She lifted her head. *Will, where are you?* For a moment she could see nothing but the trees of the wood and the blur of movement as men chased through them. Then she caught sight of a lone figure running back towards the pool.

*What is he doing?* she wondered frantically, until she realized that the bowmen were following him. They had no interest in her. As she watched, a single arrow was fired, missing Will by inches. He twisted around, raising his hands in an instinctive attempt to shield himself. Blood dripped from his left hand, staining his shirtsleeve bright red.

*He's drawing their attention off me,* she realized. Fear and rage surged up in her throat, and she felt dizzy. She had the urge to get up and run after him, but some instinct held her in place, cowering like a hare from the hunters.

At the edge of the pond now, Will hesitated, looking towards the water. Just as he turned his back, two arrows flew with cold accuracy. One hit him in the small of his back, causing him to stumble to his knees. The other struck, just moments later, into his ribs.

Time slowed down. It had all happened so fast, as though it had been planned out by some higher power.

Goldie was on her feet now, running as though she could

prevent what had already happened. The archers melted back into the forest, leaving her with their handiwork. She had not seen any of their faces, but there was little doubt in her mind as to who wanted Will dead. Even the fletching of his arrows matched; she had handled them before. *Eofric's arrows. Eofric with his companions.*

She flung herself down by Will's side, and turned his head towards her. He gasped for breath, coughing, sputtering. A dark stain spread over his shirt, and there was blood on his lips. Just a moment before, she had marvelled at the myriad injuries he had survived. *This can't be the wound that finally . . .* no, she wouldn't think of that.

*There must be some way to staunch the blood,* Goldie told herself frantically. But he would never make it back to the village; he could not even rise. If she left him to get help, he would die long before she could return.

'Will.' She patted his face, trying to get him to look at her. 'Will, see my face. Hear my voice. Listen to me!' Her voice broke, and she angrily wiped tears from her eyes. *What do I do? It was happening too fast; he was fading far too fast. Should I try to heal him? Do I have the power for that?*

Goldie raised her hands, trying to gather whatever magic remained to her. But it had been twelve years since she left her mother's abode. This magic was not meant for the human world; her mother had never laid a healing hand upon a mortal man. *The water-sprites do not intervene in mortal affairs.* Goldie had been told that, many times. *We do not interfere. Men kill men as they will, and they always have.*

'Not this one!' Goldie cried. 'This man—this one is dear to me.' *He is mine!* She stood up, facing the powers of the earth.

She called to the magic, something she had never done before. She had always denied it, rejecting everything that bound her to the world of the faeries.

*I cannot heal him,* she knew. *But I can call you. I can call you, Helya.*

She breathed the River Queen's name into the void, letting her voice travel through the earth and along its waterways to reach the other world, the shining faery realm that lay beneath the waters. Breath of a strange wind stirred her hair, and time slowed, adjusting to the pace of the immortals. At her feet, Will's heart beat slower, keeping his blood from spilling out onto the earth.

Goldie bent down and took his hand. Squeezing it one last time, she slowly looked up, her gaze going higher until she could see the stern face of the river-queen.

'A fine mess this is.' Helya's voice was as cold as the ice that she called her winter home, and raw power exuded from her, almost sending Goldie to her knees. It was pride alone that pulled her to her feet.

'I warned you, Goldwine.' She spoke barely louder than a whisper; there was no need to. There was no sound in the world where only the three of them existed. 'I told you not to go into the realm of mortals, for there you would know only pain and death. I warned you never to love a mortal man, for they can never truly know us, never cage us as they do their own women. I told you—less than two moons ago, when you sought me out—that you cannot have this man; if you *must* have a man, choose another. His destiny leads him down dark roads; you cannot hope to follow him. One might even say that he is cursed.' She looked down at the injured warrior, her mouth twisting in distaste. 'The taint of the kinslayer still lies upon him.'

'If he dies,' Goldie said, holding all emotion deep inside her, 'you lose your champion. No-one else will fight this Dark Priest of yours.'

'You think not?' Helya tossed her head. 'I have seen more of men than you, Goldwine. I have seen that they are always ready to fight, willing to die.'

'Please,' Goldie whispered, her pride finally breaking. 'Please, sister. You have to heal him. You have to help him. You set him upon this path—you can't turn your back on us now! Please.'

'It seems you only wish to call me sister when you have need of me.' Helya was as distant and cold as a faraway star. 'You turn your back on me to live with mortals, and yet when you suffer the inevitable consequences, you cry for me to help you.'

'If I was at fault,' Goldie said helplessly, 'then I should be the one who suffers. It was me who took him to this place. It should be me lying there. Not Will. Helya—I would give anything.' She saw Helya's dark grey eyes narrow in satisfaction, and everything drained out of her, leaving her empty and hollow. 'I will come back, if you wish it,' she whispered. 'I will come back and serve you.'

'Even if it meant that you would never set eyes on your lover again?'

'Just let him live,' Goldie pleaded. 'Let him avenge his family, Helya. Let him go home again. Let him return and rebuild. Even if it has to . . . has to be without me.'

Helya suddenly came forward, and there was a strange emotion in her eyes. Goldie was used to anger from her sister, as well as coldness and contempt. For the first time, there was something like warmth in the river-queen's eyes.

'For your sake, Goldie, I will restore the life of this worthless mortal if you consent to my terms. Come back to us, and live the life of a faery maiden forevermore.'

'I will,' Goldie promised tearfully. 'It has been very long, but'—she drew a deep breath—'I can learn to bide with my own people again. Some part of me has always longed to be allowed back.'

Helya stroked her cheek. 'You must consent to *all* of my terms, little sister. I offer you this for the sake of your own immortal life. Your heart is what led you astray before, for your heart speaks false and yearns for dangerous things.' She removed her hand, and turned half away. 'If you wish to return and to save this man's life, you must give up your heart forever. You must allow me to draw the love from it, as I drew the memories from Thane Wilhelm's head.'

Goldie gasped in horror. 'But I—I love—'

'These are my terms. Reject them, and Wilhelm will surely die.' She prodded the warrior at her feet. 'He fades fast. Soon he will be gone.'

*What choice do I have? I cannot turn away. I can't let Will die without having the chance to restore his honour.* A chill ran through her. *I have seen the bleak emptiness of hell, the mist-realm where cursed men go to dwell with their eternal regret. No doubt the Christian god prepares similar horrors for those who let a family member go unavenged.*

She looked down at Will's face, still and pale, eyes closed as though he were only sleeping. She was determined to remember it all. How it had felt to lie close in his arms, how the love had blossomed between them as they laughed together and how she had seen all the best of mortal man in him.

Then she closed her eyes. 'I consent.'

# Chapter Ten
# The Sword's Legacy

*Standing on the edge of the marshland, all my past life lay before me.*

*Somewhere in this land of silent mist and drifting cloud, I was born. Daughter of a noble and immortal race, spawn of a terrible faery tyrant.*

*I never knew my father. Before I was born, Helya sent him into the void of nothingness and took his place as the River Queen, casting his wickedness out of the waters.*

*Why did she come to the land of the Anglo-Saxons? Why did she leave her gloomy marsh and follow my trail to this remote western island? Surely it was not out of concern for her 'little sister,' as she calls me. I am but a pawn to her. If Will had seen her ruthlessness when* dealing with her own people, he would never have trusted her. And then where would we be?

There are only flashes of memory of the time before my seventh summer. The warm hands and sweet songs of my mother. The name she gave me, 'Goldwine,' to complement her own, Goldmeath. The brooding, silent marshland where men came to offer us their blood in exchange for magic: for vengeance, for love, for victory in war. The stern, cold queen presiding over it all, ruling us water-sprites with a fist of iron. In stark contrast to the mournful marsh, the sparkling river where my mother and I spent our summers, my favourite time of all. And always, the curiosity. Who were these men, these mortal beings who venerated and feared us, who brought us sacrifices of blood and iron to gain our favour? What could the world be like beyond our little enclaves, our pockets of eternity-in-time, the changeless realm of this lower world? What lay beyond the surface of my tame little river, and would I ever have the courage to know?

In my seventh year of life, my curiosity finally got the better of me. I left the banks of my river and followed two young boys into the woods. With the innocent companionship of the very young, we wandered far, playing together. We wandered farther until I no longer knew where to find my river again.

I knew the penalty for wandering away from my mother. It was not for us to associate too closely with humans; should we leave the immortal realm for more than a day, we would lose our faery side and become akin to mortals, with the certainty of someday death.

With my home far away and night fast approaching, Ragnar and Randalf took me home to their parents. I could not return to the faery world.

For many years, I had no reason to want to return. My human family provided all that I needed. I grew accustomed to their ways. I started to lose the side of myself that was faery and other. I thought I had chosen mortality, but I did not yet know that my faery heart would always be a part of me, whether I willed it or no.

Ragnar asked me to marry him. This union had the full support of our family. It would make me part of their tribe in truth at last. It would bring me comfort, children, status as a freewoman instead of the orphaned outsider I was. There were many reasons to agree. There was one reason not to. Although I had grown fond of my foster brothers, I did not want the kind of life they envisioned for their wives. I did not want to sit endlessly weaving, waiting for my husband to return from raiding, scratching a bare living from the bones of the earth.

I needed advice for the future, and there was only one person who could truly give it: my faery mother. She was skilled in foreknowledge. I needed to find her again.

I stood on the edge of the marshland, letting the memories of my past life wash through me. Then I took a deep breath, and plunged into the dark waters towards the other world I knew lay beneath the surface.

Deep below, the cold water closed over me. The world was dark, but I could breathe. My feet found solid ground. Sunlight shone through the water, which swirled above and all around. And my mother was walking towards me, arms outstretched, long golden hair shining in the sun.

'I am so proud of you,' she said to me, but she would not explain why. She took my hands and asked me if I was ready to see my future. I agreed resolutely.

'If you marry your foster brother,' she told me, 'you will have a happy life and die of age when your time comes. You will have children, and your sons will go on to wander the world and fight in great battles. You will know true love for your children, but never your husband. And you will never be allowed to return to me.'

I sighed. 'I knew this in my heart already, I think. Tell me then. What will become of me, if I choose not to marry him?'

'I see darkness and sorrow. Strife and suffering. Too many choices to take into account. Perilous adventure in foreign lands, yet glimmering brightly through it all—true love. One waits for you, a man you will be compelled to follow, for he will wake the love that sleeps in your heart. You will have to make a choice that you have not truly made yet. You will have to choose between your love for a mortal, and the eternal life that is yours by birth.'

'This man I love—will we have children?' I asked eagerly.

She laughed musically. 'Goldwine, if it is children and a settled home you want, why would you refuse Ragnar's offer?' Her eyes were as blue as our river, as bright and clear as the skies above, and I could not look away. 'That, I cannot foresee. Webs of time are tangled together between you and your love, between you and the two worlds to which you belong. Nothing is clear; all may change.'

Those were her words to me, that was the future she foresaw. I have journeyed far on the strength of her words. I have asked my heart to believe that I would find my true destiny. I did not know it would be like this. I did not know that the choice I made would be this bitter, the taste of my return to the faery realm poisoned by this sorrow.

When Will wakes, I will no longer love him. I will be half a woman, wandering without a heart. Without love. All I can hope for is that he lives on and forgets me. And when, one day, he breathes his last, my heart will follow him to the halls of his ancestors, or to the Christian heaven he speaks of. There, at last, it might know peace.

H E WAS DYING, Will realized, and he was powerless to stop it from happening.

Through the mists of pain and anger, he could hear a cool female voice somewhere above him. '*He fades fast.*'

He was confused. Goldie had been here, and she had held his hand tenderly. He had heard her cry out, and tried to reach her, but he could not see nor feel her now. There was only the red pain, devouring every inch of his being.

'*I consent,*' Goldie's voice whispered, somewhere in the dark. Will tried to lift his eyelids, but the darkness lay too heavily upon them. He could only dimly perceive the sunlight on the water, dancing in glimmering motes past the reach of his senses. He felt cold, and there were no hands in the darkness to warm him.

He was falling, losing the world even as it slipped away. Neither vengeance nor love would hold him here, and all his struggles availed him nothing. *Perhaps*, he thought belatedly, *after all it's better this way . . .*


PAIN SHOT THROUGH WILL'S BODY, and for a long moment he could not move, only cry out. A thousand invisible daggers stabbed into his flesh. He lay perfectly still, and ever so slowly, the pain began to ebb away. His eyes flicked open at last. He was curled into a heaving, sweating ball, covered beneath soft blankets. In confusion, he untangled his body. He was so stiff it felt that he was creaking. He stared around at the room in which he found himself. It was bare and quiet.

*I cannot be alive,* he thought, but even now he was putting two and two together. The walls around him had the same ephemeral quality as had the costume of the river-queen Helya, seeming to shimmer away before his eyes. He had the same feeling of being suspended in a dream yet unable to wake.

But the pain in his body was very real. Will put out his right hand, and used it to lift his left. A bandage was wound around the palm, and he winced as he felt a twinge of pain shoot through his ribs with the movement. Gingerly, he squirmed into a half-sitting position.

There were bandages around his chest, and now that he concentrated, he could feel the points of both entry and exit where the arrow had shot right through him. There was pain from the wound in his lower back, too, but it did not seem as though that arrow had hit anything vital. Will scowled darkly. He had caught a glimpse of his ambushers just before he had fallen, and knew at least one face amongst them. *Eofric. What was he even hoping to achieve?* When Rob got word of this, he would surely be forced to pay weregild, or more likely banished or executed. How could Will have angered him so much?

Leaning his weight upon his right arm, Will inched out from beneath the blankets. His legs seemed to be working with little trouble, besides the stiffness, but he had to hold his left arm close to his chest to prevent disturbing his wounds. There was a wooden chest next to the bed, and opening it Will found fresh clothes, neatly folded, and a shirt of ringmail.

*Where is my sword?* With a start, he remembered that he had left it in Caedwic's possession. His mouth felt dry. *How long has it been?* Given the fact that his wounds seemed well on their way to healing, it must have been several days at least. *Unless I got the wound-fever, in which case . . . I could have spent a month lying here, and the war would be decided already.*

Will's stomach twisted. Strangely, he did not feel hungry in the least, only empty. Taking the things from the chest, he began to dress, wincing with pain but determined to face the world with some semblance of dignity. Where was Goldie? Looking around at the shimmering walls, he muttered aloud: 'Where are you, Helya?'

He turned around, looking for a door, and did a double-take. Helya was standing there as though conjured by his call, hands folded serenely, grey eyes fixed upon him. She was clothed this time, resplendent in a gown of white samite, a complicated headpiece of gold and pearls woven into her hair. Will could almost smell an air of victory upon her, as though she had just walked in from a great battle of wills.

'Come,' she said, and Will obeyed her silently. The next moment, they were in a wide meadow beside of a rushing stream. Will blinked. There was no sign of the shimmering room. He turned on Helya, but before he could say anything, she held up her hand.

'You wish to know what has happened,' she said smoothly. 'And where Goldwine is.'

Will said nothing, only folded his arms, scowling.

'You will have noticed that your wounds are healed,' Helya continued. 'You have me to thank for that.'

Will glanced at her. 'I am grateful, make no mistake. But why do I have the feeling that—that all this was paid for, somehow?' He flexed his injured hand. 'How long was I here?'

'In worldly time?' Helya shrugged. 'Two or three days, perhaps. Do not trouble yourself about the Dark Priest. Rob and his warriors have fought no battles since your absence, and as far as I can tell, the priest is still hoarding his power in preparation for the final battle.' She hesitated. 'I have to warn you, however, that I can no longer protect your mind from him.' She gestured towards his injuries. 'Healing your wounds cost me power, and I still need to protect myself and the faeries who rely upon me. I fear that you will have to face the Dark Priest alone.'

Will scowled. *I'll cross that hurdle when I get to it.* He opened his mouth to ask about Goldie, but Helya was not letting him get a word in. She continued, 'I have a confession to make. I did not tell you the full truth before. Now that you are facing the final battle against your foe, however, you need to make yourself whole again.'

'What do you mean by that?'

Helya reached into her sleeve and withdrew a small bottle of clear crystal. Even through his annoyance at her, Will had to stifle his admiration of the delicate workmanship evident upon it. She passed it to him, and he saw that it held a liquid of brightest blue inside.

'These are your memories,' she said shortly.

'What?' Will whispered.

'When I chose you to bear our sword,' she explained, 'I took the memories of your past life away. I needed to see what you would become without them.'

*Just as I suspected. Why is she so smug when she should be apologizing for what she put me through?* Will clenched his fist around the bottle. He glared at the faery woman.

'What in Hell's name gave you the right to do that?'

Helya straightened herself imperiously. 'You were failing,' she said bluntly. 'You were going to get yourself killed in battle. Your grief was so strong that you couldn't think, couldn't plan, couldn't do anything but succumb to your misery and guilt.

You wandered for five years, dimly aware that someone was hunting you, but ultimately getting nowhere. All the while, the Dark Priest toyed with you, leading you this way and that, controlling your life by means of your insatiable pride. I removed the memories so that you could have a chance to heal, to right yourself. When your grief no longer clouded everything, you were able to think, and to put the anger and guilt away in their proper places.' Her eyes went to the bottle of blue liquid. 'I always intended for you to be whole again, when the time came. You are ready now. You have learned to live with what you have done and what was done to you. Drink the liquid within that bottle down, and you will be the man that you were, no longer ferreting for lost memories within yourself.'

Will tucked the bottle into one of the pockets that hung from his belt. Outrage still smouldered inside him. 'Now answer me another question,' he said, keeping his voice tightly under control. 'Where is Goldie?'

Helya's steel-grey eyes, which had been studying him intently, lowered towards the ground. 'She is safe.'

'Where is she?' Will repeated.

Helya's mouth thinned. 'She is here in the faery world, with us.'

'And why has she not come to see me?'

Helya sighed. 'You need to give her up,' she said. 'Your love for her was doomed from the start. You should never have put your eyes upon her. You faced certain death, all because you ran off with her; she distracted you from the quest at hand.' She paused as he tried to work out what she was saying. 'Goldwine paid the price for your healing, taking full responsibility for both her mistakes and yours. She willingly gave up her heart—

her ability to love—to save you.'

Will's brow creased in confusion. 'What—what does that even mean?'

'She no longer loves you,' Helya said shortly. 'In much the same way I removed your memories, I took the love from her heart. She does not deserve to lose it to you, and it is a weakness unbefitting any woman.'

Will blinked, trying to make sense of the situation. Something in him wanted to storm at Helya and strangle her, destroy that cool demeanour forever, but he knew that there was a power in the faery queen that he was helpless against. 'Is everyone your plaything?' he finally burst out. 'Or only us mortals? What could possibly be your justification for stealing such things?'

Helya's eyes darkened to the colour of a thunderhead. 'I stole nothing. She made a bargain.' As Will snorted, her eyes flared angrily. 'She is my *sister*,' she blurted out, and to his utter amazement Will could see tears in them now. 'If I let her live with you, marry you, choose the human world—she would die someday. Any immortal who comes to live amongst humans chooses death. It is the price you pay for love, children, family. No-one in their right mind would choose death over eternal life, but you infatuated Goldwine, twisted her judgment. I couldn't watch her throw away her life so easily. Though our mothers are different, we are *both* daughters of the Marsh King. Both of us belong in our father's realm, away from humans. Goldie belongs in the faery realm, with her sister. With her mother.'

There was complete silence after this outburst. Will could hardly begin to gather his thoughts, and Helya kept her stern gaze fixed upon him.

'Your . . . your sister?' Will repeated dumbly. 'Do you mean . . . Goldie is . . . that she . . .'

*Of course. I should have known. Did I not guess that she was hiding something?* He ran a hand through his hair. *I never paid enough attention. Every thought was for myself, for the things I had lost. I couldn't see what was right before my eyes. How did she know about the sword? How did she know how to get into the faery world? It should have been obvious, but I never saw it . . . the girl I loved, who loved me . . .*

'Why me?' he asked. He felt as though his heart would give in. The weight of the past months settled heavy upon him. *Goldie. Goldwine. I never knew. I never asked . . .*

'Why you? That's a question I have been asking myself all along,' Helya said harshly. 'Do you mean to tell me that Goldwine never told you that she was one of us?'

'Never,' Will whispered.

Helya shrugged. 'She probably did not trust you enough. It is always dangerous, when we share the details of ourselves with mortal men.'

'I would never—'

'You have a duty,' Helya interrupted, 'to carry out. Take your memories and go. If you do not confront the priest, your comrades-in-arms will die fighting against him. He can only be destroyed by the object of his ire—you. He would never allow another to get close enough.'

Will folded his arms. 'I want to see Goldie,' he said quietly.

'You do not have the power to make demands here.' Helya's voice was cool and calm as always, but Will sensed something stirring beneath the surface of those cold eyes. 'She does not wish to see you. Forget her. There is no chance you will ever be with her again.'

Will hesitated. He wanted to continue fighting, but at the moment he did not trust himself to think clearly. There was too much he had to do, that he needed to do . . . He closed his eyes, and wished suddenly for the steadying presence of his sword. The eyes of the young Pictish warrior laughed at him from a dream.

'Very well,' he finally said. 'I will put an end to the madness of the Dark Priest. But if I survive this . . . I promise I will return. I need to hear all you have told me from her own lips.'

He trusted himself to look up briefly, but Helya was gone. Will blinked. The stream beside him bubbled musically in its bed.

Turning, Will saw that the area was familiar to him. This stream lay just to the east of Rob's Nest, and was probably a tributary of the river beside which the Dark Priest had made his camp.

Will sank to his knees. Pain shot through the half-healed arrow wounds in his chest. With his bandaged hand, he rubbed away the tears that stained his eyes. *This is no time to weep*, he told himself. *You are in enemy territory, and you have a duty to fulfil. Everything else—even Goldie—must wait upon that duty.*

For all he knew, the Dark Priest's scouts could already be watching him from the nearby trees. Will straightened up with a wince of pain, and scanned the area around. He had to get moving. Quickly he moved under the cover of those trees. He felt almost naked; he had no weapon. And Helya expected him to make it back to Rob's Nest alive!

Scowling deeply, Will took the little blue bottle from his pocket. *My stolen memories . . .*

*I should be prepared to face him.* But what had she said? '*Drink the liquid within that bottle down, and you will be the man that you were.*'

Will put the bottle back in his pocket and headed upstream. He glanced up at the sky. There were clouds above, growing ever thicker, mist hanging over the tops of the trees. With a sense of disorientation, he realized that he had no idea what time of day it was. He scanned the sky for a ray of sunlight, but the mist barred all sight of the sun. It could have been morning, or late afternoon. There was no way of telling.

Stumbling on his feet, Will made his way through the undergrowth. The forest floor was uneven, and he could find no path. As the trees closed over him, the day grew still more ominous. The mist was starting to settle between the trees. *Thank God for the stream*, he thought. Without it, he would have had no bearings to tell him where he was going.

Will coughed. There was a strange smell to the mist, a hint of rotten eggs. Looking around, he noticed in alarm that the mist had thickened to the point where he could no longer see the stream. Luckily, he could still hear the babbling of it rushing over the pebbles, and he turned towards the sound, coming to a halt beside the water.

The silence in the mist was eerie. The light was low, but Will had no idea whether the sun was setting or rising. There seemed something unnatural about the mist, especially after the bright days of early autumn. He stayed where he was, gazing into the water for a while.

Something seemed odd about the colour of the water. Will knelt down and cupped some of it in his hands. He frowned. *Ash.* Letting the water slowly drip between his fingers, he examined the fine black powder that clung to the last drops in the creases of his hands.

*Ash.* But there couldn't be any fire nearby. Not with this mist . . .

*Not ash, you fool,* he realized in horror. *Black powder. Firepowder.*

Will leapt to his feet. *This explains the mist.* His mouth was dry. *He must have been cooking this up for a while, possibly even before we attacked him.* He began to move upstream at a fast trot, but as though his very thoughts had conjured them, hoofbeats sounded through the mist, coming fast towards him.

Cursing to himself, Will dropped into a bush and endeavoured to cover himself with it. Lying on his stomach, he managed to see through the stems of the plant. Five horsemen, unmistakably the Dark Priest's mercenaries, came into sight, moving upstream. Behind them trotted a donkey laden with two small barrels on either side. Will had little doubt of what the barrels contained.

*How much of that stuff have they got?* He twisted his lip in frustration. He needed to get back to Rob's village, and fast. Backing quietly out of the bush as soon as the horsemen disappeared from sight, he walked silently and slowly along the stream until the sound of their horses' hooves died away. Then he relaxed slightly and focused all of his attention on going faster. The streambank was muddy and uneven, slowing him up, but Will was determined not to let himself fail. Ignoring the dull aching that had started beneath his bandages, he moved forward.

HE MET NO SENTRIES IN THE WOODS, but when Will finally

reached the wooden village-gates of Rob's Nest, they were bolted and guarded, a dozen grim warriors standing behind the posterns.

When at last he got close enough for the guards to recognize him, a gasp seemed to run through the lot of them all at once. Demands were made as to where he had been and how he had been wounded. Will brushed them away. 'I need to see Rob,' he insisted. The gates were opened, and four men showed him in. One of them was in fact Elfhild, who looked at him with concern in her eyes.

'We are in serious danger,' Will explained. 'I must see Rob.'

'He's with Wulfric and the other thanes in the high hall,' Elfhild said. 'I'll take him,' she insisted to the others, raising her voice. 'Lean on me,' she whispered to Will, linking her mailed arm with his. 'They won't notice.'

The shieldmaiden was much stronger than Will would have guessed, even after he had fought by her side. She supported him with no trouble as he limped onwards, aching and out of breath.

'You look as though you've crossed the realm of Hel,' Elfhild said, as soon as the others were out of earshot. 'We've been searching for you for nearly two days; that's why all the thanes and lords are here. What happened?'

'Eofric tried to kill me,' Will whispered, as softly as he could manage. Elfhild's eyes went wide.

'Why would he do that? Were his companions with him?'

'Yes.' Will smiled grimly. 'How else would I have been shot in three different places?'

'I don't understand,' Elfhild said. 'Your weregild is worth more than any of them could pay together, and he has to know that many here would call for his execution.' She paused. 'Where is Goldwine?'

'She took me to a healer, a friend of hers, and stayed there,' Will said shortly. The cold answer, a half-truth rather than an outright lie, came easier than he had thought it would.

They were in the middle of the village now, and people stopped the business they were going about just to stare at the two of them. Elfhild said nothing more but supported him all the way to Rob's hall, where the guards all gaped at him as though he were a corpse freshly risen from the dead. Will gave them a cursory greeting, gathered his aching body together, and slowly walked inside.

The thanes, all of whom were gathered standing around Rob, who was likewise on his feet rather in his chair, stopped mid-argument as Will quietly moved into their midst and came to stand next to Rob. 'We need to get every soul out of the village at once,' he announced, mincing no words. 'You see this mist? Is it natural for this time of year? The Dark Priest has cooked it up from his magic arts, and *he is here*. He is coming, not only for us, but for the innocents, the women and children as well. I saw his patrols. He has found our location, and he means to attack. And he still has supplies of the fire-powder. It will burn even if there is a thunderstorm.'

'You're right!' one of the thanes shouted, and was echoed by another shouting, 'That's what I've been saying all damn morning!'

'Get your fighting men together!' Rob yelled above the din that had broken out. 'We march immediately!' He turned to Will. 'Where did you see patrols?'

'Due east, just along the south bank of the stream the

villagers name Sunnastream,' Will said. 'I need to see Caedwic. At once.'

'He's in his church.'

Mist was sinking over the village, turning day into dusk. Elfhild hovered near him, but Will waved her away. 'I can get ahead on my own,' he said. 'Go see to the defence of the village.'

Elfhild nodded and clasped his hand. 'I'll see you on the battlefield,' she promised, and walked away.

Will stumbled towards the little wooden chapel where Caedwic held sway. The door was open, as always. Inside, two figures knelt before the wooden altar, their heads bent forward. One was definitely the monk, in his mouse-grey robes, but the other was cloaked and muffled all in black, resembling . . . Aisha?

Will knocked softly upon the door, and the two figures raised their heads, turning around. Aisha gave a gasp of delight, and Caedwic struggled to his feet. Suddenly the monk was upon him, drawing him into a bear hug as Aisha beamed in the background.

'We thought . . . well, we thought the worst, that is what,' Caedwic explained. There were tears in his eyes.

Will patted his shoulder. 'I'm not quite dead yet,' he said, feeling Aisha's stare as she took note of his bandaged injuries. 'But someone tried. I suspect it won't be the last time, but'—he grinned—'they won't succeed without a fight.'

'Wait here,' Caedwic said, and trotted off. He returned shortly with Will's weapons, his sword and dagger, and Will breathed a sigh of relief.

'You both have to get out of the village,' Will said urgently. 'The Dark Priest is coming. No-one will be safe.'

'We were waiting for you,' Aisha said.

'But now,' Caedwic said, taking the young woman's arm, 'we go to lead the people to safety.' He clasped Will's hand. 'Take the time you need,' he said, gesturing towards the altar. 'We have to go.'

Will stood in silence as they left the church, brow creased in confusion. *What does Caedwic expect me to do in here? Pray before the battle?* There was no time to waste. He began to follow the monk out but then turned to stare at the wooden cross and the carven figure impaled helplessly upon it.

*How am I going to defeat the priest?* The thought was like a physical blow. After coming face to face with his enemy, he still had no guarantee that he would be able to stand up to him. *I relied on Helya's protection to keep my mind clear from him, and now she has withdrawn it.* The wound in his chest gave a sharp twinge, and Will bent down, going to his knees before the cross. He remembered Aisha's confrontation with the priest. She had thrown off his evil spell, simply by thinking of her temples and her god. Her foreign, heathen god.

Will looked around him, at the simple, little wooden church. Caedwic's congregation numbered no more than two dozen, and they had fashioned this building almost as though they wished to be worshipping their godhood outside instead of within walls, like the pagans did. It was made from the trees that surrounded and protected them, and seemed to imitate the arch of the forest, the hand of nature.

The pagans amongst them believed in many gods, holding none as supreme. There was no singular truth, and beings of the immortal world were as varied in nature as humans themselves. None were truly, irredeemably evil, just as none were

completely pure and good. It was easy for them to see themselves in their gods. It was easy to believe in a higher power
when magic walked in the wind, when the forests and meadows
were alive with it.

Perhaps the truth of God lay not in heavenly perfection, an
ideal no man could hope to live up to, but in the way man resembled his gods. The Christ had walked on the earth amongst
men and had shared in pain and anger and betrayal. When men
looked up to Him, they saw Him at his most vulnerable: betrayed, whipped into submission, left for dead. Will could most
certainly empathize with that.

Still kneeling, Will unsheathed his sword. The blade seemed
almost to purr with anticipation. *It is not only my imagination.* Will
laid the sword before the cross.

'You bend to *my* will, not I to yours,' he said. 'That bloodlust is something *I* control, and you will not cloud my judgment
any longer. God will be the master of our fate today, and I will
be your master if there is any tomorrow.'

Courage flowed through Will as the sword acquiesced,
backed down from an unspoken argument which, he only now
realized, had been ongoing since the first time he had ever unsheathed it. The blue-tattooed youth smiled and held out his
hand, and Will was happy to lay his own in it. There was a sense
of connection, of brotherhood. Will knew that he would not go
alone into battle after all.

There was one more loose end. *I should be whole when I face
him.* Will took the blue glass bottle out of his pocket. Helya's
words echoed in his ears. '*You will be the man that you were.*'

There was a commotion outside, a crash as though someone
had just launched a catapult upon the village, coupled with

screams and cries. Will hesitated once to look back at the cross. Wounded, weakened, and heartsore, he raised his sword in salute, then sheathed it again and slipped the bottle back into his pocket.

Outside, a group of stragglers were running past the church, fleeing a burning missile that had landed in the village common. Will gazed up. The mist had given way to a grey, grumbling sky. *Please let it rain*, Will thought to himself, though he knew that it would make little difference. He turned his attention to the straggling villagers. 'Go north until you meet with Caedwic,' he yelled at them, heading them off. 'Hurry!'

As he turned, intending to find the warriors who would be marching towards the battlefield, another flaming missile appeared in the sky before him. It was coming for him, and for the hapless villagers fleeing behind him, and there was no time to run. Will began to fling up both his arms to shield his face, a futile gesture but instinctive. However, his right hand disobediently reached for his sword. A strange power surged through him as the blade whipped out before him like a particularly impractical shield, and Will could taste metal in his mouth.

The ball of flame hit the sword, and was driven back. Holding on with both hands, Will could feel searing heat on his face, hear the amazed gasps of the villagers behind him. With all his strength he pushed, and the missile ricocheted away from the sword, crashing into Caedwic's now empty church.

The villagers turned and ran as the church went up in flames, leaving Will to gaze in disbelief at the smug-looking sword now dangling from his hand.

*I thought I was in charge here?*

If iron could shrug, the sword would have.

'But you saved my life,' Will said. 'Thank you.'

As thunder grumbled in the sky above, Will moved through the abandoned village. Well, abandoned but for the last stragglers. Will gave each of them a stern but very short lecture urging them to abandon their possessions and sent them on their way. He suddenly missed Goldie, and the thought pierced his heart. In the midst of chaos, he missed her cool competence and calming presence. She was much better than him at persuading people.

Lightning flashed violently in the heavens, and then at last the storm broke loose. A howling wind sprang up, driving torrents of rain before it. Will kept his head low and finally managed to locate the warriors, who were moving on foot towards the battlefield, slogging through the mud. Someone pressed a helmet and a round wooden shield into Will's hands, and he slipped both on, wincing at the shield's weight on his injured hand. Suddenly a familiar face was beside him.

'Are you all right?' Elfhild shouted above the rain, holding her own shield over her face to keep it off. Before Will could answer, the sky lit up in flames. The warriors scattered. Clots of flame landed all around them, beaten down by the driving rain. They moved on. The enemy host was just visible through the trees, masked by rain and smoke.

'Where's Lorica?' Will shouted to Elfhild.

'With the riders.' She gestured behind them. 'They're holding back 'till we've engaged.' She glanced at Will, whose breath was ragged, who could hardly hold his shield high enough. 'Stay close to me!' she yelled over the pounding of the rain on her own shield. 'I'll protect you. You look out for the priest!'

The two armies made contact in a flurry of blows, but after

the first shock landed and the shield-wall collapsed, Will allowed the fight to bypass him. He concentrated on getting through it all unharmed. By his side, Elfhild slew every attacker who came their way, wielding her blade with deadly competence, never misstepping. Will turned his eyes ahead. He could see the catapults now. Soldiers milled around the great machines. The fire-powder was still burning, but sluggishly, and there was more smoke than flame.

Sword in hand, Will cut down a screaming enemy soldier who ran past him, still keeping his thoughts in the direction of the priest. Only when he found himself unexpectedly in the thick of the fight did it occur to him to look for Elfhild. She was nowhere to be found. Enemy bodies bestrewed the muddy plain, seeming like her handiwork, but he could not see very far in front of him. Cutting down another boy dressed in the leathers of the foe, he stumbled away from the heat of the fray.

Will gasped in pain and faltered on his feet. The shield was too heavy for his injured arm, and he cast it loose. He was almost alone in the driving rain. A shadow ran at him, and he hacked at the enemy soldier's shield, found an opening by pure luck, and stabbed him in the throat. He was too tired to feel anything, but it was as though an outer power was propping him up, willing him to go on.

*I'll never find the Dark Priest like this,* Will thought, and he stopped, leaning against a felled tree. The rain pounded against him. He had successfully wandered away from the main engagement, and the other combatants were only shadows and muted sounds in the storm. Mounted shapes flitted here and there, and muffled war cries could be heard, but Will was on his own.

*I will find him.* Gripping his sword, closing his eyes, Will let his mind wander towards the thought of the Dark Priest. *Here I am*, he thought, *come and get me*. Surely he would shine like a beacon through the rain for the one who wanted his mind and soul. Will shivered, feeling as though dark coils had just come out of the darkness behind his eyes to trap him. Almost as though he were back in the clutches of the sea-demon . . .

Will stood up straight, and opened his eyes.

The figure of his enemy stood before him, yet somehow Will could not seem to summon the anger and hate that he wanted to inflict in return for Aedfrith's death. His eyes saw the face of the Dark Priest, smirking as he stood there, but it was the face of the boy Albert that Will remembered. The boy who had once loved Aedfrith, as Will never had.

The wind died and the rain faltered around them. It was as though they were alone in the world; nothing existed but the past and the moment of confrontation.

'You come injured,' the Dark Priest said, 'you come with no plan, no aid. I may not be able to see into your mind, but I can see that you are hopeless. You are dead.' His eyes gleamed. 'I will send you off myself. I will see the light die in your eyes, and hear the last scream from your lips.'

There was a dull ache in Will's chest, and when he looked down, he could see a dark stain spreading across his shirt. Rage and his own will had carried him this far, but now he could feel the toll of the battle settling upon him. There were more wounds he had sustained, wounds he had not even felt at the time. He was spattered in blood, and he wasn't sure how much of it was his own. Everything hurt. His sword fell from limp fingers as he collapsed to hands and knees. There was nothing left. Only guilt and the shame he could never cast off.

The Dark Priest bent and picked up the sword. 'What a re-markable blade,' he breathed. 'Forged by druids, imbibed with dark magic—this explains much.' He looked down at Will, who had forced himself upright on his knees. 'The battle still rages, Wilhelm,' he said. 'An easy victory for me, had it not been for the rain.' He waved a hand. 'But what do I care? Let the hea-thens and mercenaries die. I should be happy as long as I know that you suffered before you died at my hands.'

'I have suffered already,' Will whispered. 'I remember what you did to Aedfrith.'

'Good,' the priest said. 'And you remember how you snatched her away from me?'

'I do,' Will said. 'I remember everything.' He raised his eyes, and held the priest's gaze. 'And I am sorry. I destroyed so many lives, including yours. I will carry the guilt of that for the rest of my life. As will you. Both of us have done terrible things.'

The Dark Priest's face contorted, and he looked sharply away. 'It was *you* who taught me the most valuable lesson in life,' he sneered. 'There is no higher power of good and evil—only men like us, struggling in the mud, striving for something greater.' His eyes gleamed as they travelled up the bloodstained surface of the sword. 'You say that you will carry guilt for the rest of your life,' he murmured. 'Well, then—allow me to un-burden you!'

The priest brought the sword down in a gleaming arc, aim-ing directly for Will's head. Will reacted instinctively, flinging his arm in front of his face. The blade struck him, biting deeply into his unprotected wrist. But even as his blood spurted, fleck-ing the face of the priest, the sword struck against an invisible force, ripping itself out of the priest's hands. It flew above them both in a graceful arc, and Will stood up, his pain forgotten.

There was nothing but confusion on the Dark Priest's face; he did not understand. But Will's blood sang to the same rhythm as the magic that now burst forth from the sword, bathing him in wonder and easing his pain. It was his will to live, his longing for the sun, his love for Goldie. The blade had been forged by immortals, and they had poured all the magic of the world into it, then given it a mind of its own. No man could wield this sword unless it allowed him to, and like anything from the faery realm, the sword decided for itself whom it would serve.

Even as the priest's greedy hands grasped for the hilt again, Will reached up and plucked his blade effortlessly out of the air. With the reflexes of a practiced swordsman, he drew the long blade back with both hands, aiming for his enemy's heart. He could see the Dark Priest's eyes widen in shock; his hands wove an intricate pattern of protection as he fell back, but Will did not reverse his stroke.

The priest's spell withered against the ancient druidic magic woven into the faery-forged blade. The last Will saw of the Dark Priest was his surprised expression as he slid off the end of the sword, leaving the iron slick and red along its length. He died quietly. Thunder crashed across the blasted plain, and the rain drummed down twice as hard as before. Magic glimmered, pulsed softly, then drifted away into the driving wind, leaving Will wondering if it had ever truly been there at all. The sword thudded down to the mud once more, and this time Will followed.

'Aedfrith,' he whispered. 'Wilge.' *I avenged you. You can both rest, now. I will remember you. I promise. I will carry you in my heart for all time. But you, you can rest. You can sleep.*

Somewhere else, the battle raged on, the mercenaries of the Dark Priest meeting the swords of the men who fought for a brighter day. But victory was out of Will's hands, helpless as he was in the mud and the blood. The rain seemed kinder now, no longer a harbinger of his violent and tragic past, but a numbing power that would let him rest and sleep.

As his blood ran down, mingling with the rain, Will slipped out of consciousness. A sweet dream of the sun welcomed him, and he fell into it willingly.

# Chapter Eleven

# The Lost Lover

*In a chair next the window, a ray of sun shining through her veil onto her face, Aedfrith sits embroidering, smiling to herself as she watches the scene come together in shades of blue and green and violet. Her needle traces threads that only she knows where they may lead.*

*She has risen before me, as usual, and I wake to find my infant daughter cradled in my arms. I go to sleep most nights holding her; she does not seem to like sleeping on her own. I can scarcely blame her for that. This ancient fort is draughty, built more for defence than for pleasure.*

*When I finally dress and prepare for breakfast, my father is in the hall, with my mother, Lady Mari, beside him. He is stern and grey-*

*bearded, as he has always been, a hard unbending man whose only smiles are reserved for my mother, and sometimes for me. Sometimes, when I please him.*

*He loves my mother, even though they did not meet until their wedding day. Even though she has a streak of wildness which sometimes shames him. He likes to say that she passed this wildness, this restlessness of heart, on to me, and that is why I can never be content with the life he lives. She is not afraid to laugh with her warriors, to take me into the woods on wild nights to look for faeries. We never find them, but she tells of how, when she was a girl, she saw their witch-lights shining in the northern woods. I do not believe a word of it.*

*We sit at chapel under the direction of an ancient, grey-haired priest, and we light candles as sacrifices before the cross. Outside, the sea pounds against the cliffs, and a light rain falls over the island, over the peasants in the fields and the sheep dotting the side of the hill.*

*Perhaps I belong here, after all. The people around me have gone to the grave one by one, but this is where I spent most of my life. I was too lost and irresolute to return before, but perhaps now, when all is set right, I can come to terms with the mistakes I made and look forward to returning home. The rain falls on me, calling me back, inviting me to look back at my past.*

*Home. Who knows what I shall find there?*

THEY WERE SEPARATING THE WOUNDED from the slain, getting the former carried off to the sick-benches and the latter to the bonfires, when they found him. He was only half-conscious, speaking inaudibly to himself, but he recognized the two women; he would have known them anywhere.

Lorica and Aisha. They were doing women's work for once, patching up the wounded whilst the heroes of the battle rested.

They shouted and raised a fuss until they found men to carry the corpse of the Dark Priest to lay at Rob's feet, and they bore Will from the battlefield themselves, after they discovered that he could walk if he was being supported between them.

To their relief, they found that he was not badly wounded, just exhausted, hungry and thirsty. His arrow-wounds, though they had bled freely at some point, had managed to knit themselves again. Lorica cleaned and dried them before applying fresh bandages and then set to work on the cut along his forearm.

'You know, Will,' she said as she sewed, 'if I didn't have Elfhild, I might challenge that blonde lady of yours.' She gave him a huge wink, distracting him from the needle. 'You saved us all.' Her voice was soft, then turned flippant again. 'Fortunately for your Goldwine, I *hate* beards.' Will winced as she pulled the thread tight and tied it off. 'Done! Now let me see your face.' She raised a damp cloth to his brow. 'This one needs to be stitched as well. Battle-axe, I'd say, but luckily for you, a blunt one.' She smiled. 'Well, you'll have several new scars.'

'So do you,' Will said. Lorica chuckled, touching the bandage wrapped around her upper arm.

'Nothing much—an errant arrow.' Looking into her eyes, Will could see that she had an old scar just above her brow, almost a twin to the one she was cleaning. 'You have more scars than what I do. Been at battle for longer.'

Will grunted in acknowledgment of her remark, then flinched and bit his lip as she inserted the needle.

'I'm done with war, at least for now,' he said, seeking to

divert himself.

'What will you do, then?'

'Go home, I think,' Will said. That sounded good. He was no longer a beggar come to trouble joy, but a man who had been through much and deserved to return home at last. There were secrets from his past that still awaited, things he needed to see for himself. He remembered the way back now, and his heart was set on returning. Even if it were to be without Goldie by his side.

'It is sweet to return home,' Lorica was saying, 'but sometimes, Will Nobody, home can be a person. I have never returned to the place where I was born, but Elfhild is all the home I need.'

WILL SIGHED AS HE LOOKED DOWN at the corpse arrayed for a funeral befitting a battle-hero. 'Eofric.'

'He died fighting for this place,' Rob said, folding his hands behind his back. The bandit chieftain's bushy moustache quivered. 'Whatever sort of man he was, Eofric was a good fighter.' He glanced at Will. 'If you wish to press the trial and have him shamed—'

'No,' Will replied wearily. 'I will keep my peace. He fought to defend the innocent—I will not have that taken away from him.' He rubbed at the bandage wrapped around his left hand, felt the twinging pain of the healing wounds in his back and breast. 'But he hated me.' He scowled. 'I wish I knew why.'

Rob hesitated. 'You did not happen to catch a glimpse of the others who were with him?'

Will shook his head. 'It was misty, and they were in the trees.

I caught only a fleeting glance; Eofric was the foremost, and the only one I recognized.' He sighed in frustration.

'May I ask how you managed to escape?'

'They thought me dead,' Will replied, 'but . . . but Goldwine saved me. She brought me to a—friend of hers, a . . . a woods witch.' He shook his head as if it could cast loose the memory of that day. 'I would have died without her.'

'And that's where she is now? With this woods witch?'

Will nodded.

'She always has been an unpredictable girl. Wild as a fox. Do you know, last time she disappeared, she told no-one that she was even thinking of leaving?' Rob guffawed softly, then sombred as he looked down at the fallen warrior. 'I need to confess,' he said. His eyes were upon Eofric's still countenance. 'He came to me the night of the revel, the one we had with Wulfric. The night before he tried to murder you.' Rob paused. 'He was drunk, but coherent enough. He wanted me to put you on trial. I refused, but he kept insisting that he needed vengeance. I tried asking him what he meant by that, but he only—obliquely—mentioned the death of a relative.' Rob shrugged. 'Do not ask me which relative, or even whether he imagined you had killed them or not. I cannot hold trials for things that happened years ago under someone else's rule, and I told him that. He was fuming when he left.' Rob looked up at Will apologetically. 'I thought he might try and confront you, but I never imagined that he would ambush you. I did not think that he had murder in his heart. I am sorry.'

'You did nothing wrong,' Will said. 'If I had kept my weapons with me like I should have, they would never have been able to best me.'

Rob raised an eyebrow. 'They had bows,' he said, and abruptly changed the subject. 'You know that he was not alone,' he stated baldly. 'The others may also be slain, or some may still be alive. If you wish to stay, I cannot have discord amongst my men. I would have to find them . . .'

'There is no need,' Will interrupted, seeing Rob's request for what it was. 'I am going home. I have no wish to remain.'

'You understand, I am not chasing you off—'

'I know that,' Will said. He gave a short bow. 'You have been a good lord to me, Rob Lightfingers.'

'I don't want you to feel as though you have done so much for nothing,' Rob said. 'Ask me for anything, and you shall have it. You need a horse, a battlesteed. I can give you one.'

Will shook his head. 'A horse would be nought but a liability. I need to travel across the water ere I reach home.'

'Armour, then? A vest of chainmail. *Two* vests. A short sword.'

'I have no use for more armour nor another sword.' Will hesitated. 'Give me a pack-mule and enough provisions to last me the journey home, and I shall be grateful.'

Rob sighed. 'Let me send one man with you as an escort, at least, and take a horse on loan until you reach the kingdom of Rheged,' he said. 'You are ruining all my attempts to be a generous lord. When will you be leaving?'

'Tomorrow,' Will said. He paused. 'Rob—I need to go somewhere tonight. I need to see her. Goldie.'

'Will she be leaving with you?' Rob asked neutrally, even as something like amusement played in his eyes.

'Perhaps.' Will turned. 'Can I have a horse?'

Rob grinned. 'Certainly. Anything to help you win your fair lady.'


IT WAS EVENING BY THE TIME Will reached the meadow where Helya had left him. Dismounting, he paced up and down the stream for a while. 'Helya!' he called. 'Helya!'

Of course, she didn't answer. Will felt foolish. Goldie had been able to slip freely into *their* realm of existence, but after all she was one of their own. He was a man and nothing more. Will stroked his beard, thinking.

Inspiration came to him as he rested his hand upon the hilt of his sword. Will drew it from its scabbard. It was strange to think back to the way it had behaved during the battle, and even now he wasn't sure that he hadn't imagined most of it. It seemed like a perfectly ordinary blade, to the untried eye. Will scowled. *I know you are so much more.*

Leaning back, Will threw his sword overarm into the river.

Before the spinning blade could hit the surface of the water, a silk-clothed arm reached up and caught the hilt in mid-air. Will smirked to himself as Helya's face appeared above the water, the sword held steady in her hand. One moment she was rising from the river, the next she was standing before him.

'What is the meaning of this?' she asked, her eyes flashing.

Will shrugged. 'I've come to return your sword. My mission is complete.'

Helya proffered the hilt of the sword. 'I have no use for it. It was a gift, not a loan. Keep it, as a token of our gratitude towards you.'

'To be honest,' Will said, folding his arms, 'it's not about the sword.'

Helya's face darkened. 'I told you before, you have no business poisoning her life.' Her eyes narrowed. 'You didn't drink the potion. You refused the gift of your own memories?'

'I had no need to remember anything more before I faced the priest,' Will said coolly. 'Your gifts are poisoned. Why should I trust your counsel?'

Helya stuck the point of the sword into the ground. 'All right. You survived the fray, against all odds. It pleases me. Now what will it take for you to go away and stop bothering me?'

'Goldie.'

'I told you, she does not wish to see you.'

'I would hear that from her own lips.'

'It would avail you nothing.'

'Then what are you so afraid of?'

'Not *you*,' Helya snapped. She stepped back. 'Very well. But do not blame me if this upsets both of you.'

Will picked up his sword and slid it back into the scabbard at his belt. Helya turned. There was an instant of absolute darkness, and then Will saw that they were standing on a high bank that rose over a meadow with a lake at the far end. Witch-lights, greenish and strange, floated across the meadow, illuminating a lone figure by the side of the water.

Will's breath caught in his throat, and he started forward. She did not turn, even when he had descended the bank and stood not ten paces from her. She was leaning down, cupping the water from the lake in her hands, as slender and graceful as the sighing willow that grew on the bank beside her. Clad in a gown of blue and white cut from fine silk, with pearls round her neck and silver at her wrists, it was as though she had just risen from the sparkling waters of a summer stream, her cascading hair as golden as the sunlight that glinted from the water.

Will had never seen her wear such finery before. There had always been something in Goldie that was strange and wild, but for the first time, she seemed alien, untouchable. To besmirch her with his lowly mortal hands seemed almost an act of wickedness. In the silks and jewels of a princess, she was even more beautiful than she had been in wool and leather, but it was an aloof beauty, like a sculpture carved from stone.

He half-considered turning around and walking away, but there was something in him that needed to know the truth at all cost. Softly he called, 'Goldie.'

She whipped around, nearly losing her balance, and stared at him, eyes wide with panic. Will held out his hands in front of him as he approached, as though to steady a wild animal. 'Do you remember me?'

'Of course I remember you,' she said in a low voice, moving a step backwards so that her feet were in the shallows of the lake. She glared at him. 'You shouldn't be here.'

Will flinched. Her eyes looked the same, and yet very different. He had never seen such derision in them before. Before he could speak, however, she did.

'It's strange,' she said. 'I can't understand what I saw in you.' Her eyes swept over him from head to toe. 'What did I see in you?' Her tone was curious, rather than contemptuous.

Will shook his head. 'I don't know,' he whispered.

'You're just a mortal,' she said, 'nothing more than a strong man who fights. There is more of the mercenary in you than the nobleman.'

'That did not seem to trouble you when you knew me.'

'I do know you,' she said. She turned her head as though she would have liked to dive into the water.

'And I know you—or at least, the woman that you were.' Will kept his voice as gentle as he could. Longing washed over him, and he wanted nothing more than to go over and seize her, to pull her from the water and take her forcibly into his world. 'You would never have allowed yourself to be controlled like this! Why are you letting Helya do this to you?' He took a step forward, stopping when he saw her eyes flare in alarm. 'You fear me,' he realized. 'Why?'

For a moment it looked as if he had managed to touch her, but then she closed her eyes and turned away. 'The spell cannot be broken,' she said softly. 'Some curses are unbreakable, Will. Some magic cannot be wished away.' The lake rippled around her feet. 'You think that I am being controlled, forced? By what? Truly, I have been freed from the control of my own heart. Helya was right all along. Now that the plague of love no longer clouds my eyes, I see it clearly. Why should I choose death? Why should I choose you?'

'You did, once.' All the world seemed quiet save for his speaking, and the sun was vanishing into the hills behind him, throwing amber-dark shadows across the surface of the lake. 'You said that you chose me. That you loved me. That you needed to follow your heart.'

'That was before.' The breeze shifted through the willows on the lakeshore. 'I cannot love anyone now, nor will I ever again.' She looked back at him as she moved further into the water. 'It was the bargain I made for your life. Only a great sacrifice could have paid to heal your wounds. Believe me, we are both better off this way. You can go home now. You can marry again, have children and live out the rest of your life in peace. I will remain here,' she ended quietly. 'Where my kind belong.'

*How do I tell her that none of those dreams—home, love, family, peace—mean anything without her?* 'Don't do this—' Will began, but she smiled with a haunting sadness that made the words catch in his throat.

She turned away from him and dove into the water. Will ran towards her, reaching the lakeshore and stumbling to his knees in the shallows, but she was already gone. The wind died in the trees, and the water lapped indifferently at his clothes. The ripples from her passing shivered briefly before him, then smoothed away to nothing.

Will would have liked to reopen his wounds—all his wounds—and remain here, bleeding out the rest of his life into the indifferent water. But there were people waiting for him, and duties, and so many unanswered questions, and he knew there was nothing to do but trudge back up to the bank.

He quickly wiped his eyes, determined that Helya should not see him weep. To her credit, she only hovered for a moment, and when she spoke, there was no malice in her voice.

'I tried to spare both of you from this,' she said.

'How do you live with yourself?' Will shot at her.

'Better than you do with *your* other self, Thane Wilhelm,' she snapped. Darkness fell before his eyes for a moment, signalling the end of their conversation. Will turned to retort, but she was gone and he was alone beside the river, the sun disappearing over the treetops.

Exhausted, Will sank down upon the grass and buried his face in his hands. Now that Helya was gone, he gave himself up to the grief in his heart. The rushing of the river masked his sobbing, and the oncoming night hid the tears that fell.

But at the end, he emerged with clarity, looking forward on his path. *At least she is safe,* he thought. *At least she is with her people.*

He picked up his sword, feeling its stalwart presence in the back of his mind. Something in the trees whispered to him, *Don't give up.*

AISHA BADE HIM A TEARFUL FAREWELL, her father smiling by her side. Caedwic was stoic as always, unharmed by the battle and twice as determined to bring the gospel to the heathens. Lorica and Elfhild were there to bid him a stern warriors' farewell, clasping his hand in comradeship. There were even a few that Will had never actually met, or only met in passing.

Ed had been badly injured during the battle, and lay only half-conscious, yet there was recognition in his eyes when Will sat beside him, and the grip of his hand was firm when they bade farewell. Will left him to the ministrations of young Gerd, alongside a village woman who was obviously more than just a casual acquaintance, to judge from the way she hovered over the dauntless mercenary, dabbing at his brow and inspecting the dressings on his wounds.

Wulfric and his son, who had both made it through the battle largely unscathed, saw him off with the customary horn of shared mead. And when Will rode out, weighted down with the golden arm-rings Rob had presented to him, he was accompanied not only by the strongest pack-mule to be found in the region, but also by one of Wulfric's most trusted warriors, who had volunteered to be his guide until he reached the Welsh kingdom of Rheged that lay on the western coast.

'This is disputed land,' Wulfric had said, frowning over the north-western part of the map. 'Are you sure this is the route you wish to take?'

'It's the quickest way across the sea,' Will insisted. 'I'm sure we had some sort of agreement with the Welsh chieftains about travellers.'

Wulfric had regarded him dubiously, but not gainsaid him any further. The warrior acting as his guide was a dark, taciturn sort of fellow, for which Will was glad. Their journey to the border of the Saxon kingdom was a largely silent one, and Will had plenty of time to dream and think, which he alternated depending on how the mood took him.

Luck was on their side, and the road north, leading across wide moors and through deep valleys, was uneventful. At last, they arrived at a broad meadow running alongside a mighty river flowing as blue as the autumn sky above. Wulfric's man cast an unhappy eye over the forest that brooded upon the opposite bank.

'This is as far as I take you,' he announced. 'Beyond that river, the land is treacherous. The Welsh devils would shoot you full of arrows as soon as look at you.'

'Is that so?' Will dismounted from his horse, handing the reins back to Wulfric's man.

The warrior was muttering something about 'barbarous hordes,' but Will interrupted him.

'I should be on my way. There may be a crossing nearby, and you'd best be getting back to your lord.' He took hold of the mule's lead-rope. 'Give Thane Wulfric my thanks. Any request from him or his son, I would gladly carry out.'

Once the other man had left, the evening was very quiet. The sun was sinking into the forest, caressing the land with golden fingers. *The colour of her hair.* Will sighed.

'You'd like to rest, wouldn't you?' he said to the mule. She nosed at his shoulder.

'All right,' he laughed. 'I guess this is as good a place to sleep under the stars as any.' The mule was swiftly unloaded and hobbled, and she tucked into the sweet grass of the meadow. Will made his way down to the water, his hand resting upon the hilt of his sword.

Summer was drawing to a close, but there was still a month to go before the festival of the Hallows, or the night of Walburga, as some Saxons still called it. The days were noticeably shorter, the breeze colder. The wind blowing from the water was nothing less than bracing.

After the rainy weather that had plagued them since the battle, the sky was clear at last. It was the last breath of summer, calm and quiet, a night for faeries to dance in the silent meadows, for young lovers to sleep naked under the stars . . .

Will sighed again, and rubbed his eyes. *I'll never forget her, will I? I might as well learn not to weep whenever I think of her.*

He raised his eyes to the forest. Somewhere beyond, closer now than he had dared to realize before, waited the place where he had been born. *Home.* He was returning as a man made anew.

Standing by the water's edge, Will drew from his pocket the tiny bottle Helya had given him.

For a long time he simply gazed at it as it rested in his palm, assuring himself that what he was about to do was the right thing. Finally, he lifted his hand. The glass bottle glinted in the setting sun as he unsealed it and tossed the stopper into the water.

Carefully, he raised the bottle and tipped the blue liquid into the river. Like rippling, beaten gold in the sunset, the waters swirled around and took the liquid memories into their embrace. The glass bottle followed as Will hurled it into the current.

'Are you listening, Goldwine?' he murmured, giving up her name to the rushing of the river and the soughing of the wind through the trees. 'I am a man who follows my own path, much like you. I swim against the current of the river.' He paused, thinking for a moment that he felt her presence, but the wild wood was silent, and the wind blew over the meadow the same as it had the moment before. 'Whatever I am to become, it will be on my own terms. It will be as Will Nobody, as the man you loved. The man who looked at you that day of the wedding, and saw everything he ever wanted.' He sighed, and closed his eyes, brushing a last tear away from his cheek.

Stretching himself out on a blanket, he looked up at the stars until sleep took him. Just for now, there was peace within his mind. He did not doubt for a moment that he had done the right thing. Thane Wilhelm was gone, and it was time for Will to build a new life for himself.

*The Broken Knight will return in Part 2 of the magical series,*

# THE RIVER'S DAUGHTER.

AS THEY BOTH STARED OUT over the grey sea, the wind whipping the waves into a white froth, Dernhelm's oarsmen finally finished adjusting the sails on his boat, and beckoned for the two noblemen to board. They strode through the shallows, water sucking at their boots, and clambered awkwardly inside as another man pushed the prow of the little boat off the sand. The wind was strong, and Will's mouth was dry with anticipation. It was the last stretch towards home.

Dernhelm's smile was back, and his eyes were shining with excitement. 'Are you ready for your homecoming?'

Unable to say anything in the moment, Will grinned back at his cousin as the little sailboat crested the first waves and skimmed out onto the open sea.

Hi! I'm Emmylou Kotzé, a poet and writer from Mangaung, South Africa, and I hope you enjoyed reading my debut novel, which I wrote whilst I was meant to be working on my Ph.D. in Germany. Feel free to come pick my brain at my website, www.amphipolitan.com, where I  post most of my poems and shorter works. I'm not too hung up on genre, and my work spans literary, fantasy, sci-fi, and romance, with my main focus on three-dimensional characters with an inner life and the ways in which they relate to each other. In my stories, people like assassins, kinslayers and sex workers navigate their complex lives in magical worlds and fall in love—as often as not, queer love. I have a long history of questioning everything: religion, sexuality, gender, history— and I strive to reflect that stance in my writing. The two themes that make me practically quiver in delight are feelings of otherness, and clashes of culture. I love narratives where things get messy and complex, and where it all comes with a heaping side of intense, gory pulp-style action. Outside of writing, I did get that geoscience doctorate in the end, and I can confidently explain the terms 'buttress' and 'orogeny.' I currently live on the border of Lesotho, with the sight of my favourite mountain range, the Malutis, in the distance.

ILLUSTRATIONS

Chapter One: The Golden Girl — 'The Knight at the Crossroads,' 1878. Artist: Viktor Vasnetsov, Russian, 1848–1926.

Chapter Two: The Christian Wedding — 'Leilah,' 1913. Artist: Gaston Bussière, French, 1862–c.1929.

Chapter Three: The Sea-Demon — 'The Sirens,' 1874. Artist: Wilhelm Kray, German, 1828–1889. This snippet becomes highly symbolic with regard to Will, but the original painting tells a fascinating story of its own and thus is definitely worth seeing.

Chapter Four: The Faery Sword — 'Vercingetorix Throws Down his Arms at the Feet of Julius Caesar,' 1899. Artist: Lionel Royer, French, 1852–1926. This snippet of the original painting completely cuts out the real focus of the work so I highly recommend checking out the original. If you're an Asterix fan, you'll definitely want to see it since Uderzo redrew it a zillion times.

Chapter Five: The Burning Town — 'Memory of a Wooded Island in the Baltic Sea (Oak trees by the Sea),' c. 1834. Artist: Carl Gustav Carus, German, 1789–1869.

Chapter Six: The River Queen — 'After Igor Svyatoslavich's fighting with the Cumans,' 1880. Artist: Viktor Vasnetsov, Russian, 1848–1926. This painting depicts a military disaster from which only 15 men walked away.

Chapter Seven: The Deserters — 'The Unfaithful Knight,' inscribed with lines from Keats's 'La Belle Dame sans Merci' (although the artist himself seems to have misremembered and attributed the poem to Tennyson). Artist: Albert Goodwin, British, 1845–1932. Not to be confused with the British-Canadian labour activist who was shot dead by a policeman in 1918 for supposedly resisting arrest. The charge? Evading the World War I draft.

Chapter Eight: The Dark Priest — 'Queen Guinevere's Maying,' 1900. Artist: John Collier, British, 1850–1934.

Chapter Nine: The Secret Pool — 'Tristan and Iseult,' 1911. Artist: Gaston Bussière, French, 1862–c.1929. These lovers were part of a tragic Arthurian romance.

Chapter Ten: The Sword's Legacy — 'Siegmund the Walsung / Thou dost see! / As bride-gift / He brings thee this sword,' 1910. Artist: Arthur Rackham, British, 1867–1939. This was created to illustrate Wilhelm Richard Wagner's epic Ring Cycle. If you want to know why Western fantasy is so deeply in love with things like valkyries, magic swords, and talking animal sidekicks, I highly recommend you check out this influential opera trilogy in some or another form. Yes, there is a reason why I chose *Wilhelm* as the name for my protagonist and not something that was verifiably Anglo-Saxon.

Chapter Eleven: The Lost Lover — 'Ruth and Boaz,' 1863. Artist: Walter Crane, British, 1845–1915.

www.ingramcontent.com/pod-product-compliance
Lightning Source LLC
Chambersburg PA
CBHW020402120726
47904CB00002B/667